Also by Keith Lee Morris

The Greyhound God

The Best Seats in the House and Other Stories

The Dart League King

Keith Lee Morris

TinHouseBooks

This book is a work of fiction. Names, characters, places, and incidents either are products of the author's imagination or are used fictitiously. Any resemblance to actual events or locales or persons living or dead is entirely coincidental.

Published by Tin House Books, Portland, Oregon, and New York, New York Distributed to the trade by Publishers Group West, 1700 Fourth St., Berkeley, CA 94710, www.pgw.com

Library of Congress Cataloging-in-Publication Data
Morris, Keith Lee, 1963-
 The dart league king / Keith Lee Morris. -- 1st U.S. ed.
   p. cm.
 ISBN 978-0-9794198-8-1
 1. Darts players--Fiction. 2. Psychological fiction. I. Title.
 PS3613.O7735D37 2008
 813'.6--dc22   2008020391

First U.S. edition 2008
ISBN 10: 0-9794198-8-3

Interior design by Laura Shaw, Inc.

Printed in Canada

"The Trouble with Liza Hatter" originally appeared in *Tin House*.

www.tinhouse.com

FOR MY MOTHER AND FATHER,
WHO MADE SO MANY THINGS POSSIBLE

For my part, I have walk'd about the streets,
Submitting me unto the perilous night,
And, thus unbraced, Casca, as you see,
Have bar'd my bosom to the thunder-stone;
And when the cross blue lightning seem'd to open
The breast of heaven, I did present myself
Even in the aim and very flash of it.

—SHAKESPEARE, *Julius Caesar*

Men at some time are masters of their fates.

—SHAKESPEARE, *Julius Caesar*

Table of Contents

Dart Night in Garnet Lake, Idaho   11

Jack the Fucking Dude   29

The Trouble with Liza Hatter   37

An Intellectual Conversation   49

Goddamn Clouds, Fucking Rain   57

And All the Stars That Never Were   65

Give Me Darts or Give Me Death   81

A Thing of Beauty   89

Stupid Assholes   99

A Dartboard Is a Perfect Circle   107

¿Como Se Dice?   119

Candles   127

Where We Put Our Socks and Shoes   139

A Fucking Perfect Opportunity   149

The Music of the Spheres   159

Whirlpools and Sea Monsters   165

One Last Dart in Hand   183

The Point at the Center of the Universe   201

Distance   211

Velocity   217

Weight   225

Gravity   231

Release   241

Epilogue   245

Rules and Regulations for the 2007 Garnet Lake Dart League   271

Dart Night in Garnet Lake, Idaho

Tonight was Thursday, and Thursday night meant dart league, and Russell Harmon was the Dart League King. For that reason, and for others, Thursday night was Russell's favorite time of the week. His least favorite time of the week was Friday morning, when he would have to step down from his role as founder/commissioner/team captain/ individual champion two years running of the Garnet Lake Dart League and resume his job on a logging crew, a type of work for which he was unenthusiastic and ill-suited.

But this was Thursday night, not Friday morning, and in just a couple of hours dart night would be in full swing, and the thing for Russell Harmon to do now was to lay out a few lines of coke for himself and his boss/best friend Matt down in his mother's basement, where he'd been living for almost a year now, as a kind of preparation for and celebration of another excellent evening of darts and various related activities.

Dart night had become a big thing in the community—bigger, for instance, than country/western dance night on Fridays at the Elks Lodge. In the two years since he formed it, Russell had seen the dart league expand to ten teams from four, and darts, rather than pool, which Russell had never been very good at, had become the game of choice at most of the local bars. Even the Garnet Lake Monster, the most upscale bar in town, now sponsored a team. Russell's team, the 321 Club, was hosting the Monsters tonight, which meant that Russell had his work cut out for him—he would be playing Brice Habersham in singles. Brice Habersham was the only other undefeated player in the league this season, and Russell feared, when he got down to the very bottom of his soul and started being honest with himself, that he couldn't beat Brice Habersham, who had once been a professional.

But Russell wasn't much of a thinker—more of a doer, he liked to imagine—so it hadn't been hard for him to go around all week telling everyone how he was going to kick Brice Habersham's ass come Thursday night, and even now, consulting with Matt over four lines of coke spread out on the glass of his framed high school diploma, Russell felt reasonably sure of himself.

"I figure we win both the doubles," he said, "and you win your singles match and I beat Brice Habersham and that's it. We're champs, no need to wait till next week."

Matt nodded, perhaps a little uncertainly, it seemed to Russell.

"You go first," Russell said.

Matt rolled a twenty and snorted two lines, one up each nostril, and handed the bill to Russell, who did the same, pocketing

the twenty when he was through. That was the customary price
Matt paid for these Thursday nights—that and Russell's beers.
It didn't actually cover half the amount Russell had to pay, considering he had a second bindle in his pocket for later in the
evening, but it was close enough, because Matt was his friend,
and Matt was his boss, and he probably wouldn't even have a job
if Matt hadn't put him on his logging crew, and Russell wasn't
as handy with a chain saw or as easy at the controls of a skidder
as he was with a set of darts. Tomorrow morning would be hell,
like it always was, and it helped to have Matt a little indebted. It
had helped a little bit last Friday when Matt found him sleeping
on the seat of the backhoe while he was supposed to be clearing
brush.

So he put the twenty in his pocket and called it good, and
he and Matt both took a swipe at the glass with one finger and
rubbed their gums, and Russell folded up what was left of the
first bindle and slipped it into his pocket with the twenty, and
he hung the diploma back on his bedroom wall. Then they
left the basement and went to the den and played Xbox for a
while and headed out the front door without saying good-bye to
Russell's mother, who was in the kitchen cooking a dinner that
Russell wouldn't wait around to eat.

In the parking lot of the 321 Club Russell flipped open the
glove box and got out his darts.

"You bring the heavy ones tonight?" Matt asked. He was
standing outside the passenger door thumbing through his
wallet.

Russell nodded, checking his leather case to make sure he'd
brought a fresh pack of flights. You didn't want old, ragged
flights when you were playing Brice Habersham. "These ones

feel better to me lately," Russell said. He knew Matt liked the lighter set with the thin tungsten barrels, but Matt always played with the same set Russell used, regardless—hoping the good luck would rub off. But there wasn't any luck involved when it came to Russell's dart playing. He took out the darts and held them in his hand, stuck a flight on one and held the barrel with his thumb and first two fingers, his third finger edging down toward the point, and he moved his wrist back and forth slowly. These ones were fit for a dart king; they'd cost well over a hundred bucks at the Pastime Sport Shop, where Russell had bought them on credit several months ago and hadn't paid yet. "Fuck Brice Habersham," he said, and got out of the truck and locked it.

"How much money you got?" Matt asked, putting away his wallet, eyeing Russell from beneath a strand of long brown hair.

"Enough," Russell said.

"I mean if Vince shows up," Matt said, still not raising his head all the way.

"Enough," Russell said. But there wasn't enough to satisfy Vince, he knew. That was a possibility he didn't want to think of—Vince Thompson showing up on the most important night in recent memory.

In the bar they warmed up for a while, and the throwing felt good to Russell, smooth and easy. He would be ready with the help of a couple of beers to get rid of the last little tightness. He shared a line with Bill, the bartender, back in the kitchen, because it was good form and because Bill was a good guy. He worked on the matchups for dart night. He and Brice Habersham had agreed to play the final singles match—that

way, no matter what the outcome as far as the league championship went, there would still be some suspense at the end,
because he and Brice Habersham were undoubtedly playing for
the individual championship—they were the only undefeated
players in the league, and neither of them was about to lose
to anybody else. Here's what Russell was thinking—he'd split
himself and Matt up in doubles, pairing himself with Tristan,
and Matt with James. That was risky because it was spreading
the real talent—him and Matt—thin, but if they could pull off
both the doubles then he would have Matt scheduled first in
singles, and if Matt won, they would be guaranteed at least a tie
for the evening when it was Russell's turn.

Russell worked out the calculations on a sheet of scratch
paper and then transferred them to the official dart league sheet
that Tristan had made up on his computer, and he paused for a
moment to look at this sheet with satisfaction—he had started
the league, and without him there would be no such sheet,
with its official look and regular lines.

It was just past seven o'clock, and the match didn't start
until eight, and Russell and Matt more or less had the place to
themselves. A couple of guys from some office downtown sat
up front at the bar, their ties loosened, drinking dark beer. The
host musician for open mike night was setting up for later on,
turning his little dials and knobs, testing out various beats with
that fake electronic drum thing. Russell hated open mike night,
which started at nine thirty. He usually scheduled himself first
in singles so that he would be through with his matches before
the fake drum banged out its annoying rhythm, which always
interfered with Russell's own rhythm at the dartboard. But
tonight he was playing last, which meant he would have to face

Brice Habersham with that awful *da da boom, da da boom, da da boom tisk boom* coming from the front of the bar. It didn't matter what the guy was singing or playing, it was the fucking drumbeat that stuck in Russell's head, tempting him to speed up his throwing motion. If it weren't for the cool 321 T-shirts—depicting a beer mug lifting off from a launchpad shaped like the state of Idaho—that Randy, the owner, provided the team, Russell would have taken his business elsewhere.

The dartboard was at the back of the bar, and when the fake drum started up Russell called time-out from the 301 game he and Matt were playing and went to look out the window. Back behind the bar was a little cedar deck with wooden chairs and two big birch trees and beyond them the hill sloping down to Sand Creek with the boat slips at Garnet Lake Marina. To the left was Sand Creek bridge, which Russell and his friends used to jump from when they were kids, eyeing the bridge traffic for cops before slipping off their T-shirts and climbing the bridge rail, plunging down through the air and the summer sunshine to hit the cold water. But Russell wasn't the nostalgic type, and even though it was summer now and the weather was warm, the perfect season for fond recollection, he didn't dwell on the memory. The birch trees, the water, the bridge—they were there, just like they'd always been, and that was it. Russell left the window and sat down at a table with Matt and their pitcher of beer.

"So what if Vince shows up?" Matt said. He was looking at Russell the way he had been lately, kind of half disgusted and half concerned.

"It's not a problem," Russell said. He poured himself another glass and took a couple of big swallows and licked foam from his upper lip. "Just quit with that shit already."

"It *is* a problem, Russell," Matt said. "What are you gonna do—run out the back and jump in Sand Creek?"

"What the fuck," Russell said. "Why are you going on with this shit? He comes in, I deal with it somehow. I came here to play darts. No problem."

But it *was* a problem, and as that fucking musician started messing with the drum thing again, Russell felt a tension in his gut and his foot started tapping when he didn't want it to. He wanted to go do a line in the bathroom before too many people started showing up, but he hadn't had enough beer to find a proper equilibrium yet—an absolute essential for dart throwing, a proper equilibrium—or enough to make him forget about Vince Thompson. He owed Vince Thompson over two thousand bucks for the coke he'd bought over the last nine months, when it went from being a pastime to something resembling a habit. He was buying from someone else now, a precocious high school kid, and it was embarrassing to call the kid up at his parents' house with some pretext for a meeting somewhere, but what could you do? Start doing meth, which was cheaper and easier to get, but which Russell associated with lowlifes living in rundown houses on the edge of town? Certainly not buy more drugs from Vince Thompson, who had become the scary figure in Russell's dreams, chasing Russell through the downtown streets with the gun Matt claimed he—Vince—had been carrying lately.

So Russell pushed the thought of Vince Thompson aside, leaving it for the nightmare hours. The thing to do now was prepare for Brice Habersham. But when the open mike guy had finished setting up and gone to the bar for a beer, and Russell and Matt had resumed their 301 game, Russell experienced a strange kind of heightened feeling, a feeling that the colors of the dartboard and the dart leaving his hand in that smooth motion and the solid thunk of the dart entering the board at just the spot he'd intended it to and the taste of the beer and the coke at the back of his throat were all just a bit more precious when there was a man with a gun hunting you. It was similar, perhaps, to the feeling he'd had when he rolled the skidder down a cliff last month and nearly killed himself.

James and Tristan and the first couple of guys from the Monsters team showed up at about seven thirty. Russell had just the right edge on by then, so he excused himself to the men's room and let the other guys warm up. He locked the door behind him and pulled the first bindle and his keys from his pocket. He unfolded the bindle carefully, dipped the end of his house key into the coke until he'd accumulated a satisfying little pile, carefully lifted the key to his right nostril and inhaled, then repeated the procedure with his left. His eyes watered a little bit, and he rubbed them with the back of his hand, feeling the coke pass through his nasal cavity. He ran water in the sink and got his fingers wet, then put his fingers in his nostrils and breathed deeply, letting the water push the last of the coke up his nose, then he checked the mirror to make sure there wasn't any white stuff showing. Someone knocked on the door and he called out just a minute. He splashed his face with water and yanked paper towels from the dispenser and wiped his face. Then he dropped the paper towels in the trash and unlocked the door. It was Tristan waiting outside.

"You ready?" Russell said, and fake-punched Tristan in the ribs, and Tristan eyed him funny. Back at the dartboard he slipped the bindle out of his pocket and tapped Matt on the arm and placed the bindle in Matt's hand, and Matt's hand went to his pocket and he headed to the bathroom.

Russell watched the Monster guys warm up. He knew them all—an older guy named Tim who bartended at the Monster and a guy named Slade who was the same age as Russell, twenty-three, but who had graduated high school a year ahead of him because of Russell getting held back in first grade, and some dude named Kurt who worked for Brice Habersham at the gas station he'd bought when he moved to town six months ago or so. None of them were any good. Russell wondered when Brice Habersham would show up. It was fifteen minutes until the match was supposed to start, and they needed to go over the lineups.

He watched the Monster guys throw at bull's-eyes and miss outside the triple ring until he couldn't stand it anymore, just the sheer ineptitude, the embarrassment for the dart league as a whole, the very idea that a player as good as Brice Habersham would even allow such people on his team. He looked at their stupid shirts. They looked like bowling shirts, old man shirts—Habersham had probably picked them out of some catalog. They were red with button-up fronts and collars, and stencils of the Garnet Lake Monster, which looked like a cross between a blue whale and a dragon, across the back. The Garnet Lake Monster didn't look anything like that. Russell knew; he'd seen it once, when he was out in a boat fishing with his uncle Roy. According to local legend it was something like the Loch Ness Monster, but Russell thought it was more like a giant sturgeon, some ancient relic from days gone by. He'd seen old photographs of a sturgeon they'd fished from the Snake River long ago—a massive fish hauled up from the bank by a chain attached to the rear of a flatbed truck. It would be some strange creature like that, living in the deep water of the lake, far down there where only the glaciers had ever reached. He hadn't *seen* the monster, actually, that time with Uncle Roy—just the long ripple in the water without explanation, the strong impression that there was something huge underneath.

Russell bought a couple of pitchers of beer and brought them back to the table. That would get the camaraderie going, and camaraderie was one of the main things about dart league. It didn't matter if it cost a little extra money every week to promote that. James and Tristan were warming up now, and it was almost eight o'clock, and Brice Habersham still wasn't there. Russell watched Tristan throw. He was the new guy on the team, just joined this spring when he came home from college. They had known each other since grade school, Russell and Tristan, but never that well. Russell was a jock, mostly, a second-string tight end on the football team, while Tristan was the intellectual type, but cool intellectual—into cool music and movies and books. He'd always wished he'd known Tristan better, to tell the truth, and this year's dart league had been his chance. And yet he still didn't know Tristan very well. He showed up on time for the matches and took his playing seriously enough and drank beer with the rest of the team and laughed every once in a while and generally took part in the conversation. But when the matches were over he'd shake hands with everyone and leave, or, if it was a home match, go up front to listen to open mike night, sometimes sitting with the open mike host himself, who was teaching Tristan how to play guitar.

So it had been a little disappointing, having Tristan on the team. But he had gotten pretty good, hadn't he, Russell thought. He watched Tristan cluster a nice group at the 20—two in, one just outside the wire—and noted again how if he would just shorten his throwing motion, keep the dart in front of him instead of pulling back to the side of his head . . . but then he'd gotten pretty good anyway. Better than James now, who'd been on the team since last year, and getting to the point where he could just about challenge Matt. Russell supposed it had something to do with intelligence—how even if his motion was a bit off, Tristan had the power of concentration to *will* the dart to the spot he wanted. In fact, when he watched Tristan's dark brown eyes focusing on the board, he became a little reluctant to point out to him again the thing about the throwing motion—no telling how good he might get if he fixed his mechanics and practiced more.

Eight o'clock on the nose now, and still no Brice Habersham. The guys on the Monster team had no idea what might have happened to him. Technically, Russell could call for a forfeit. Technically, the dart league championship could be wrapped up for a third year right here, right now. Russell just had to say the word—you forfeit. But he didn't want to, didn't have even the least desire to, even though taking that route would offer the additional advantage of allowing Russell to slip out of the 321 before Vince Thompson came looking for him there, if in fact Vince Thompson planned on tracking him down tonight. All week long Russell had thought of nothing but his match with Brice Habersham. Out in the woods he had thought their match through, visualized the outcome, convinced himself over and over that what he saw on the inside of his head (shaking hands with Brice Habersham after he'd nailed the bull's-eye in Around the World—"Hey, man, I got lucky," he'd say, trying not to smile too big) would become a reality. In Brice Habersham's gas station, you could see them up on the wall—big trophies from Cincinnati, Cleveland, Louisville. Not the kind of lame trophies they had made up at the sports shop for the dart league award nights—*real* trophies, heavy mother-fuckers, the kind they handed you along with a check. Beating Brice Habersham would make the Garnet Lake Dart League legitimate—*Local Boy Beats Former Professional, Whole Town Basks in Glory.*

And so Russell resolved to wait fifteen minutes, and he informed the assembled dart league members of his decision, and he had James note the time on his watch and appointed him official timekeeper.

Two things happened before the fifteen minutes were up. First, while Russell was checking the entrance every ten seconds or so for Brice Habersham, Kelly Ashton came in. Russell hadn't seen her in maybe a year, and he hadn't talked to her in maybe two. She had dark brown hair and breasts as large as grapefruits, and Russell knew certain things about her—that she cried out very loudly when she reached orgasm, which she did easily, and that she liked to hold you tight when you slept together, and that in the morning she wasn't very good at making pancakes, the mix still adhering in spots where she hadn't stirred it enough and the bottoms slightly blackened. This had been back when he had his own apartment, when he worked for the satellite TV company, long before he'd had to move back in with his mother. Kelly Ashton's arrival complicated things. The fact that her eyes were very blue and her bottom teeth were just a little bit crooked in a cute way when she smiled and her breasts were as large as grapefruits—that she looked really *good* in the way women looked really good when you hadn't seen them in a long time and were suddenly reminded—created an additional distraction. She sat at the bar and ordered a glass of wine and saw Russell right away and smiled at him ruefully, and it was enough to drive Russell to the bathroom for another bump, even at the risk of upsetting his equilibrium, even though he had to open the second bindle because Matt still had the first one in his pocket.

The second thing that happened was that Brice Habersham showed up, breezing in at 8:13, according to James's watch. Brice Habersham claimed there had been a little incident of nonpayment at one of the gas pumps, and he had needed to wait around to describe the offending vehicle to the police. Russell doubted it. He had a tendency, in fact, to doubt virtually everything Brice Habersham ever said, unless it had to do with darts specifically, an area in which he never doubted anything Brice Habersham ever said, having seen all the trophies, having seen Brice Habersham once accept reluctantly, after much prodding, a gentleman's bet (because, he said, he only played for money in officially sanctioned tournaments) that, given three darts, he couldn't step up to the line with his eyes closed and hit a bull's-eye, and then having seen him hit not one, but two. But there was something about Brice Habersham that made Russell feel he was otherwise full of shit. Maybe because he was a little guy, no more than five-six tops, and because unlike most other little guys Russell knew, he didn't seem to feel the need to talk big. Maybe his appearance—his graying hair so short and neat, the gold-rimmed eyeglasses he wiped with a clean white handkerchief every minute or two, the pressed slacks, the polished shoes, the aforementioned primly collared team shirt, with his name stenciled in script above the pocket. Maybe how he was so calm all the time, maybe how he drank his beer so slowly, never finishing more than one or two, maybe how he never laughed at anything but always smiled politely, maybe how he always shook his opponent's hand and said so sincerely, "Nice game." Russell didn't trust the son of a bitch as far as he could throw him.

But he was here now, and the match could start. And that— he was going to have to admit it to himself here in a second or two—made Russell nervous. And Russell was not the nervous type. He went over the lineup sheets with Brice Habersham, then swallowed half a mug of beer in two long gulps and excused himself to the bathroom. Taking another bump from the second bindle, he stared at himself in the bathroom mirror, the curly brown hair, the face gone slightly pudgy, the cool blue eyes that had won him most of his girlfriends, and told himself that he would be fine, that he would be back in here two hours from now having a celebratory line to mark another championship, but he couldn't quite make himself believe it.

When he returned to the board, the situation was even worse. Because he'd been late, Brice Habersham refused to take warm-ups, so the first match, with Russell and Tristan paired against Brice Habersham and that Slade guy who couldn't hit the board if he were shot at it from a cannon, was on *right now*, and Russell had imagined loosening up with another half glass of beer or so. And then there was Kelly Ashton, seated with her legs crossed in a short skirt at a table just behind theirs, apparently there to watch the dart match, and Tristan was sitting next to her in a way Russell didn't particularly like.

He hadn't seen Kelly Ashton in a long time, probably because she'd had a baby a while ago, he couldn't remember exactly how long, and there'd been some trouble with the father, he'd heard, some guy from out of town who apparently had decided to stay out of town more or less permanently after the baby was born, and so, Russell suspected, Kelly Ashton probably didn't have much chance to get out and about anymore. Which was sad, because she looked damn good, and because she looked damn good he didn't quite like the sight of her huddled up there with Tristan, and he started wondering if maybe Tristan had invited her downtown for dart night, if this might be their idea of a *date*, and so he said to Tristan in an unusually angry tone, "Tristan, you playing darts tonight, or what?" And Tristan glanced up from his conversation with a look of either surprise or amusement on his face, Russell couldn't tell which, and said, "I'm here, *El Capitan*. Just call me when it's time." A serious breach of dart league etiquette—it was a *team* game, dammit, and you sat with your *team*, not some brunette with nice legs and slightly crooked lower teeth and breasts as large as grapefruits. Russell tried hard now not to look at or think about Kelly Ashton at all.

So he and Brice Habersham threw a cork to see who went first in cricket, and Russell lost, and Brice Habersham stepped up nonchalantly and hit a triple and a single 20, putting Russell and Tristan one number down and 20 points in the hole to begin with. And then Russell stood at the line and it was like something strange and new was happening inside his head, it was almost, for a second, as if he could feel or hear a sort of grinding, like unoiled gears rubbing together, and he shook his head slightly to clear it, clear it of Brice Habersham and Kelly

Ashton and Vince Thompson and whatever else was causing that *screeching* noise inside there, and then standing at the line he wondered, for the first time in his life, how it was that a person was supposed to throw a thing such as a dart anyway—it was as if his motor memory had suddenly been erased. You put your fingers around the barrel like so, he seemed to remember, and you made a little circle with your thumb and forefinger to indicate exactly where you wanted the dart to go—that had always been his own little trick, the secret to his success—and *then* what the hell? You were supposed to make the dart stick in that tiny pielike sliver under the 20? Jesus fucking Christ—it seemed impossible all of a sudden, and sure enough his first dart went just wide and the next two were worse.

And so his heart struck up against his chest like a little hammer and his fingers pulsed strangely, and throughout the first game, while Tristan kept them in it, throwing better than he ever had and sauntering over to the table to talk with Kelly Ashton between turns, Russell missed and missed and missed.

Somehow, with Tristan nailing bull's-eyes and Slade shooting just about the worst darts Russell had ever seen thrown in the Garnet Lake Dart League, they managed to win the cricket game. Tristan won the cork from Slade for 301 and doubled in on his first dart and again held up Russell's end of things with Brice Habersham breathing down their necks despite his worthless partner, so that finally the score stood at 32 for the 321 Club and 42 for the Monsters, and it was Russell's turn to shoot. There was about a fifty-fifty chance that Brice Habersham could finish the game off from 42, and Russell had three darts in his hand to make the chances zero, and Tristan had left him double 16, the perfect out in 301. Russell had hit double 16 a thousand times, but now his first dart stuck in the 8 about four inches from where he'd aimed. He shifted to double 12 then, with 24 remaining, and his next dart missed the board entirely.

It was perhaps the most embarrassing moment in Russell Harmon's life—for Russell, at least, although anyone who knew him well could probably have picked out any number of events that *should* have been greater sources of embarrassment—and for the first time ever he broke rhythm and stepped back from the line. The back of the bar was entirely silent. From up front, he could hear the music from the stereo, some old country shit that Bill had put on. Out the window the sun had crept down and Russell saw the branches of the birch trees in silhouette against the orange sky and on past that the evening light on Sand Creek. Everyone was waiting. He could feel the eyes of Tristan and Kelly Ashton boring into his back, their conversation stopped now, and to his right Matt stood there looking at him, eyebrows raised, hand in his pocket fingering the bindle he hadn't given back to Russell yet. To his left stood Brice Habersham with his arms crossed, eyes still on the board as if there hadn't been any interruption of play, as if nothing unusual were occurring, darts in his right hand, the flights clacking together, waiting to see if he would shoot again this game. In his own right hand Russell held one dart, and if he hit a double 12 he could put an end to the stupid fucking doubles match and go outside to his truck for a good long line and a chance to get his head together. With nothing more than that in mind he stepped up to the line and threw, and just like that the first match was over and he was receiving handshakes

all around and downing a beer and smoking a cigarette someone gave him while the other guys warmed up for the second
doubles match, and it was almost like he had never panicked
at all. Strange.

James and Matt were still in the early stages of their cricket
game when Kelly Ashton got up to go to the ladies' room.
Something occurred to Russell, what you might call a plan.
He walked over and sat with Tristan at the table. Tristan was
holding one of the crappy house darts he threw with, examining the design on the flight as if it held some interest for him.
"Why were you looking at me funny when I came out of the
bathroom?" Russell said.

"What?" Tristan asked, looking Russell up and down like he
might have to fight him in a minute.

"Why were you looking at me that way?" Russell said again.

Tristan shrugged. "You were in there an awful long time."

"And?" Russell said.

"And I guess I wondered if you were holding," Tristan said,
leaning over the table.

Russell scooted back his chair, grabbed his mug off the table,
chugged what was left of it, and set it down empty. "I am," he
said. "Come on."

Tristan glanced toward the restrooms.

"She'll be here when you get back," Russell said.

Jack
the
Fucking
Dude

Vince Thompson was forty-two years old and he lived all by himself in a one-bedroom apartment above Gillespie's Hardware on Third Street, and that was good enough for him. Problem was that the new Home Depot on the outskirts of town had run Gillespie's out of business finally, and now his friend Chuck, his fucking supposed *friend* Chuck, who owned the building, was leasing the fucking apartment right out from under his ass because the new people who leased the downstairs, some computer firm that developed software or some such shit, some of this new high-tech crap that Vince knew absolutely nothing about other than how to find porn on the Internet, wanted his upstairs apartment for "executive office space" and were willing to pay double what Vince paid in rent. And so fucking Chuck, this is the same Chuck who, when they were in sixth grade, hit Vince with an iceball on the playground after school and scratched the cornea of his left eye, and then his fucking dad, Vince's fucking dad, the hardcore Vietnam air force colonel asshole, had said Vince was being a baby and didn't need a doctor, and before he changed his mind the eye was infected and next thing you know Vince is half blind for the rest of his life and it probably caused his fucking hard-ass father about two goddamn seconds of actual fucking sorrow and worry when he was away on his monthly duty down at the base in Mountain Home and found out about it when he called the house to make sure his goddamn wife, Vince's mother, the perpetually aproned maternal unit, the goddamn dinner-cooking, floor-sweeping, dish-washing, feather-dusting, vacuuming-the-carpet-to-within-an-inch-of-its-fucking-life *fool*, was holding down the so-called fort while he was gone—now this same Chuck, who you have to admit pretty much ruined Vince's life with the goddamn iceball, I mean think about it, because how's a twelve-year-old kid supposed to hit a baseball with no goddamn left eye to speak of, how's he supposed to see a pass coming on the fast break, how's he supposed to run a crossing pattern when a) if he's going left to right he can't see the defender, and b) if he's going right to left he can't see the goddamn *football*, and now he has to make new friends because he's not on the goddamn high school sports teams, not a big-ass jock motherfucker, and so he has to start hanging out with the potheads in the parking lot and smoking dope at lunchtime so his grades go down the shit hole and he can't get into college and he'll be *damned* if he'll go into the service, and not even to mention the self-confidence factor, which pretty much goes down the goddamn tubes when he's sitting on his bicycle seat and trying to pick up on some adolescent girl with fresh nipples poking through a bikini top and legs as long as sunshine down at City Beach, Vicki Ashton her name was, and now she's a drunk-ass single grandmother if you can believe that who lives across town but at the time she was a fine piece of teenage ass if ever there was one, and then his goddamn left eye starts doing some goofy shit, he can feel it like *drifting* around uncontrollably in the socket, and consequently he pedals away on his cheap-ass bike that his cheap-ass dad grumbled about buying him for his eleventh birthday and it's already too goddamn small for him now but the old man won't buy him another one till he's at least fourteen because where the fucking hell does money grow, on trees? And then he's never quite the same. So right, this goddamn Chuck who ruined his life in the first place, who he was decent enough, who he was *white* enough, to actually forgive and become friends with, is now going to set his ass out on the street after ten fucking years of model citizenship with the goddamn rent always coming on time, not late even *once*, and now he's got the nerve to look at Vince out of the corner of his eye—which Vince can barely see him doing, by the way, because he's standing to Vince's left— has the nerve to say to Vince that it's too *risky* to have him here anyway. *Fuck* him.

So now Vince Thompson would have to clear his shit out— his guns, first of all, the Beretta and the Lugar, the Bushmaster semiautomatic and the Winchester 30-30 and the Winchester 12-gauge and the Japanese Nambu pistol from the Korean War that his father, the son of a bitch, gave him on his eighteenth birthday, and the other ones he couldn't remember at the moment, along with the assorted knives and sabers and shit, and the various paraphernalia, the scales and the razor blades and the baggies and the baby laxative, and what little furniture he owned, the old beat-up couch and kitchen table and shit he'd inherited from his dead grandma, or not really inherited, because no one wanted the cheap-ass shit and his asshole father wouldn't give him any of the good stuff, anyway, saying how he, Vince, didn't *deserve* it, and then giving all the good shit to his motherfucking brown-nosing older brother Douglas, named after General Douglas Mac-fucking-Arthur no less, and the futon he slept on in his bedroom and the computer and the three thousand or so CDs that took up pretty much every square inch of the apartment along with his bitching stereo, his incredibly awesome music collection, all the old classic stuff, sure, but also kick-ass new stuff that even these fucking kids around here hadn't heard of with their goddamn Britney Spears and their *boom-de-boom* hip-hop, like some sad nigger off the street with no musical ability whatsoever and a stupid name like DJ Tony T or some shit could hold a candle to, would be fit to wipe the *ass* of, some major musical genius like Miles Davis or Coltrane, truly revolutionary dudes who changed the fucking world, who made it into a proper badass place where things were called by their fucking right names, where a spade was a fucking spade, and then afterward you could *have* your kick-ass rock and roll, your Stones and your Nirvana, and more and more kick-ass motherfuckers who also knew what the world was about, violence and anger, and the best you could do was set it to a beat and a hummable tune and they weren't afraid to say so, now he was going to have to take all his shit, all this valuable shit, across town to live in the apartment complex he managed part-time, where the goddamn landlady, the wheezy old half-dead bitch with her respirator and shit, Mrs. Krum, who lived across the street and was always riding over on her little four-wheeled moped contraption, what did they call the thing, My fucking Buddy?—yeah right, her little goddamn four-wheeled friend, he practically had fucking *dreams*, I shit you not, about the old biddy forgetting to look both ways and being plowed over by a dump truck, always riding over to make sure he was keeping busy, clipping the hedges or fixing a toilet or posting late-rent notices, he was going to have to move into the goddamn complex, into apartment no. 2 right next to the kid with his pregnant girlfriend and all the goddamn yelling and abuse, he'd had to call the cops on them just last week, and the old goddamn landlady was going to take his rent out of his paycheck, which would make it seem like, disregarding the logic here, because it was the *feeling* that mattered, he was working practically for free, even though the job was just a front, basically, a way to explain how he had some cash while the *real* business, the real fucking *business* he ran, the narcotics operation responsible for the fucking forty thousand dollars he had stashed in a locked box in a closet in his old room at his goddamn parents' house, and which was eventually going to get him the fuck *out* of this piece-of-shit town, went along its way, although things were making Vince Thompson nervous lately, there was a shitload of stuff going back and forth across the border, and his goddamn supplier, Fred, this dude he'd been getting his shit from for upwards of ten years, suddenly seemed to be getting, like, delusions of grandeur, like talking all the time about how his business was fucking *expanding*, and how he wanted Vince to *come on board* more than he had been, *get inside the loop where the big money was*, where what Vince wanted was to just keep on toodling along his merry fucking way, not taking the big risks, the shit that would get you caught again, like he was back in the early nineties when he'd had to do a six-month stretch at the state pen and he *didn't ever* want to go back there, no *fucking* way, especially since the old man's lawyer wouldn't get his ass out of the proverbial sling next time around, the old man had assured him of that, he would be doing serious time, so shit no, no thank you, you could just leave old Vince out of the big money, he'd just go on making his money slowly, slowly, because that way he could sleep nights like he hadn't for a while, partly because of all the fucking meth on the streets now, this homemade cheap-ass shit that Vince wouldn't touch with a ten-foot pole, all these amateurs cooking up this shit in their trailers out in the fucking boonies, but primarily because of this dickwad Russell Harmon, this goddamn addicted fuzzy-brained numb-nuts who wouldn't pay his legitimately accrued debts, and who Vince Thompson was starting to get the idea, was starting to see the signs, was just the sort of limp-dick motherfucker, chickenshit, pantywaist, to go blubbering in a goddamn fright to the police and make a confession that would send Vince Thompson up the river, and *then*, since he *couldn't go back there*, he'd have to sell out Fred, no fucking choice in the matter, and then the shit would get *majorly* serious, we're talking witness protection program, no fucking lie, and Vince could just see his lower middle class ass parked in some fucking vinyl-sided nightmare in the middle of goddamn Nebraska, working at the elementary school as a goddamn janitor the rest of his life, cleaning up after the fucking first-graders who didn't know to lift the goddamn toilet seat, and when things got *this* bad, when they got so bad that you actually found yourself *hoping* that your friend Fred was a big enough supplier to get you into the federal witness protection program when you ratted on his sorry ass, Vince Thompson figured it was time to make a decision, time to make a fucking move, and as far as he could see the goddamn limited options were these: a) cancel Russell

Harmon's outstanding debt, say good-bye to Fred, and get out of the business alto-fucking-gether or b) take his 9mm Beretta and find a good way to just jack this Russell Harmon dude, and then get the fuck out of town. And right now, on this particular Thursday night, watching the sunset out of his upstairs apartment window, Vince Thompson was leaning toward the latter.

The
Trouble
with
Liza
Hatter

On the evening before his college graduation, Tristan Mackey walked into the campus library, probably with the notion of trying to steal or deface a book or two—he couldn't seem to remember exactly now, but probably to do something of the sort, something to make him feel more like *himself* and less like the other self, the one that seemed like a version of Tristan borrowed by other people in order to suit their own purposes. At any rate, he was bent on making some sort of trouble, probably because he was a little drunk already, and the library, because it was quiet and secret, offered the sort of trouble he seemed to be looking for, which was quiet and secret trouble, the kind of trouble that would only be known to himself, that would have no consequences outside of his own head, that wouldn't keep him from graduating.

The trouble he found there was Liza Hatter, a girl from his political science class. He found her in the second-floor reading area, wearing shorts and a sleeveless top that showed her long limbs to advantage, thumbing through the latest issue of *Lucky* magazine, bored, killing time, her flip-flop sandals clicking softly on the floor. Liza Hatter had a thing for him, Tristan happened to know, in the same way he almost always knew, was almost never wrong, almost never made a false move or assumption when it came to love, or sex, or however you wanted to refer to it, as if Tristan cared one way or another, the object generally being the same.

In Liza Hatter's case, it hadn't been difficult at all to figure out, the signs having been there from the first day of spring semester when he walked into the classroom, and readily apparent on the few occasions when he had run across her in the downtown bars of Moscow, Idaho, and readily apparent now, also, here in the library, the darting eyes and flickering lashes and the rising color in the neck and cheeks, particularly noticeable because Liza Hatter had a pale complexion inclined to a ruddiness that matched her auburn hair, and the nervous agitation of the fingers flipping the magazine pages, and the feet shuffling constantly in the sandals. Tristan had long ago noticed the signs, but he had up to now filed Liza Hatter away for future reference, labeled her as a girl who would do in a pinch, never feeling any urgency in connection with her due to a) her obvious and therefore not very interesting availability, as it was always more gratifying to have to wade through a layer of subtle oppositions to get to the ultimate goal, and b) the fact that, from Tristan's perspective, she lacked the one quality he valued most highly in the opposite sex, that being a pretty face. She was no dog, certainly, and in fact her high cheekbones and widely spaced greenish eyes and rather full lips and her svelteness and her prodigious height—she was easily five-ten, almost as tall as Tristan—qualified her as *hot*, a term that Tristan detested but also knew applied in this case, at least where other guys would be concerned. But not so much for Tristan, who found her looks a bit over-refined, a bit cold and aloof, very similar in fact to the pictures of the women in the magazine she thumbed through, and none of the women in the pictures met with his particular approval. No, he'd rather have a good, buxom country girl any day, which was a good thing when you'd grown up in Idaho, where there were plenty available. But as noted, the shorts and blouse Liza Hatter wore in the library accentuated the positive, and there wasn't any other action around at the moment, the idea of stealing or defacing books having receded all of a sudden, and Tristan was definitely in a pinch.

He had moved out of his apartment in Moscow the week before, back to Garnet Lake, where he was renting a duplex with money he'd inherited from his grandfather, who, in Tristan's view, had been a lunatic, full all the way up to his white hairline with patriotic zeal and religious nonsense, but who had also been filthy rich and very kind to him, so that he felt badly in his less charitable moments toward him. But now he was back in Moscow for one night only, by himself, having talked his parents and his two older sisters out of coming down for his graduation by threatening not to walk in the ceremony if they attended, claiming it was a waste of time and effort on their part, but for no better reason really than that he hoped to get laid one more time in Moscow before returning to his home-town, where the selection of women was more limited and less interesting, although he hadn't entirely admitted his motives to himself. But with the apartment unavailable, the apartment in which he'd had sex with so many girls that it had become almost embarrassing, more for the girls themselves than for him, because he had started to feel toward the end that they probably should have known better, he had no place to sleep for the night, and had either to crash in the car, fall back on the hospitality of one friend or another whom he didn't really want to see, or find a girl to shack up with, which was, of course, Plan A. And Liza Hatter was looking like a good candidate.

It had taken virtually no coaxing whatsoever to get her out of the library, where she had come simply to escape the heat, an unusual heat for Idaho in the middle of May, and over to her apartment, where she drank margaritas and he drank beer. And it took only two margaritas to prompt from Liza Hatter the sort of confession that Tristan dreaded hearing—that she had been infatuated with him for months now, and not only that, but her roommates, too, who would both be *so jealous* when they found out, which, as it happened, they never would, or at least Tristan would soon come to hope not.

Liza Hatter had in mind for the evening something she called "nesting," which involved a trip to the grocery store to get more beer and margarita mix, and a trip to the video store to pick up movies. By the time she'd reached the part about "cuddling on the couch" Tristan had begun to grow bored, and he hated boredom more than anything else, probably because it was the state at which he arrived more often than not when he was with other people, because when it came right down to it he didn't find people all that interesting, as they all seemed more or less to have the same kind of thoughts, perform the same sort of actions, very little variation occurring between the experience he had with one person or group of people and the next, and this was disturbing to him, because he was a conscientious person in the large ways and the deep ways if not in the small and everyday, and so wanted to think of himself as someone who tried to be helpful, someone who cared, even while he realized that he wasn't very helpful and usually didn't care, at least not until long after the fact, so that he passed up new opportunities for helping or caring due to his preoccupation with the missed opportunities of yesterday or the month before or last year. Right then, in fact, he was thinking about a girl named Kelly Ashton whom he had slept with last weekend at his parents' lake house and never called afterward, which was more than a little puzzling to Tristan, since he had been in love with Kelly Ashton as far back as junior high. He mulled this one over, this surprising lack of feeling for Kelly Ashton, while Liza Hatter ticked off in an excited voice the potential choices of new releases on DVD, and in thinking of last weekend Tristan's mind got settled on the lake house for some reason, and a potential avenue for escaping his increasing boredom started to take shape, an avenue that seemed to offer the possibility of at least being able to tolerate the several-hour prelude to sex with Liza Hatter, and so he laid out to Liza this plan—grab a twelve-pack and make the three-hour trip to the lake house, spend the night there, come back the next morning for his graduation.

Thirty minutes later they were driving north on Highway 95 out of Moscow. It was from this point on, Tristan decided over and over again in the following weeks, that he had been home free. Of greater concern to him were the meeting at the library, the entry to and exit from her apartment, the stop at the convenience store for beer and snacks, although she hadn't gone inside with him.

Of the trip to Garnet Lake Tristan had very little memory, a not uncommon problem for him since the events of that night, the very last event of which his mind dwelt on obsessively, so that the time following the event and the time preceding the event, the rest of his whole life, in other words, seemed to be shoved aside in either direction, like the waves that constituted a boat's wake, until like those waves they had diffused and disappeared.

He remembered the familiar landscape better than the conversation. He remembered that Liza Hatter had begun to talk, and that he had begun not to listen, because to listen, to really pay attention, would have been to become that other self, the one that smiled and nodded, the one that seemed to be on loan to someone else, the one that had completed his four years of college education, the one that had tried for years to please his parents and succeeded very well in doing so, the one that had made him popular, admired, and envied by virtually everyone he'd been around every day for the last half-dozen years, so that he felt a huge chunk of his life had been used up by this other self on loan to these other people, answering their demands, giving pleasantry for pleasantry, joke for joke, sage advice for the asking, while the self he wanted to be and felt most comfortable with, the self that thought and acted boldly, erratically, somewhat dangerously on certain occasions, was a private self that had not gotten all it asked for, ever, and could seldom go about its business unhindered, and it was that self, there in the car, that tried to shake loose from Liza Hatter's conversation, sought escape through the windows into the woods and the wheat fields, the fireworks stands and the casinos on the reservations, the dusty streets and violent taverns of the reservation towns themselves, and then later, after it had turned dark, into a little game that this self liked to play, and in which Liza Hatter had joined to the best of Tristan's recollection, a game that involved leaving the brights on and drinking from a whiskey bottle, kept always under the seat for this purpose, each time another driver on the lonely highway flashed them, which was often enough that Tristan felt fairly dizzy by the time they pulled off the highway and onto the road to the lake house.

The details of the ten-mile drive from the turnoff to the lake house at Garfield Bay presented themselves to Tristan's memory more clearly, as if in moving closer to the event things became sharper due to their proximity, like a kind of foreshadowing, or maybe just the opposite, that the event itself in its startling vividness had shone a light backward over the preceding hour. Even now, warming up for dart night at the 321, thinking about how Russell Harmon had been in the john for such a long time and what sort of drugs he had in his possession and whether he might be willing to share, because something like that might help him relax, he could recall the sight of the lake that night as they drove, visible through the cedar trees, sparkling with moonlight. He could recall also how the night had turned colder, how the wind curled in through the open window and helped to sober him as he took the winding turns, how from the stereo Mick Jagger had sneered his way through "Midnight Rambler." And he could recall the conversation then, too, or not so much his own words, if there had been any, but Liza Hatter spilling out her life to him as she had been for the last three hours, poor dizzy Liza Hatter, dumber than a post, dumber even than Russell Harmon with his dart league and his score sheets and his puffed-up pride in his trivial abilities.

Liza Hatter, he recalled, had talked for several minutes about her plans to switch her major to veterinary science. She had already begun to take courses in preparation for the switch, and although she was sure she'd made the right decision because *she just loved animals so much*, she had been disturbed by a class in which her professor dissected a dog, and Tristan hadn't felt much but disdain for her at the time, disdain for her squeamishness at the opening of the sternum and the examination of the viscera, disdain for her sentimentality and lack of professional rigor, for her teary-eyed assertion that "this was someone's best friend, this was once someone's little puppy." It seemed pretty nigh hopeless for Liza Hatter ever to become a veterinarian, but he allowed her to believe in his sympathy and understanding even while he was starting to hate her a little. And yet this conversation came back to him now daily, hourly, with a kind of poignant irony.

They arrived at the lake house. They carried their things inside. He searched through his parents' CD collection, which wasn't much to shout about, and put a Ray Charles disc in the player, the old Ray Charles stuff from the time when he still wrote his own songs and hadn't yet become a clown. He showed her around the house, listened to her *ooh* and *aah* at the view of the lake from the tall windows, a view that he could have appreciated more himself if he'd been in the house alone. They sat out on the deck and drank beer and Liza Hatter scooted in close to him and kissed him and he lit a cigarette, because he didn't want to kiss her then, was still finding her slightly repugnant, even despite the perfume she'd dabbed on in the upstairs bathroom.

It was her idea to go skinny-dipping. He agreed reluctantly, bored, bored, bored with the predictability of the suggestion but agreeing to play along, and preparing himself already for the iciness of the water at this time of year, an iciness that he knew would surprise her and probably send her swimming frantically back to the dock as soon as she dived in, so that he could escape for a few minutes and swim out into the lake alone.

They stripped at the end of the dock. The moon was almost new, and even with the lights shining down on them from the house there was a swarm of stars. To left and right were the rocky cliffs of the cove, the pine trees rising up and up in the night air, whispering faintly in accompaniment to the music from the house. They were entirely alone, he and Liza Hatter, he had to keep reminding himself of that these days, that there were no houses close enough for anyone to see or hear. Liza Hatter stood before him naked, as if she were backlit on a thrust stage. The long legs, the auburn hair, the coy smile, the soft and rather dainty breasts, the thin line of dark pubic hair—again he found something unsatisfying about her looks, and wished he'd had the patience to wait around longer for someone else.

"You know what I like about you?" she said.

He told her no, he didn't.

"You're so calm and quiet," she said. "It makes me feel safe."

And that pleased him, because he had cultivated for a long time a calm and quiet outward appearance, all the way back to art class in junior high school when he sat next to Kelly Ashton, quiet then because he was too shy to talk and not much worth looking at, an exceedingly skinny kid with a mouthful of metal braces and a fairly bad case of acne, and Kelly Ashton had told him much the same thing one day that Liza Hatter had just told him now, that she liked how he was confident enough not to have to make noise all the time like the other guys, and right then he had decided that, if Kelly Ashton liked it, this calm and quiet thing was worth looking into, especially since he had the quiet part down already and could master the calm part over time.

So he was feeling a little more kindly toward Liza Hatter as he ambled toward the dock, unselfconscious of his body because he knew women liked it, and dove easily into the water, counting away the freezing seconds as he went underneath, saying to himself *a thousand one a thousand two a thousand three* as a way to get through the part where the cold went to the bone and then could start to work its way out again. When his head popped above the surface he heard a splash behind him, and then just seconds later a high squeal and Liza Hatter saying, "Oh my God oh my God, it's freezing," and he smiled, knowing he had been right, that she would retreat as fast as she could to the dock and probably run to the house for a towel. So he went under again, pulling with long strokes against the water, and he started thinking in Spanish, which he did occasionally— *agua fria, agua negra*—and when he came up he let out his breath and shook the hair from his eyes and started swimming in long strokes out into the lake, thinking *lago oscuro, una noche de estrellas.*

He could not recall hearing anything as he swam, nothing other than his own sounds and the music still audible over the water, Ray Charles singing faintly "A Fool for You," and he allowed himself to enjoy the thin sliver of moon high in the sky and the way it was reflected in the tiny waves always just ahead of him, and he thought he could go on swimming like this for hours, though he was already numb under the water.

Then he heard her say, "Tristan." And he heard her actually laugh a little, a nervous laugh, a shy laugh, as if she realized she'd been caught doing something stupid. He turned to her in the water, saw she had followed him all the way out, was maybe fifty feet or so behind him, the dock and the house a long way back, the cliffs of the cove actually closer on either side, he noticed quickly, because he knew what was wrong even before she said so, was already calculating the difficulty of paddling to the rocky bank with her arms around his neck. "Tristan," she said again, with a desperate edge to her voice this time. "Tristan, I'm out too far. I can't feel my legs."

And quietly, calmly, he began swimming back to her. He came closer, closer, close enough to see her now clearly, and when he was within several feet of her, he stopped. He could see her try to come toward him, but she managed only a kind of rough, jerking motion, and she went in up to her forehead and then lifted her face again, choking and coughing. She managed to say the word once more—"Tristan?"—the last thing she ever said to him. He was perhaps two arm-lengths away, treading water, watching her intently. Because something had happened to her face. The moonlight shone on her directly, and he could see the water in her dark hair and on her cheeks, and her mouth opened and closed in little gasps. Her green eyes were huge, almost glowing. In the black irises, he could see the white crescent of the moon. Very pretty, he thought. He could even love her, maybe, if she looked that way all the time. But then she went under the water, softly, and did not come up again.

Standing back on the dock, naked under the stars and shivering, he could still see her pretty face almost perfectly, as if it hovered near the moon.

An Intellectual Conversation

In the truck Russell Harmon slid in his Led Zeppelin CD, hoping that would impress Tristan, who was, after all, even if he was trying to hook up with Kelly Ashton right under Russell's nose, the coolest guy Russell knew. At least that was what everybody in town seemed to think. Russell skipped tracks to his favorite song and heard the familiar dirge-like opening while he slipped the bindle from his pocket, and he wasn't sure what the hell instrument those guys were playing, but it sure did sound fucking great.

"'Kashmir,'" Tristan said, his head nodding slightly, his lips kind of screwed up to one side. "A classic, of sorts."

Of sorts. What the fuck did *that* mean? Russell unlatched the window to the canopy and felt around back there until he had hold of the mirror. He shook out most of the blow from the bindle and chopped it up with his maxed-out credit card and severed it into two long lines and handed the mirror to Tristan and pulled a ten from his wallet and passed that to Tristan, too, holding everything low and scanning the street and the parking lot for cops.

Tristan held the mirror on his lap and the bill in his hand and didn't move. "To tell you the truth," he said, "I've never done this before."

This confession surprised and pleased Russell. He took a certain pride in introducing people to this, his new hobby, but he hadn't expected to have the pleasure with Tristan. So now, in an almost avuncular fashion, he instructed Tristan to roll up the bill and hold the mirror up with his knees, take half the line up one nostril and then switch to the other, wipe his finger across the mirror and run it along his gum line when he was through.

Before Tristan passed the mirror over, Russell had a chance to inspect the world outside the windshield again, and he wasn't so much looking for cops, he realized, as he was looking for Kelly Ashton, and as a dark-haired woman passed by on the sidewalk his heart did a little hop, skip, and jump, and he wasn't sure whether that meant he had hoped the woman was Kelly Ashton (it wasn't) or hoped the woman was not Kelly Ashton. On the one hand, if it were Kelly Ashton leaving the bar, that would mean, first, that she wouldn't be around to watch him shoot darts against Brice Habersham, and that would be a good thing, he supposed, because he couldn't quite not think about her as he stood at the line, couldn't quite not imagine what he looked like to her from her place at the table. But wouldn't it be nice to have her there if he won? If she understood the significance of his beating Brice Habersham, that is? But he definitely couldn't beat Brice Habersham if he kept shooting the way he had in the doubles match, with that awful tight feeling in his arms and that constriction in his chest, and maybe Kelly Ashton had been partly responsible for that. And so yes, he thought, a little wave of fear and anxiety taking him at the realization that, soon now, he would have to go back in there and play Brice Habersham again, this time *mano a mano*, with the singles championship at stake and maybe the team championship, too (although that seemed less likely, Matt and James were probably in there right now putting the finishing touches on the second doubles game, which would mean the Monsters had to win three of four singles matches to tie the match overall, which was impossible given the fact that the other guys on Brice Habersham's team were what amounted to dart retards, so that the team thing really wasn't a factor), it *would* be a good thing if Kelly Ashton weren't there. And, also, if she left the bar now and went home, it would mean she hadn't cared enough about talking to Tristan to wait around. But wouldn't it also mean she didn't care enough about the possibility of talking to *him*?

Russell cut down the volume on the tunes—it was a great song, but it sure went on a long time—and took the mirror from Tristan, watching Tristan run his tongue along his upper teeth, listening to him sniff. "How's it treating you?" Russell said.

"Can't tell yet," Tristan said, and the look on his face made Russell laugh his big, jolly laugh, the laugh that made people like him more than they probably would have otherwise.

"Give it a minute or two," Russell said. Tristan didn't say anything. Russell took his line in one swift snort up the right nostril, shut his eyes tight when they started to water, wiped the mirror clean and put it back through the canopy window, got his nose spray out of the jockey box because he'd need it later.

"Mind if I have a smoke before we go back in?" Tristan said.

Russell said sure, and bummed one for himself. He didn't smoke very often, but he could get used to it if he had to. They sat there smoking and not talking and staring out the windows at nothing, more or less. Matt was probably on his singles match by now, which meant that Tristan had to get back inside pretty quick, since he was up next. Russell rarely missed any part of one of the league matches, and he tried to remember why he'd asked Tristan to come out to the parking lot in the first place. Something to do with Kelly Ashton, of course, but what had he hoped to accomplish just by getting Tristan out of the bar for ten or fifteen minutes? It wasn't all that clear.

"You ever think about living somewhere else?" Tristan asked. He blew a steady stream of smoke from his mouth, his head tilted slightly toward the side window, maybe glancing out at Sand Creek and the marina.

"No," Russell said. But actually he had, once. That was back when he was working for the satellite TV company, traveling around the Northwest to put up dishes for hotels and restaurants and other businesses. They had been in Seattle, and the job was installing a huge dish on top of the Bank of America Tower, the tallest building in the city. They worked close to the edge, seventy-six stories above the ground, and Russell was scared to death of the wind, of the almost limitless space he felt around him, the sheer height, the feeling of being so far up in the world. Several times he'd been afraid of blacking out and falling, imagined floating unconscious toward the pavement, dreaming pleasant dreams on the way down, and he had refused the temptation to shut his eyes tight. Only after they'd finished the job had he been able to relax and breathe. He wiped the cold sweat from his forehead and felt the crisp air go in and out of his lungs and suddenly found himself calmly looking around. He was on top of everything. All the buildings of the city stretched out below him, moving far away and up and down the hills, and there was a ferry out in the Sound, and Mount Rainier high and proud in the haze, and the Space Needle, miraculously, somewhere down below. And he thought for a moment that it was a hell of a city, and that one day he might like to live there. But fifteen minutes later, drinking his first beer at a bar down the street, he'd already forgotten all about it, and he hadn't remembered until just now, when Tristan had asked. "Or not really," he said. "Why?"

"Just wondering," Tristan said. He dragged on his cigarette and flicked the ash out the window, still not looking at Russell. "What do you plan to do here, I mean. You going to work for Matt your whole life?"

"Fuck no," Russell said. "Logging's bullshit." He took a deep puff on his smoke and held it in, feeling his head buzz pleasantly. He should definitely take up smoking. It went very well with cocaine. "Die fucking young out in the woods, man. Dangerous shit."

"Why do you do it, then?"

Russell shrugged. "Job's a job." What he meant was it was the only job he hadn't been fired from. "Pretty soon I'm gonna be working out at Evergreen. Good benefits. Work four tens, get Fridays off. None of this Friday-morning-work-with-a-hangover shit." A couple weeks before, he'd gone and talked to a guy he knew out at Evergreen Lighting Designs, a place where they made expensive wooden lights for landscaping, but no one had called him yet and, to tell the truth, he had been just as afraid of the band saws and the jointers as he was of the chain saw and the skidder. When he was walking out of the building, the hum of the saw still reaching his ears in the parking lot, he had thought it was time to admit, maybe, that he just wasn't very mechanically inclined, and it might be a better idea to sign up for an Internet course in business administration.

Tristan stared at the dash, his jaw clenched. He was feeling the coke now, Russell knew. "So that's it?" he said. "Russell Harmon, guy who makes lights for peoples' circular driveways? You're happy with that?"

"Sure," Russell said. "Why not?" He tossed the question out casually, or that word that meant you weren't really expecting an answer, but then he wondered if maybe there *should* be an answer, an answer from Tristan, a smart guy who'd graduated from college with a degree in what was it, some kind of foreign language. But Tristan didn't say anything. "What about you?" Russell asked.

Tristan laughed through his teeth, kind of a hiss. He sat up straight in his seat and looked at Russell for the first time in about five minutes. "I don't know," he said. "I've been thinking about hanging around here a bit longer."

"And doing what?" Russell asked.

Tristan shrugged. "I don't know," he said. "Nothing. At least not until I have to."

That made sense to Russell, since it had basically been his own philosophy for quite a while now. It was enjoyable to have this sort of discussion with Tristan Mackey, to figure out areas where they saw eye to eye. Still, he had a hard time seeing Tristan with his ass parked in Garnet Lake, Idaho. It was Russell's impression that Tristan was meant to do unusual things in places that Russell had never heard of. "But if you *were* going to do something," he said, "what would it be?"

"Around here?" Tristan asked.

"Anywhere."

Tristan tossed his cigarette butt out the window. "Could do a lot of things. Go to South America and teach. Join the Peace Corps. Go to graduate school."

Russell nodded eagerly, as if he understood all this. "Fuckin' A, man," he said. "Sounds like a plan." But then he figured he'd better shut up. South America—that was the country down below Mexico, or a *continent,* it was. It had countries *in* it, Brazil and Argentina and a couple other ones, and lots of trees and one of those really big rivers, like one of the big three, *los tres riveros humungos,* the Amazon or the Nile or the Mississippi, but not the Mississippi. Tigris-Euphrates—he remembered that from social studies, but what was it? Did it have something to do with South America? Better not ask. And the Peace Corps—that was where they sent you to Africa to feed the starving kids. It was like the army, only without guns. He'd talked to a girl once, in a bar in Boise, whose parents were in the Peace Corps while she was growing up. She told him they ate roasted beetles for snacks. He'd fucked her, too, that same night at his friend Rick's apartment on the hide-a-bed. She was wild, he remembered, like she still had some Africa in her. Graduate school—that was where you went to learn how to be a professor. That much he knew. "But hey," he said, "it's a good thing you're around now." He smacked Tristan on the thigh with the back of his hand. "Good to have you on the dart team. Thanks for making up those score sheets."

Tristan sighed, and then sat there looking out the windshield with his lips puckered, blowing out air. "Russell, Russell, Russell," he said. He combed his hair back with one hand. "I could tell you some shit."

About what, Russell thought. The score sheets? It looked like more than that, and Russell didn't really want to know. That was the thing about smart people—they always had shit on their minds, and whatever it turned out to be never made much sense to Russell. Kelly Ashton had been like that, sort of, Russell remembered. One morning after she'd stayed at his apartment, probably before she got up from bed to start burning the pancakes, she'd started talking to him about what was the meaning of life and was there a God or whatever, and he'd had to try really hard to just keep nodding his head like he was agreeing with her all the time and not fall back asleep. The thing was, though, he liked smart people for some reason, and he was always hoping he'd get better at this shit someday, at having these kind of intellectual conversations, but he usually just found himself nodding his head—it seemed like the safe thing. So that's what Russell did now—sat in the seat and nodded his head, and he could feel Tristan looking at him, so he kept his gaze fixed to the windshield. "Yep," he said after a while, still nodding. "Definitely some shit to tell." He started to open the door. "We better get back inside."

Tristan tilted his head up slightly. "Can we do another one of those first?" he said.

Russell laughed his big, jolly laugh and reached in the back for the mirror and started unfolding the bindle. They were going to be better friends from now on, he and Tristan. Russell could tell.

Goddamn Clouds, Fucking Rain

Vince Thompson had a beer and looked at porn on the Internet and listened to the Velvet Underground and afterward lay down on the bed and jerked off and took a shower and put on his asshole father's old camouflage pants and a long T-shirt and slipped the 9mm Beretta into a side pocket and a hunting knife into the sheath on his belt and three bindles of coke into the secret hip pocket in case anybody wanted to purchase anything. Then he headed down the stairs and out into the evening. Goddamn rain clouds on the horizon to the west, big fucking massive things that looked like they'd picked up the whole goddamn ocean and were prepared to dump it on him, Vince Thompson, specifically. He'd never seen clouds so tall, tall as fucking death, man, like the grim reaper dressed up and coming over the hills, and even at this distance you could see the fucking lightning rippling in sheets, Mother Nature was ready to make some shit go down, so he'd better take the car. It was a weird deal when you thought of it, making decisions like that based on the fucking weather, take the car or no, when you were getting ready to shoot someone in the head maybe, maybe not, depending. Depending on what, though? He'd figure it out when the time came, he thought, getting into the car, clearing the shit out of the passenger seat, the couple of beer cans and the copy of *Spin* magazine and the month-old *USA Today* and the flier from the new pizza delivery place that they'd stuck on his goddamn windshield while he was at the fucking bar and there hadn't been a trash can around, go figure, and he didn't like to litter and shit if he didn't have to, what with the hole in the ozone layer and that goddamn garbage scow from New York twenty years or so ago that couldn't find a place to dump its load, he figured it was the least he could do, not litter, to help the world on its merry fucking way, but cleaning off the passenger seat right now because why, because he was thinking maybe he'd force Russell Harmon at gunpoint into the car and drive him out to the middle of fucking nowhere and waste his fucking ass and he didn't want to inconvenience him by having fucking trash on the seat? He was being goddamn *polite*? Whatever. He tossed the shit in the backseat and cranked the car, pumping the accelerator because his goddamn battery was starting to go, goddammit, what a fucking car to have to make an escape in, Jesus Christ, what would he do, shoot the motherfucker and then stop at the service station on the way out of town? Fuck it though, the car would start, and if not he had jumper cables. The thing to do was to stay rational here, he hadn't thought this out all that well, he could just leave all his shit at the apartment, the clothes and computer and stuff and even the guns, he didn't care, but all the CDs and the records and the stereo, that fucking hurt, no lie, but if he left it all everyone would think he was dead, he'd decided this much, because anyone who knew Vince fucking Thompson would know he'd die before he'd leave all his

music, so it was a sacrifice he was going to have to make, goddammit all to hell, and what the fuck, he had forty thousand
dollars in a box at his goddamn parents' house to buy more
music with, he'd have to go and get the box afterward, it would
be late and he could slip in the back door and be real quiet and
no one would know, but Jesus Christ beyond that he hadn't
given the goddamn thing much thought, he was letting his
anger get the best of him again, anger at this dude Russell
Harmon who, well, let's be honest, he had thought of as a
friend at one point, and this friend had fucked him, used him,
sat around his apartment and talked to him about shit, about
everything under the sun and moon, really, or Vince had done
the talking mostly while this Russell Harmon sat there with the
shit-eating grin on his face saying *fucking right, man*, etc., *that's
some serious shit, man*, etc., snorting lines off Vince's goddamn
rickety kitchen table. All right, all right, but it didn't have to be
right *now*, did it, not *tonight* that he'd jack the dude, but he'd
been telling himself the same thing every night for a month,
not *tonight*, not *tonight*, and the thing to do was to have some
balls, be a man, show people what it meant to fuck with Vince
fucking Thompson, because if he shot the motherfucker he
could choose his own time to get the fuck out of town, whereas
if he waited around long enough for Russell Harmon to get all
chickenshit and go to the police he'd never see it coming when
it came and there wouldn't be any time to hit the road, just the
knock on the door, the fucking warrant, the fucking Miranda
rights and what have you, so OK, OK, staying rational was the
thing, but it was fucking hard with this shit about the apartment eviction was what it amounted to and fucking Fred getting all gung ho, all Mafioso or some shit, Mr. Big-Ass Drug

Lord Kingpin, and his goddamn father the asshole who should have helped him more, helped him get his shit straightened out but wouldn't even fucking *talk* to him these days, all right, all right, stay calm, Vince Thompson thought to himself as he drove two blocks down Cedar Street toward the center of town. Russell Harmon, the dumbshit, would be at the 321 playing darts, that much he knew, that the goddamn penis-head freak wouldn't even know enough not to show up as advertised by the dart league schedule Vince had seen in the window the other day. So that was where to go ultimately, OK, but maybe the thing to do first was stop into PJ's for a drink, sit down, have a fucking drink or two, get *rational*, goddammit, because why, all of a sudden, was it so hard to *think*. It might actually be a good idea, when you thought of it, to dip into the stash, open a bindle, because you would get that kind of heightened concentration that would at least make things fucking *clear* for a goddamn *while*, but no, he'd given that up, it didn't lead anywhere good and you couldn't make any money that way Vince Thompson had discovered a long time ago. A couple of drinks, then, at PJ's, and some time to get things straight. So he saw a parking space on the other side of the street and whipped over there in front of oncoming traffic with the drivers honking at him and shit, like *Oh my God, there's an insane person*, the fucking weenies, and he went ahead and parked pointing the wrong fucking way because fuck 'em if they can't take a joke, and he got out and looked up at the goddamn clouds again, big and black as a fucking old-time freight train, goddamn puffing and puffing, maybe an hour or so away, tops, and he walked into PJ's hitching up his asshole father's camouflage pants because they were after all too big for him blah blah, go ahead and admit it, his father the big fucking muscle man whose pants Vince could never fill, fine, whatever, and *there was his goddamn father sitting there*, what were the chances, pretty fucking good, actually, he knew that, but sitting with of all people Clint Harmon, Russell fucking Harmon's dad, who he was friends with because Russell Harmon's dad, Clint fucking Harmon, was a veteran of the "Gulf War," which in Vince's estimation wasn't much of a goddamn war at all but was apparently enough to make his father and Clint fucking Harmon, who was only a few years older than Vince, drinking buddies. This meant trouble, no fucking doubt. But OK, check the Beretta in the pocket, give it a little pat, sit down and have a drink or two, think, think, think, and ignore the motherfuckers, his goddamn asshole father who saw him come in and couldn't even be bothered to glance more than a second or two. Order a Jack and Coke, lift it off the bar and make a toast, say, "Workers of the Fucking World Unite!" sitting all by himself with the fucking bartender, Gus, looking at him wary, just because he'd had an argument with some college-educated tourist shithead last time he'd come in about George W. asshole Bush and the motherfucking Iraqis and Palestinians and Israelis and the goddamn UN and the fucking Democrats and the asshole motherfucking U.S. military and this college-educated dude getting all whiny and shit, *You're self-contradictory, you're self-contradictory, you're contradicting yourself all over the place and I can't talk to you anymore,* and Vince Thompson had taken a bite out of his beer glass and spit it at the dude and all hell had broken loose, whatever, with the guy going *He's totally out of his mind* and shit. And then another Jack and Coke and lift it high above the bar with his motherfucking father there trying to ignore him, trying to talk to Clint fucking Harmon about their goddamn bowling league, this Clint fucking Harmon who didn't even have the decency to raise his own kid, even barely acknowledge his own fucking kid, ran away like a chickenshit when he knocked up Russell Harmon's mother, which Vince Thompson knew because Russell Harmon had done some talking, too, right, that was why Vince made the mistake of thinking they were friends, so he knew about Clint fucking Harmon who had been just a few years ahead of him in high school, knew about him in a way he didn't know about the other asshole fathers his own age whose children showed up at his door to buy drugs from him, motherfucking Vince Thompson, because even though he knew, I shit you not, some of them just by sight, just by the goddamn family resemblance, they were all—except Russell Harmon, who had actually hung out with him, hadn't he, because maybe he fucking wanted to a little bit—they were all like *Cool, dude, thanks for hooking me up* and shit, *This is my friend so-and-so*, and then friend so-and-so showing up next week on his own, saying *Cool, dude, thanks for hooking me up*, cycle, cycle, cycle, fucking cycle, the same shit over and over, so that after a while he'd started pulling out the fucking guns and shit just for variety's sake, just to throw a fucking scare into the motherfuckers like that goddamn Matt, Russell Harmon's friend who'd shown up a couple times when Russell didn't know it. Fuck it, raise the glass and look right at that asshole son-of-a-bitch father and say, "Chairman Mao! Nikita Kruschev!"—why not, and then after a while another Jack and Coke, and raise the glass and say, "Ronald Reagan takes it up the ass from fucking Jesse Jackson!" and oh yeah, he'd hit a nerve there, there was the goddamn military asshole father unit out of his seat all puffed up and coming at Vince, *You're just a lousy piece of shit* and whatever, and Vince not even stopping to think, goddammit, there still hadn't been a goddamn second to *think* about all this shit like the Beretta in his pocket and the plan to jack this Russell Harmon dude, he needed to *think* for one goddamn second if that was possible, but stepping up right off the bat and getting ready to plow the old man with a wicked right-hand cross, only Clint fucking Harmon, mister tough guy in his muscle shirt— how old was this dude anyway, like sixteen did he think he was with his muscle shirt and his gym shorts and shit?—this Clint fucking Harmon dude stopped him, and he didn't even see it coming because as mentioned before about the goddamn eye thing, and *wham!* there came stars dancing and motherfucking shit and Vince was sitting on the floor, laughing and shit, and then he got up and did this karate thing like you see on TV, like saying *hee-yaw* and *ah-so* and waving his hands around and *wham!* there it came again, and sitting on the floor this time with blood coming somewhere from his face and he heard the old man saying *That's enough, that's enough, it's all right, he's not going to do anything to me, all right*, etc., he's just a mess, and then Vince fucking crying because the old fucking man didn't know this might be the last time they'd ever see each other, but still getting up and raising his fist like to hit him, but then thinking the old man looked too goddamn old now, didn't he, he'd never noticed before, all wrinkled and shit, too old to beat up and Vince wanting to hug him instead, say *Dad, Dad*, and shit, motherfucker he needed some space to *think*, but Clint fucking Harmon hustling him out the side door into the alley, and him, Vince, saying *Asshole cocksucker, you didn't even have the guts to take care of your kid, be a fucking man*, etc., thinking of Russell Harmon and how they'd sat there sometimes in his apartment and watched football on TV, and how this goddamn Clint fucking Harmon wouldn't even acknowledge his own son and how maybe Russell Harmon *needed* someone to acknowledge him before he got shot in the fucking head, and then blood, blood, blood, he was getting the shit kicked out of him for real now back in the alley by some dickhead forty-five-year-old muscle man who obviously thought he was still in high school, and Vince Thompson told him these things while he was being beaten. And then it was raining. And then he was walking down the street, holding his head up to the mother-fucking hard rain, hoping it would wash his face clean. And then he was outside the 321 with the lightning coming down, and there was Russell fucking Harmon trying to make a run across the parking lot from his truck with that Tristan dude he'd met once at the record store and the Tristan dude knew a lot about music but if he knew what was good for him now, because Vince Thompson was tired of this shit, he'd better get the fuck out of the way, which he did, running on into the bar out of the rain, not seeing Russell fucking Harmon stopped dead in his tracks behind him, looking wide-eyed and shit at Vince Thompson, whose head hurt, who had no idea what he looked like standing there with the blood and whatnot. But he did know this, or suspected it—that Russell Harmon would be just fucking stupid enough to come on into the bar and play his fucking dart game even if Vince was there, even if the hand of motherfucking God was about to smite him right in the side of his goofy goddamn head, so Vince Thompson decided he might as well go inside and get out of the fucking rain.

And
All
the
Stars
That
Never
Were

Above Hayley's crib was the sign, black magic marker on white poster board, *The fault, dear Brutus, lies not in our stars but in ourselves, that we are underlings.*

In sophomore English class, Kelly Ashton, along with the rest of the students, had been forced to memorize and recite lines from *Julius Caesar.* Her own lines had been the entirety of the *I come to bury Caesar, not to praise him* speech, which she hadn't paid much attention to, and had delivered in a monotone that reflected the desperate chore of remembering all the words. The other kids were the same. As they recited their lines one by one she began to fall asleep. There was some excitement when Russell Harmon, whose only role in sophomore English had been to provide comic relief, attempted to disrupt some other kid's speech, sitting in the back of the room with a spiral notebook wire shoved up his nose to make the kid laugh, but the kid didn't laugh and when Russell Harmon tried to get the wire out of his nose he couldn't, twisting the pointed end into his skin so that he had to be led, bleeding, down to the nurse's office. But after that the dull routine reestablished itself. Then Tristan Mackey got up with his partner, a kid named Boyd who labored through his lines like he was digging them up with a shovel. But when Tristan Mackey spoke she began to wake up. He wasn't remembering, he wasn't reciting, he wasn't trying out a British accent like some of the more ambitious ones. He was just *saying*, just *talking*, and she leaned forward at her desk and rested her chin on her hands and started to listen, and all of a sudden Shakespeare started making some kind of *sense* to her, because Tristan Mackey was *good*. And then at one point he looked at Brutus, this kid Boyd whose nose was pointed to the ground, whose face was beet red, and Tristan Mackey let out a long sigh and his eyes went to the window, to the melting icicles dripping along the roofline and the slushy snow out in the street, the sparkling of the snow in the bright morning sun, and for a second she could hear truck tires hissing down the road and she could hear the radiator at the back of the classroom ping, and then Tristan Mackey said as naturally as if he were talking about the weather or what he was going to do after school, "The fault, dear Brutus, lies not in our stars but in ourselves, that we are underlings." And her eyes filled with tears and she pressed them hard against the knuckles of her thumbs. And that night in bed she opened her English textbook and by the light of the bedside lamp, hearing on some level the dog scratching at her door and her mother cackling in the next room at something on TV, she read the words over and over, and she understood in a deeper way than she'd ever understood anything before what it was that Tristan Mackey, not William Shakespeare, meant: that it was up to them, to

Tristan and to her and to Boyd if he could pull his head out of his ass, and to Russell Harmon down in the nurse's office with a wire stuck up his nose, and to anybody else who might be alive enough to listen, to find their own way to get the fuck out of this life, get the fuck out of this town, get to a place of their own devising where there wasn't any fate and there wasn't any God and there was only a clear, clean space above it all, a breath you could take and a windowpane you could look through to a world where everything below, everything boring and stupid and sad, melted away.

And so when Hayley was born, when it looked to everyone around Kelly Ashton—her drunk mother and her brainless friends and her boyfriend, Aaron, who had already stuck around longer than he had any reason to and whom for that reason she could no longer respect, and to Russell Harmon no doubt if he even knew anything about it, and to Tristan Mackey too if there was anyone to tell him down there at college—like she was stuck in this town forever and she was never going to do anything with her life and would just stay there and drink too much and lose her looks like her mother, she wrote out the words in black magic marker and taped them above the crib.

And so tonight, as always, she read the words, and she changed Hayley's diaper, thinking how, soon, Hayley would be in the Pull-Ups, and telling her so, saying *Big girl, big girl,* and tickling her tummy. Then she dressed Hayley in her pj's and transferred her to the playpen, banging her knee on the bed frame in the crowded room for the thousandth time as she did so, and then to make sure Hayley was happy in there, she squeezed the squeezy doll several times until Hayley got interested and started doing it herself, sitting there in the playpen with her blond hair dangling in her eyes. She put the picture books in there carefully too, leaving them open to the pages Hayley liked so they would get her attention when she tired of the squeezy doll, so that she wouldn't start crying before Kelly was safely out the door, because if she did that, if she started crying, if she kept crying, it wouldn't be until after Hayley was safely asleep that Kelly could convince herself to leave. Then, holding her breath, she snuck out of the room, closing the door about halfway, and then real quick went to the refrigerator down the hall in the little apartment, the fucking apartment she'd lived in with her mother since she was fourteen, and mixed up a bottle with the formula, even though Hayley shouldn't need a bottle anymore but then there would be hell to pay come bedtime if not. She had to do it herself because she couldn't trust her mother to do it right—measuring the right amount of formula into the water, shaking it, shaking it, putting it in the fridge. Then checking herself one last time in the bathroom mirror, one last time, running her tongue over the uneven bottom teeth and thinking goddammit at her mother for never getting her braces, and she had to get out the tweezers again because the eyebrows just weren't *even*, not quite, and then her hair, toss it a little this way, lower her chin, look at the eyes, and was this blouse getting too tight on her, could she still wear it, because the bathroom mirror wasn't any good for seeing that and she didn't dare go back down the hall to the bedroom. She could hear Hayley talking in there—*Sam I am, green eggs and ham.* She'd better get the hell out quick if she was ever going at all, so she explained everything to her mother one more time, her mother there in the easy chair with the Coors Light next to her on the table, like some drunk old man, was she sure she knew the cell phone number, did she understand that the bottle was already made up in the fridge, did she know when bedtime was, would she make sure to take Hayley out of the playpen in no longer than half an hour, tops, and was she going to *stop after this beer*, mother, *this* one, not the next one and not the one after that, all right she didn't have time to argue, she would call to check on Hayley soon. She opened the apartment door and stepped out onto the landing in the warm summer dusk and she took a deep breath and thought *not in our stars but in ourselves*, because there was still time and opportunity to be something bigger than she could be in Garnet Lake, Idaho. She had the looks and brains to make it happen.

She was going downtown to meet Tristan Mackey, who was turning out to be an asshole when you got right down to it, not at all the Tristan Mackey who had liked her all those years, not at all the Tristan Mackey who had created a new world for her that day long ago in English class. He'd fucked her and now he wasn't all that interested. She knew the type, but hadn't pegged him as that particular kind of disappointment. She was angry at herself more than him. It had been a long time since she'd allowed anyone other than herself to get her hopes up. But, so, he'd asked her to a dart match, not a nice restaurant in town, not on an actual *date*, just *maybe she could come to the dart match to drink beer with "the boys,"* as he'd called them condescendingly, too good for them all obviously, whoever they were, but all right, it wasn't too late to show him the mistake he was about to make.

But when she walked into the 321 and looked toward the back of the bar the first person she saw was Russell. Russell, cheerful Russell, good sweet Russell, silly Russell, stupid

Russell, my God what could you do with him and what could you tell him about himself and about who he really was and how would you go about it anyway. Poor Russell whom her heart went out to, who drove up Baldy Mountain with her one time to get a good view of the northern lights even though he really didn't care anything about them, who told her how his father left him, whom she told about how her father left her. Russell was a dead end. Russell was a loser. He was Hayley's father, but that didn't count for much in his case, and she'd never had the heart, or maybe not the necessary lack of common sense, to let him know. But then she hadn't seen him in a long time, either.

Her father had been the manager of a men's clothing store. He dressed, she could still remember, in crisp gray slacks, in a clean white-collared shirt, in a square-shouldered jacket, a blue tie, and he smelled of good cologne. His socks were sorted in a dresser drawer from lightest to darkest. His shoes were on a shoe tree. His face was smooth and his thin blond hair was just so. He was quiet and he smiled a lot and he did the best he could even though he was relatively poor. Then one day when she was ten he had fixed her breakfast and he had laid out her clothes and helped her get ready for school (her mother was never up for that sort of thing), but when they walked out the door to get in the car he was still dressed in his boxer shorts and undershirt. She'd laughed—*Daddy*, your *pants*—and then she'd seen something like terror in his eyes, and after that nothing had ever been the same.

There had been times when he was all right, sure, sometimes months on end when he would get back to the old routine, the socks lined up neatly in the drawer, which she checked whenever he wasn't around, as if it were a medical chart of some kind or the psychology test with the inkblots, and the ties and the neatly pressed suits in the morning, the eggs and bacon cooked just so, the drive to school during which he never exceeded the speed limit, the same comforting words when he dropped her off, the *See you this afternoon, honey*, the *Have a good day*, but then, inevitably, more and more, there would come the day when he went to the grocery store four times to buy bread, the day when he would canvass the neighborhood, go door-to-door asking the neighbors to show him plat maps of their property lines, even the neighbors who were several doors down, the day when he would suddenly exit the house naked to go grab the newspaper, or, once, to adjust the idle on the car. The doctors disagreed—was it the onset of Alzheimer's? A brain tumor? Schizophrenia? Manic depression? He showed up at the doctors' offices dressed perfectly every time, perfectly in control of himself. The CAT scans were negative. He passed all the standard tests. At times Kelly Ashton suspected that it was all a performance of some sort, and it was only when she remembered the look on his face that first time when he stood at the door in his boxer shorts that she could put aside the suspicion.

Then there had been the Saturday when he left the house to go to work, his suit pressed, his tie perfectly even and tight, his socks chosen carefully from the lined-up pairs in the drawer, and did not come home. A Forest Service employee found his car parked along the High Drive, far up in the Cabinet Mountains, and he was never seen again.

Russell Harmon could disappear that way. Or not exactly that way, not in a way that was so complicated and sudden, was more mundane and predictable and slow, but it was something to keep in mind. So she smiled at him only slightly, no matter the feeling she had all of a sudden, the same one she always had when she first laid eyes on Russell, that he needed her protection, no matter the feeling all of a sudden that his simplicity could be a way of protecting her, that what she saw as Russell's simple good nature might be a way out, a way to reconcile herself to living in this town, with Russell and Hayley, forming a pleasant little family that would let her leave behind thoughts of big things and deep things. But she was here now to meet Tristan Mackey, who represented something entirely different, which was genius, which was possibility, which was the stretching of her life beyond the confines of this town out into the greater world, a world in which she had not been very often or for any length of time, but which promised the chance of recognition, of being able to find the self you dreamed of and make the dreamed self and the actual self one and the same. That couldn't happen for her in this town. And so she held out some hope—based on the fact, she knew, that he had been pretty crazy about her at one time—that despite his recent indifference there was still a way to hitch a ride out of here with Tristan Mackey. He was going places, and she could too.

And yet this was nothing more than "dart night." She swore to God, men had no imagination sometimes, not even the smart ones. You couldn't help but be an underling if you didn't even know, or weren't able to keep in mind, that you *had* any stars. So tonight would be to remind him.

And so after sitting at the bar for just a while, really not long enough for Russell to be going to the bathroom twice—Was he doing it to get a look at her? Was he drunk this early? Did he have some sort of medical problem?—she took her glass of merlot and headed to the back, past the Red Hook sign and the framed photos of Garnet Lake in the old days, the muddy streets, the towers of felled timber at the old landing along the lakeshore, the old schoolhouse that had been razed to make room for the commerce park, and she liked the warm glow from the overhead lights hung from the high ceiling and the sound her heels made on the hardwood floor and the view of Sand Creek out the window, and she was glad to discover, because she'd never been in here before, because she'd hardly been to any bars in town, having been saddled by the time of her twenty-first birthday with a baby to nurse and then a full-time job to pay for rent and child care afterward, that at least the place wasn't a total dump. She could forgive Tristan Mackey a little bit.

And there he was, sitting alone with a glass of beer at a little table surrounded by wooden chairs. And there was a moment—too short, but definitely there—between them in which she could tell he was glad to see her. He leaned back in his chair, his eyebrows went up, and a slight grin spread across his face. His eyes went for a second from her tight shirt to her bare legs, but then just as quickly back up to her face, he always looked at her face and she liked him for that, and she remembered then being with him at the lake house, the moment after she'd first undressed, when he'd had a chance for appraisal after wondering all these years, and even then he'd seemed more interested in her eyes. That had been a nice moment, before he'd seemed to drift off, and now there was a nice moment again.

He said hello, she said hi. "It's a good night," he said, whatever that meant. And then he just sat there. He looked out the window. This was both the attractive and the unattractive thing about him, his tendency toward silence. It was nice not to have to say something all the time, just to be able to sit with someone, not have to fill up the space with words. But sometimes you wanted to talk. And when he was quiet it was as if you couldn't say anything, as if you weren't there at all, as if only Tristan were there, Tristan and the world inside his head. He could go away for minutes at a time, so that the only thing that seemed to exist was whatever went on in his head, and you were just a sort of absence waiting to become present again. It was this sense of having vanished that explained why she'd never gone out with him back in high school when he'd been so in love with her—that and the fact that he'd never asked her to.

So this was how it was going to be—hello, hi, it's a good night, stare out the window, start all over again at square one, as if they hadn't been together for the first time just a month and a half ago, as if that shouldn't have meant something or didn't amount to anything after all these years. She wasn't hurt by this, just exasperated. Tomorrow morning she would have to go back to work, drop Hayley off at day care and drive up the mountain to the ski resort, sit at a desk while the summer sun shone out the window and make phone calls, try to sell condos, try to sell family ski passes, try to sell vacation packages, try to convince people in the outside world she longed to go to that they in fact needed to come here, and she would want to scream into the phone *Don't be stupid!* She didn't have time for silence tonight.

But she couldn't think of anything to say. So she looked out the window too, because what was out there was more interesting than the people throwing darts at the dartboard. Out the window were birch trees, and Sand Creek, and boats, one boat with green and red lights on the bow slipping quietly up to a dock right now, the waves gentle behind it like a soft stream of air, and on the other side of the creek the small parking area, and then past that the lights of the city beach, and beyond that, even though you couldn't see it from here in the bar, the lake itself, the reason all these people first came here, the reason there was a town here at all. And then she could see way off in the distance the Cabinet Mountains, black against the fading sky. What if you could just fly off, what if you could just lift yourself up from the table and go right out that window, fly off right above the creek and the beach and high up over the water, sailing through the evening sky with the mountains coming closer, growing bigger, and what if you could soar above the peaks of that range until you found a skeleton in the trees, maybe in the thick brush by a stream, a skeleton wearing a coat and tie, wearing just the right socks to match. Would that accomplish anything? Or what if you could sail on past those mountains, what if there weren't any skeleton at all, what if you could trace where that man had walked over the mountains, where he'd walked into Montana, where he'd grown a mustache maybe and renamed himself Rupert, moved on to Chicago, started a chain of clothing stores, and was waiting right now for something he couldn't put his finger on, the name of something he'd left behind, a daughter he'd somehow forgotten? Would that make a difference?

Out of the corner of her eye she saw Russell, back from the bathroom and approaching the dartboard. And Tristan, she saw, was watching her now. "You get that look on your face," she said to him. "Where *are* you when you're like that?"

"I could ask you the same thing," he said.

Russell was talking to a little man with gold-rimmed glasses. The man took a handkerchief out of his pocket and wiped his forehead. "Maybe," she said. "But I asked you." Russell and the man went over to a table and looked at some sheets and Russell laughed, not his natural laugh, not the one she knew.

"*El hombre que desaparece,*" Tristan said. He picked up the pitcher in front of him and poured himself a glass of beer but didn't take a drink. *El hombre*—the man. But what was that last word? She'd taken two years of Spanish. She should know. Tristan leaned in closer to her, raised his eyes to her, looked like there was something he wanted to say.

"Tristan, you playing darts tonight, or what?" Russell called out. He sounded angry, and Russell was never angry. What was wrong with everyone tonight? Maybe it had something to do with her and maybe it didn't.

"I'm here, *El Capitan*," Tristan said, smiling, still looking at her and not Russell. "Just call me when it's time." He took a drink of beer and set the mug on the table. *Desaparece*—what was it? "Let me ask you something," he said. "Do you want to get out of here?"

Now maybe they were making some progress after all. "Out of this bar, you mean, or out of this town?"

"Either," he said.

"All the time."

"Really?" he said.

Really. Now Russell threw a dart and the man with the glasses threw a dart and then there was some kind of brief discussion and she was afraid any second Tristan would get called away from the table. "All the time," she said. "You don't know what it's like. You've been gone for four years."

"But still—"

"No," she said, "you don't know." She leaned in closer. "Are you saying you want to *stay*?" She didn't mean to sound angry, but if Tristan Mackey thought for one second that he intended to stay in this town, she was going to slap him. If there was one person in her whole life whom she'd ever been sure about, ever known for sure would move on to bigger and better things, it was Tristan. She wanted to make sure he stayed put long enough to get accustomed to having her around, to grow fond of Hayley, to come to think of them as a family, and not a second longer.

"Most of the time I don't even realize I'm here," he said. "It's like I'm not anyplace at all, I mean it's like I'm somewhere in my head but not actually in a physical space." He took up a cigarette pack and a lighter from the table, lit a smoke. *Desaparece.* He sat there smoking for a few seconds, his foot tapping. "Does that make sense?"

"Sort of," she said. "Not really." What else was she supposed to say? He could sit there and stare at her accusingly all he wanted to, but if she didn't get it, she didn't get it. And she wanted him to sound comprehensible.

"I get focused on one thing inside so that I can't see the things outside it," he said, "and then I feel like that one thing inside is the only real thing, and that outside of it I'm not really anyplace."

"OK," she said. "Got it."

"And then there's a night like this. Everybody's just hanging around, and I'm in a pretty good mood and not thinking about a lot of things, and then you come walking in"—he motioned toward her with the cigarette, the cigarette taking in the hair she'd fixed just so, the eyebrows she'd plucked just right, the tight blouse that maybe wasn't too tight after all, the skirt and her legs underneath—"and you look good, and I remember what you're like, and it's like I'm coming up from under the surface somewhere, like I haven't been able for a long time to breathe and look around." He looked down at the floor, took a drag, cleared his throat. "And so, yeah, then it seems like life has possibilities."

All right, so he wanted her to rescue him—a good start on the personal commitment front, if not the emotional and psychological. But she could work with that. She leaned in to say something and then Russell called to him in an irritated tone. "Hold that thought," he said.

And so she did. She wanted to go places and do things, and she had decided that the person to go places and do things with was Tristan Mackey, and even though he sounded a little depressed and not quite like himself tonight, she wasn't going to give up due to some slight trepidation on her part, was she? She should look at it as an opportunity—he was feeling a little low, and she could be the one to raise his spirits. She thought of this while they threw their darts, while she found herself for some reason watching Russell more than Tristan, maybe because there was something wrong with Russell tonight, too, Russell who might be stupid but was always relaxed and easy, never tense, never *intense*, like he seemed to be tonight, but thinking of Tristan, and wondering if she could say to him, maybe say, *Do you remember that time in English class, the time you talked about the stars?* Oh, she'd practiced lines like that, she'd practiced, there in front of the mirror, staring straight ahead, not a single muscle of her body or her face moving, saying lines silently and with no expression, filling the script of a hundred movies simply with the thoughts in her head, a secret performance undertaken in a little room with a fucked-up mother outside the door, a father nowhere to be found, and then when a baby was napping, her baby breathing lightly behind her somewhere in the room, maybe sensing her mother's dreams.

Once she had gone so far as to attend an audition for *My Fair Lady* at the community theater, convinced that she would make the perfect Liza Doolittle. She sat there in a seat in the old converted movie theater, and she said the lines in her head, knowing exactly what they would look like and sound like onstage, but she left before the director called on her, sensing that if she went on that stage and uttered a sound there would be some gap, some violation of the perfect form she imagined, either in her execution or the shabby nature of the whole production itself. Maybe she wasn't destined to do something like that in her life. But every life should be its own drama, and hers, such as it was, thus far had the unhealthy feel of budding tragedy rather than romance. Tristan Mackey could help change that. But could she tell him about all these things? Could she trust him to have enough imagination?

When he came back to the table he had completely forgotten their conversation and simply sat there staring out the window. And then she started thinking to herself how ridiculous it was that she needed anyone at all, a Tristan Mackey or anyone else, to get the hell out of here, but she couldn't do it alone with Hayley, had known that for a long time even though she'd imagined scenes of she and Hayley driving, just the two of them going down the road, just she and Hayley like water flowing out into the whole wide world.

And when Tristan was entirely done with his silly game he came back over to her and sat in the chair but he might as well have been on the moon. His eyes were that far away, that far gone. He didn't even know she was there. "Tonight," he said suddenly, "might be perfect." Perfect for what? He reached in the pack on the table for a cigarette and put the cigarette to his lips and lit it without ever looking at anything. He grimaced for a second, as if he were frustrated at not being quite able to get hold of something. Then his eyes were blank again, and she was sure he didn't even know he'd been speaking to her.

She felt that tingle she'd felt in English class, but not a good tingle this time, not at all. The root, what was the root? *Desapara* . . . *desaparacer*. To *disappear*. Tristan Mackey, the disappearing man. It was true. He'd vanished right before her eyes. She grabbed her purse and headed to the bathroom. Safely inside, the door locked, she fumbled for her cell phone, called home, made her mother get Hayley, made Hayley say, made her say it three times, *Hi momma*, *Hi momma*, *Hi momma*, made Hayley make everything OK, made Hayley make sure that everything at home was the same as it always had been.

Give
Me
Darts
or
Give
Me
Death

So there was Vince Thompson. It was raining like bejeezus, and Russell Harmon wanted to get back inside and get back to his match, to get back to Brice Habersham. But here was Vince Thompson approaching in the rain. And what was more horrifying, what really stopped Russell in his tracks, was that Vince Thompson was *bleeding*. You could see it in the streetlights—the puffed-up face, the black-looking blood from the mouth and nose. And if Vince Thompson was *bleeding*, then that meant he would be *angry*, bleeding and angry, and Russell remembered all the times Vince Thompson had talked about how he would *blow motherfuckers' asses away* and *waste those goddamn pieces of shit*. Russell knew he was one or the other, a piece of shit or a motherfucker, and he could easily be wasted or blown away, right here, right now, on First Street.

So he thought it best, under the circumstances, to stop. He also thought it best to cower, to duck, maybe to run away, but he didn't, possibly because he couldn't seem to get his body to work very well all of a sudden, couldn't seem to find his legs there under his stomach. There went Vince Thompson, bleeding, looking at Russell. There he went toward the door of the 321, and the rain made a rasping noise on the pavement, not much different from the noise that had gone on in Russell's head when he tried to throw darts just a while ago against Brice Habersham. Vince Thompson looking at Russell, Vince Thompson walking and not shooting even though his hands were in his pockets and *Jesus*, he was wearing the camouflage pants, that was a bad sign Russell knew, *that* meant he was in his motherfucking-goddamn-asshole-military-father mode. Vince Thompson appeared to be walking right into the 321, and there was Tristan too, running, getting farther and farther away from Russell, like someone fleeing the scene of a crime, or running directly into it. It was like a math problem, Russell had time enough to think, strangely, since he had never been much interested in math problems before—if Person A, Vince Thompson, walked to the bar at the rate of such and such and Person B, Tristan, Tristan-who-now-owed-Russell-something-because-he-had-snorted-Russell's-cocaine, ran toward the same bar at the rate of so and so, would Person C, Russell Harmon, have time to address a question to Person B, running away in the rain at a certain speed, before Person A killed Person C? "Tristan," Russell shouted. "Could you get Matt to come out here?" And then Tristan disappeared into the bar and then Vince Thompson, still looking at Russell—and was he smiling, shaking his head?—disappeared into the bar, and Russell was alone on the street. And *man* was his heart pounding. And he was getting his ass wet, too.

And he stood there and got his ass wet for a while, it seemed to Russell, and Vince Thompson did not appear in the doorway to shoot him, and so Russell, tentatively, eventually, moved under the awning at the 321's entrance, taking a peek now and then through the front door but never seeing much of anything. Fucking Tristan. Fucking Matt. Russell pictured the two of them in the bathroom snorting up the rest of the bindle he, Russell, had handed Matt, what . . . an hour ago? It seemed like about two days.

There was a flash of light in the sky and then a few seconds later thunder, and the rain began to pelt the awning with even greater intensity. Russell watched the rain hissing down under the streetlights and the wind whipping the birches by the parking lot. Maybe it would be best to just make a run for the truck and go home. He could say he'd gotten sick. They could still win the championship next week if they played up to par. But then what if they didn't? And could he live without knowing if he could beat Brice Habersham? He turned his attention back to the bar. No Vince Thompson anywhere, which meant that he must be at a table back by the dartboard, the only area of the bar not visible from the street. And then he caught sight of Matt, sitting right there on a bar stool talking to Kelly Ashton. Kelly Ashton's back was turned to him, but Russell thought he could see her head turn a little to the right while Matt talked, as if she were looking around for someone else. Him, Russell? Tristan? Probably Tristan. But now wasn't the time to think about that. Trying not to look too much like a fool, he began waving one arm over his head, even jumped up and down a little. He was just about to lean in the door and shout or whistle when Matt looked up suddenly and saw Russell's face almost pressed against the window, and Russell motioned to him frantically to get his ass outside.

Matt excused himself, trying to look suave or some shit, practically *bowing*, for God's sake. Then he came out the door and stood with Russell. "Holy shit," he said, looking at the rain.

"You see him?" Russell asked.

"See who?"

"Vince," Russell said.

"Vince Thompson?"

"Yeah," Russell said.

"No."

Russell craned his neck around to see as much as he could toward the back of the bar. Nothing. "He's in there somewhere."

"I don't think so," Matt said. "I would've seen him."

"I *saw* him go in the door."

They stood and looked in the window together. There was no sign of Vince Thompson anywhere. "So, what does that mean, then?" Matt said.

"The fuck you mean, what does it mean?"

"I mean, does that mean you quit? You gonna get the hell out of here?"

Russell scanned the faces, the backs of heads, leaning close into the window, which was getting speckled now with water coming in through gaps in the awning. Still no sign of Vince Thompson anywhere.

"We lost, by the way," Matt said, stuffing his hands into his jeans pockets.

"*What?*"

"We lost."

"What do you mean, 'we lost'?"

"We lost the doubles."

"You *lost* the doubles?"

"We lost the doubles."

"To those guys?" Russell said. "How?"

"We didn't throw too good," Matt said. He kept looking in the window—at Kelly Ashton, Russell realized now.

"What, you got a thing for her now, too?" Russell asked. "You and Tristan both? No wonder we can't shoot worth shit."

"No," Matt said. "She just looks good. If you're going to look at something, why not look at something that looks good?" He tilted his head up and squinted. "I'm getting wet," he said. He sniffled. "You bring your nose spray?" he said.

Russell dug the nose spray out of the pocket of his baggy shorts and handed it to Matt. Matt turned his back to the window, glanced up and down the street, and took a hit up each nostril.

"You're not wasting all of that, are you?" Russell asked.

"All of what?" Matt said.

"All of what-do-you-think?" Russell said.

"I don't know," Matt said. "'All of what' meaning the coke or 'all of what' meaning the nose spray?"

"The *coke*," Russell said. "Who gives a shit about the nose spray."

"I don't know," Matt said. "I thought you might."

"No," Russell said. "The coke."

"No," Matt said. "There's still plenty." He put the nose spray in the same pocket as the bindle and turned back to the window. A couple of guys Russell recognized vaguely made a run for the bar entrance from across the street and ducked inside. "So what are you gonna do?" Matt asked. "I don't think he'd shoot you right in front of all these people, would he? I mean, he wouldn't just stand up and waste you while you were throwing darts or anything."

"He's bleeding," Russell said.

"He's what?"

"Fucking *bleeding*," Russell said. "From like his nose and his mouth."

Matt turned his head toward Russell. "How do you know?"

"Because I fucking *saw* him," Russell said. "I told you that already. I saw him come right up the street in the fucking rain and his face was covered with blood and he was wearing his camouflage pants."

Matt looked back in the window and started craning his neck like Russell had before. "That's not good," he said.

"No shit," Russell said. "Not good at all."

"He might shoot you if he's wearing the camouflage pants," Matt said.

"And *bleeding*," Russell said.

"And bleeding," Matt said. He looked at Russell for a second, looked at him closely as if he were trying to see him for the first time all over again, maybe. "I don't think I'd go back in there if I were you," he said.

"Aren't you supposed to be playing singles right now?" Russell asked.

"We were waiting for you," Matt said.

"Why?" Russell asked.

Matt shrugged. "You're the captain," he said. "You've always been there before."

Matt would win his singles. There was no way he'd lose to that lame Kurt guy. That would put them up 2-1. But then what if Tristan, or more likely James, lost? Russell's forfeit would mean a tie, which would mean that they'd have to win next week against the second-place team, Big Ed's. If they lost to Big Ed's—which wasn't very likely, but still—that would mean a tie for the championship overall, and in the case of a tie, according to the dart league rules, the championship went to the team that beat the other in head-to-head competition, which would be Big Ed's. If Russell skipped his match with Brice Habersham, he would lose the individual championship, and possibly the team championship, too. And if he ran from Vince Thompson now, what would stop him from just coming after Russell next week? And if he wasn't going to play Brice Habersham, what did he have to look forward to anyway? He didn't have any money, not to speak of, and he hated his job and he wasn't very good at it, and he lived in the basement of his mother's house, and he didn't even have a father, really, not one that would count, and he didn't have a girlfriend, either, and the one girl he'd probably most like to have for a girlfriend was in there now, getting up from her bar stool, he saw, and headed to the back of the bar, probably looking for Tristan Mackey. Russell wiped the rain from his face, his cheeks feeling hot despite the rain, his hand shaking a little bit. If he was going to get shot, he might as well go ahead and get it over with.

"I'm going in," Russell said.

"Your funeral," Matt said, opening the door.

A
Thing
of
Beauty

The night Liza Hatter drowned in Garnet Lake, Tristan Mackey did not dream of her at all. He didn't dream anything that he could remember. In the morning, the lake house was bone cold, and he went out to the woodpile and brought in an armload of cedar to start a crackling fire. He made a pot of coffee. He sat on the couch and put his coffee cup on the table and looked out the picture window at the lake, and it was only then that the fear caught up to him. It was a sunny day, the morning sun dancing on the water. And other than that there was nothing. Everything looked the same as always. But it was as if he could sink beneath the waves, recall his underwater swim of the night before, and underneath the water now he could sense the body of Liza Hatter, as if she were suspended beneath him, rising slowly, ready to tickle his feet. And in imagining her beneath the water he thought of her face, the way she had looked before going under. And it occurred to him that, in some odd way, he missed her already, even though he'd really never known her at all. Liza Hatter—she'd wanted to cuddle, she'd wanted to rent movies, she'd wanted to take a moonlight swim, she'd wanted to be a veterinarian. Liza

Hatter, whose eyes caught the moon as she slipped down into the lake.

He cleaned up, got rid of the evidence that they'd been there. He did it indiscriminately, stupidly, dumping her clothes and her purse into a trash bag without even checking for identification, money, a cell phone, and took the bag to the Dumpsters behind the vacation cottages at Garfield Bay Resort, then drove to his duplex in town, and, feeling heavy and dull, fell asleep again. But he woke very quickly from a half dream, half thought of her body floating ashore. Then he was back in the truck, driving to the lake house as fast as the narrow road along the cliffs would let him, and realizing now that he'd already made one big mistake, that today was his college graduation and he wasn't there, and that that would certainly look suspicious if he were linked in any way to Liza Hatter's disappearance.

But he wasn't. Out at the lake house, there was no body. Over the next few days, there was no visit from the police, no phone call from a roommate or a friend who might have found some evidence of her whereabouts. When an article finally appeared in the Spokane paper, one day short of a week since Liza Hatter had drowned, there was no mention of anyone seeing her with a tall, good-looking, shaggy-haired young man, no mention of her in the passenger seat of a black pickup truck headed north out of town. There were no clues whatsoever. The time of her disappearance had been placed at Thursday afternoon. The last person to report seeing her was a psychology professor, to whom she had turned in a late paper Thursday morning. There was speculation that she might have found a ride to her hometown in southern Idaho for the weekend. A photograph accompanied the article—it showed the Liza Hatter Tristan didn't particularly care for, her features a bit too sculpted, a bit too aloof.

At times fear hit him in a gust. His head spun into some weird orbit, usually when he woke from dreams. Then he would throw on a pair of shorts and a T-shirt and drive to the lake house. Once there, he slammed on the brakes in the gravel driveway, took long breakneck strides down the trail to the water. But again there would be no body. And standing on the dock looking out at the sun-bright water his hands would start to shake, his fear passing from his heart into his fingers, where he could almost feel it tremble into the air.

He did a hundred little things wrong, he knew. He quit going to his guitar lessons, though he managed to show up for dart nights. He hardly talked to anyone, including his family. He used his computer to look up information on forensics, on the rate of decomposition of bodies in water, files that the police could find. He was seen at the county library perusing certain books. He drove back and forth to the lake house obsessively. He smoked more than he ever had. He spent a lot of time swimming, diving underwater to try to reach bottom at different depths, particularly over a certain spot. Eventually, he moved his things out to the lake house, told his parents he needed some time alone, asked them to stay away. They indulged his whim in the way they always had. He stood for long periods at the end of the dock, looking out over the water. He read the newspapers every day. He failed to get a job. He kept spending his money. He didn't fill out applications for the Peace Corps or the international teaching program he'd spent so much time looking into. He didn't touch base with his professors or his friends. He didn't shave. He had an aimless look about him. Some days he didn't get out of bed. On several occasions, he picked up the phone to call the police, but, phone in hand, he failed to come up with an explanation for why he hadn't called before. Liza Hatter had looked pretty. He had been tired. Everything had seemed so quiet. There hadn't been anything wrong.

He drove to Moscow. On a cloudy day he walked around town, stopping before telephone poles, stopping before streetlights, stopping before bulletin boards, stopping before store windows, looking at the posters that named Liza Hatter a missing person. Surreptitiously, he took one of the posters down, and later taped it to the inside of a closet door at the lake house. He went to the library, lingered at the table where he'd talked to her. He drove by her apartment, slowing almost to a stop. He went to the convenience store, made small talk with the clerk about Liza Hatter's disappearance. He'd done all these things wrong, he knew, but no one suspected him. Not yet. But he prepared himself for the day when someone would, opening the closet door each morning to reveal Liza Hatter's picture—the same one they'd used in the newspaper, her head tilted back, her red hair flowing, the version of her he found distasteful—and standing naked in front of his mother's mirror, studying his breathing for signs of agitation, observing his facial expressions, practicing the words he would use when someone, anyone, finally asked him, *Are you a friend of Liza Hatter's? Have you seen her recently? Do you know she's disappeared?* But the longer he stood there the more the words refused to come, and he wouldn't think of anything, staring at the picture and then staring at himself, watching his chest rise and fall with air.

Strangely, though, he felt pretty good most days. He was,

almost always now, Tristan—almost always himself. When he sat or stood at the end of the dock, sometimes for hours, waiting for Liza Hatter to appear, because according to the statistics it might be days, it might be weeks, it might be never if the water were cold enough and deep enough, the world moved by peacefully, the sun rising or the sun going down, the waves pricking up in the wind or the lake lying flat and calm, the temperature rising or falling, the slow passing of a cloud, and he could be Tristan, just Tristan, apart from everything, one moment to the next.

But really there was just one moment, a moment that all the other moments kept getting sucked back into, the moment before Liza Hatter went underwater. It was a moment that seemed to hold itself in suspension, isolated from time, as if it hung just briefly on some precipice before dropping. There was Liza Hatter's face above the water, there was the moonlight. There were her glowing eyes, there was the word she said—*Tristan?* He couldn't think of anything else for very long.

Two weeks after Liza Hatter's disappearance, he came back to the lake house from a trip to town for groceries. He loaded up the refrigerator and the pantry and then headed to the dock. It was the last day of May, not a cloud in the sky, and the air felt warm enough to be called summer. There was barely any wind. The knotty pines on the surrounding cliffs were vigilant and still, like silent witnesses. The sun on the water was blinding, the popping of a thousand flashbulbs. He stood mesmerized by the dancing of the lights, and he was thinking of Liza Hatter, almost remembering right then the sound of her voice when she'd said his name—*Tristan?*—so softly. He could almost catch the sound, almost re-create it in his head, but something was pushing at the edge of his thoughts, his vision. He cocked his head slowly, and, down at the waterline off to his right, there was Liza Hatter. His hands trembled, though he could still feel himself breathing evenly, the draw and release he watched in the mirror. Liza Hatter, her bare feet on the rocks of the shore, her red hair adrift in the lapping waves. For some reason, he looked around at the trees and the cliffs of the cove, the sun high in the sky, its reflection in the water, the tree-covered hills leading up to the road, the house nestled there, and then Liza Hatter's body at the shore, as if he could make an engraving of all this somewhere in his head.

But soon he stood ankle-deep in the cold water, monitoring himself and her for several minutes. In one sense he was strangely calm, in another strangely agitated. His body seemed to work fine, the trembling stopped despite the cold water, as if it had passed out of him in that first moment, but his mind insisted on playing tricks. Several times he thought she moved voluntarily. Each time he bent toward the water, as if to lend her a hand. Once he said something to her—"Liza." But she was simply moving on the waves. Nevertheless he thought of other things to say: *I'm sorry. You* are *actually very pretty. I understand about the dog.*

He had not touched her yet. To touch her, it seemed to him, would represent the crossing of some plane. He didn't know right now if it had to do with time or space, whether he would be reaching across to the past or to the future or to the other side of something more physical. It wasn't a violation of time or space that he felt willing to make. And yet he had to move her. There was something in the world that insisted on it. He couldn't leave her body on the shore. For a wild moment he considered not doing it—he considered, instead, going to the lake house and calling the police. Female body washed up onshore, no knowledge of the victim. He gripped his forehead tightly, closed his eyes, tried to explain to himself once again why it wouldn't work, and even though he couldn't, he knew better than to try. Sadly, in trying to consider such an action, he felt like the old Tristan again, the one who felt compelled to do things he didn't want to do.

But Liza Hatter herself was pure. She was beyond any compulsion. After a while he grew calm again looking at her. He knelt and turned her body over. The arm he held felt clammy and cold, barely registered with him, not the sort of violation he'd thought it would be. But it was as if he saw her again for the first time—saw *her*, the Liza Hatter who had called his name. Her eyes were as large as he remembered them, maybe larger. There was a film over them now, a veil. He felt the trembling start again, a panicky reaction that had already started to seem ancient, part of him for a long time. He did his best to gather himself. He had, after all, prepared himself for this. The preparation was as old as and fully equal to the panic.

So there she was. He tried to look at her scientifically, the way she said she'd been unable to look at the dog in the class. He'd criticized her, secretly, for not being able to achieve that inner calm. There was no color in her face. She looked as if she'd been preserved in formaldehyde. But the face was bloated and sore-looking, the body bloated and sore, her thin limbs warped somehow, her belly thick and distended. He made his eyes move away from the erect nipples, the strip of pubic hair. He was glad that there wasn't an overpowering smell. He thought of his mother and father and sister and his grandfather, and he thought of the years he'd spent in college and the plans he used to make, even though he had never wanted to make them, not really. Now he was into something different, there was a different life he was living here, and he wasn't sure to what degree he'd chosen it. But he knew no matter what it was that it was going to be hard and that it would take everything he had and that it wouldn't go away. He'd better get started living it.

He grabbed Liza Hatter's ankles and pulled her all the way onshore. He looked at her there on the rocks. Those eyes— almost the same as he'd remembered them. He touched the lids and closed his own eyes while he tried to close hers. But they wouldn't close, the eyes too distended, the lids no longer pliant. He heard himself breathe in through his teeth. Not looking at her, he began to drag her up the rocks, onto the dirt of the trail, up the thin path through the weeds and the wildflowers and the underbrush. He was aware that her ass and her back made a scuffing sound. Partway up the trail, he paused to consider. "Liza," he said, still not looking at her, "what to do with you." He spoke to her as he had in the library. He couldn't take her any closer to the road. He couldn't take her any closer to the house. He couldn't bury her along the path. Up the cliff then, partway between here and the neighbor's property. But there was no way to drag her there. He'd have to pick her up, carry her.

He was surprised to find himself crying, suddenly—nervousness, a sense of something lost. The sun was high in the sky. It was, by all conventional measures, a perfect day, and he tried to think of that, how there was this business to dispense with and then he could return to being himself, the self he'd enjoyed being lately. He finished with the crying.

But when he tried to lift her she was impossibly heavy. Fluid leaked from her, in ways he didn't want to imagine. She was a human-size sponge, the body slick and not slick, the flesh cold and, he had to admit, a relief from the heat and exertion. At one point he lifted her cold hand to his cheek and then dropped it. Finally he went to the house for a blanket and came back and wrapped her in it. He pulled the ends of the blanket together and squatted and lifted as hard as he could, until he stood there trying to balance with Liza Hatter slung over his shoulder. He proceeded uphill, falling down often, landing on his knees, sometimes his elbows, sometimes resorting to dragging her, though he feared leaving a trail through the undergrowth. He stopped when he dared go no closer to the neighbor's property. The lake house was below him, the cliffs of the cove below him, the water far, far down there. "Liza Hatter," he said, as if he would ask her a question.

He left her in the blanket and went to the shed behind the house and grabbed a shovel. In the midday heat he cleared a small space and dug a grave, a shallow one. It was hard work. He dug it just deep enough to bury her in, and it took a long time.

He took the blanket off and laid her as gently as possible in the earth. There was a kind of turning. Of what, he didn't know. His thoughts, the time. And there she was, Liza Hatter. Her reappearance would be an ending and a beginning. "Stay calm," he said, to her or to himself. "We'll get through this." You were worth it after all, he wanted to say to her, and he wasn't sure later whether he didn't or he did. Everything was as still as a painting in the hot afternoon. He looked up into the sunshine. He looked far down at the water. He took notice of the trees. *El sol. El agua. Los arboles.* Now there would be new words for everything.

Stupid
Assholes

Bleeding like a motherfucker Vince
Thompson walked into the low light of the 321, keeping his
head down. Fucking bartender, Bill, would kick his ass out in
a heartbeat if he saw him all bloody. Make his way quick to
the bathroom then, look at himself in the mirror. A black eye
tomorrow, probably, a cut on the upper lip—it didn't show up so
much with the stubble, though—that made Vince Thompson
wince at the feel of the cold water he ran from the tap, the
hot water not fucking working, of course, nothing happening
when he turned the knob, so he had to use this freezing shit to
get the blood off, and then the lip didn't want to stop bleeding
and the goddamn bloody nose to deal with too, so he had to
grab paper towels and stuff them in his pocket, the one with
the drugs, not the Beretta, and he ran a hand through his thin-
ning hair and tried to get the swollen eye to open all the way
but it wouldn't, no big deal considering he couldn't see out of
the son of a bitch anyway, and then, looking more like shit than
he usually did even, definitely not the sort of person anyone
would want to talk to, would they, it was his own fault in some
ways, his goddamn solitude, he pressed a paper towel to his
mouth and went back out into the bar, looking every direction
for trouble.

So far, so good, except there was no Russell Harmon. Not anywhere at the front of the bar, and so he took a peek around the corner toward the dartboard but no Russell Harmon there, either. Maybe he'd figured wrong, maybe Russell Harmon was even more of a pansy ass than he'd supposed, but then coming toward the front again he saw him out the window, talking to his goddamn friend Matt, some sort of heated conversation concerning Vince fucking Thompson, no doubt, whether Russell Harmon should risk getting his ass shot or no, the two of them huddled there under the awning like fucking bridge trolls, Matt taking a hit off the old nose spray, his back turned toward the camera, so to speak. Nothing to do but wait it out, then, let them stand out there in the rain. Vince Thompson pressed the paper towel to his bloody lip and pulled it away and looked at it, still bleeding profusely, more or fucking less, and he pressed the towel against his lip harder and made his way back toward the dartboard, not even bothering to order a drink, like they'd give him one anyway, the fuckers. He sat in a corner out of the way. Reconnaissance, that's what the asshole father would call it, check out the space and determine the general fucking flow of the action, the potential traps, the land mines waiting for you at every turn, because Vince fucking Thompson definitely didn't belong here, not in this place, not ever since the night he'd caused the goddamn supposed commotion during their weenie-ass open mike night a few months ago, got his ass kicked out by Bill when all he was trying to do was suggest that *maybe*, just *maybe*, it might liven up the quote "show" if they introduced a little goddamn electric guitar, you know, a little fucking honest-to-God rock and roll, and OK, maybe the nature of the suggestion was a little bit disruptive, he could

maybe see his mistake there, how he'd stood up from the bar
during the hippie dickwad acoustic player's set and started
wanking on his air guitar, going *wow now now now wee nee nee
neer neer wow now* really loud to the tune of something he can't
remember but it sure pissed people off at the time, especially
when he wouldn't stop and kept on going *weer neer neer* on the
fucking air guitar all the way out of the bar with asshole Bill
shoving him, and especially not tonight with the half-wiped
blood and the pieces of paper towel he was stuffing up his nose
now and pulling out when they got all saturated and shit with
his fucking blood and dropping them on the floor and how he
was all wet and shit and dripping everywhere, but fuckin' A,
was it his fault all hell had broken loose with the goddamn
rain, were we going to start blaming him, Vince fucking
Thompson, for the fucking weather along with everything else,
let's hope not, although in his estimation it wasn't outside the
realm of possibility, and then there was the fact that he wasn't
even drinking because he was too afraid to walk up to the goddamn bar because of goddamn Bill and was still maybe considering it best to just sit here in his corner out of sight. Anyway,
the thing to do while waiting for Russell Harmon to reappear
was a little fucking reconnaissance, take stock of the situation
and formulate a plan, because how did he figure he was going
to shoot Russell Harmon anyway on Thursday night at the 321,
what with all the stupid assholes hanging around, let's see, you
had the open mike guy who he could hear at the front of the bar
going *testing, testing, fucking testing* and Bill the goddamn bartender and the eight or ten yuppies he'd passed up front on his
way in, all real estate agents or builders most likely like practically every other person or so in the whole goddamn town was

now, if he was to take his fucking Beretta out on the street at
noon on any weekday and start taking potshots with his fucking eyes closed he'd hit a goddamn real estate agent within 7.5
seconds, everyone in town, every lame-brain jerk-ass he'd
known for half his life getting their fucking real estate license
for the money, money, money, *Come build your goddamn man-
sion on the lake! Piss the whole town to hell, who cares!* so that even
if he did find a way to shoot Russell Harmon's ass and get away
with it he'd have to drive fucking fifteen miles out of town just
to find a decent place to dump his fat ass, whereas twenty years
ago he could have practically just dragged his carcass out the
back door and dumped it in the goddamn weeds next to Sand
Creek and nobody would have found his fucking corpse till
Christmas, and when you actually thought about it, it was *him*,
Vince fucking Thompson, who should have been the fucking
real estate agent anyway, it was him who knew every goddamn
square inch of this town, but oh, they'd say, you've gotta get
your goddamn license, like you need a fucking license to show
someone around a goddamn house, here's the fancy fucking
kitchen, here's the goddamn toilet where you piss, you rich
California motherfuckers, and oh you've gotta cut your hair,
Vince, you've gotta shave more regular and quit carrying a gun
around and scaring the shit out of people and acting antisocial
and shit, and oh by the way what about that felony conviction
and oh by the way would you please piss in this jar. Assholes.
But goddammit keep your mind on what you're doing, performing that reconnaissance, boy, like the old man would say.
So you had your two losers over there on the far side of the back
room, faggots probably, look at the way they were sitting so
close, there was a time when there wasn't a fucking fag in the

entire town of Garnet Lake, Idaho, but not the case today, no, they'd probably start groping each other any minute, and then there were the six or eight freaks with their silly dart shirts and their little pointy darts—Vince Thompson could beat their ass, he'd played some darts in his day—tossing them and saying shit like, "Nice grouping, James," and "Where's Russell?" and shit, well, he could tell them where the fuck Russell was probably, still out in the fucking rain getting his ass wet, that's where, trying to decide whether to be a chickenshit, and Vince fucking Thompson was still guessing that his little dart match was more important to Russell Harmon than a small consideration like a bullet in the fucking eye socket, and then there was that Tristan dude sitting at the table with a dark-haired chick with nice hooters and *holy shit* he was seeing ghosts now, it was the ghost of fucking Vicki Ashton from down at the beach twenty-five years ago, Jesus Christ, he could feel his eye going crazy right now just with the memory, Vicki Ashton's daughter, it must be, son of a bitch. Take a look at those legs take a look at that hair take a look at those knockers. My God, you didn't get that kind of quality entertainment even on the Internet, hardly, not the sites Vince Thompson looked at, anyway, before he laid on his bed and jacked off, where he could imagine the moment he looked at the women actually taking off their clothes in front of him, actually putting their naked bodies against him in the bed, a soft thing, really, nice and slow and talking to him sweetly, *You're a good man Vince* and shit, *There's a side of you people don't see* and shit, he didn't even want to think about it it made him feel so pathetic, older women, women his age, the pictures of them undressing from their fancy clothes in fancy houses, jewelry and shit, he liked the classy-looking older women because, come on, really, the younger ones wouldn't ever want anything to do with his fucking ass anyway and with the older ones he could at least pretend, *I love you Vince* and shit, taking their clothes off and then spread naked with the soft skin of their kind of saggy breasts and the little paunch and the loose skin of their legs and then their pussies spread open with their fingers, their asses bent over waiting for him, their eyes closed like they were coming or smiles on their faces like they were glad to be with him, Vince, he was making them so fucking happy, and he could memorize every fucking tiny detail, the mole just to the left of the vagina, the red stretch mark on the left tit, and while he lay in the bed after looking he could feel himself running his hands over them, soft, it was an intimate thing, not dirty at all when he did it, not dirty at all, and now, son of a bitch, he was almost crying, wasn't he, thinking about his pathetic life and how he loved those women on the goddamn screen and looking at Vicki Ashton's daughter and how the line of her tits showed from her shirt and Russell Harmon, too, goddamnit, how he didn't want to shoot him but he *had* to somehow, because Russell Harmon wasn't his friend anymore, because not a goddamn person in this bar was his friend, not a goddamn person in this town, not one fucking person in the town he'd lived in all his life to say that Vince fucking Thompson was fit company, but he could have been one of them, he could have been one of them except for his asshole father and his fucking supposed friend Chuck with the goddamn iceball, and except for all the fucking choices, all the fucking wrong decisions such a long time ago, maybe he had to admit, and then the fucking thing in his brain that made him think so much and fucking hate everything, no, you couldn't bring him around nice people like these. Then a booming sound, shit, and he about jumped out of his skin, fucking thunderclap, more fucking rain and so much sadness, looking at Vicki Ashton's daughter and watching her smile a sweet smile for someone else, and now there he was, *there* he was, finally, Russell Harmon, goddamn right he'd been, old Vince, there was Russell and oh, now they were all so glad, now they could get their little dart match rolling again, Russell and Matt were back, fucking hallelujah, and Russell laughing laughing laughing, the jolly fat boy, but peeking at Vince fucking Thompson out of one eye too, which made Vince laugh right along, quietly, to himself. And here was how he'd do it—make Russell think everything was cool, say he had some coke for him, he was back in Vince's good graces, whisper to him to wait five minutes and meet him at Russell's truck, no one would see them leave together that way, then tell him the coke was in his car down the street, have him get inside to do a line, drive someplace quiet and shoot his ass right then and there, plaster his fucking dimwit brain all across the window, then drive his dead ass out of town and dump him. Vince Thompson could fucking *feel* it. His finger squeezing that trigger, the blast as big as thunder. No time for crying. Vince Thompson, the bringer of the lightning and the light. Let the stupid assholes see.

A
Dartboard
Is
a
Perfect
Circle

A dartboard was a perfect circle, the center of which, the bull's-eye, measuring just over an inch in diameter if both the green single and red double were taken into account, was suspended at exactly five feet eight inches from the floor, if the establishment in question could be trusted to hang it right. The foul line, from behind which one was required to throw, was at a distance of seven feet nine and a quarter inches from the board, so that Brice Habersham, who was five feet six exactly in the shoes that he wore to dart matches, and who held his dart at precisely eye level prior to releasing it, his eyes five feet one inch from the floor, approximately (he'd resisted many times the urge to measure the exact distance between his eyes and the top of his head, though he estimated it to be five inches) had to throw a dart (the release point nine and a quarter inches from his eye, he calculated, though he realized the calculation was rather convenient) at an angle that would achieve a one-inch rise in its trajectory per one foot distance to the board (a 1:12 vertical/horizontal ratio, in other words) in order to hit the bull's-eye at its center. This calculation could only be correct, though, if one assumed the dart traveled in a straight line from the release point to the board, a result that would necessitate throwing the dart much too hard to maintain pinpoint accuracy, given the dart's relatively light weight. The one extrinsic force that Brice Habersham had to figure into his finely tuned calculations, then, was gravity. Everything else could be determined logically; gravity you had to feel.

Brice Habersham took none of this as seriously as he used to. Gone were the days of the tournaments, when he could focus his attention on the game and the comfort of his sci-entific approach to it. Gone were the days of practicing long hours in the basement, all alone with Bach or Mozart on the stereo, while upstairs Helen lay in bed with the blinds drawn and the blindfold over her eyes and the jar of skin cream near at hand and the bell on the nightstand in case she wanted to ring him for something, which she often did—a glass of water, an offensive ray of evening sunlight that pierced the blinds, an aching in her limbs or a prickling in her skin, for which he could do nothing but say, "I'm sorry," and stand silently and weather her abuse.

Now it was just a game he played every Thursday night, not nearly as well as he once had, but still well enough to beat the likes of the members of the Garnet Lake Dart League, Russell Harmon included, though Russell might think otherwise. He wouldn't be able to play at all if not for the fact that he could consider it mildly work-related, and so explain it to Helen, who grudgingly accepted his absence for two hours' time.

For over thirty years now Brice Habersham had worked for

the Drug Enforcement Administration, and his career was winding down, more the result of Helen's illness than any deficiency in his work. He had always been an effective if somewhat unspectacular and uncreative member of the agency, and his relocation to this small town in Idaho, away from the busier and more high-profile cities of the Midwest, had come at his own request. He needed to travel less, on account of Helen.

His traveling upset her and aggravated her condition, or so she said, or so her doctors said. Brice Habersham supposed it couldn't be denied, since during his last few extended trips Helen had barely been able to function on her own in the most basic respects—cooking meals, taking a shower, monitoring the amount of pain medication (or alcohol, at times) she was using to relieve her various ailments. Brice Habersham believed that, in fact, Helen could manage just fine on her own if she chose to. She sometimes did choose to—when her sisters came to visit, for instance—and when she had made the choice to do for herself rather than have Brice do for her, it would have been hard for anyone unfamiliar with Helen to find anything wrong with her at all. She had seen a veritable army of physicians and psychologists over the years, and there was wide disagreement among them regarding the degree to which Helen's illnesses were real or psychosomatic. Brice Habersham didn't doubt for a moment that they were real to *Helen*—she was far too proud a woman to carry on a sham year after year. But he believed deep in his heart that the roots of Helen's illness lay not in any physical condition but in a deeply held conviction that her marriage to Brice—her life with him from the time she agreed to a union that she did not want from the start but merely accepted as inevitable—had been a terrible waste, a slow, relentless desiccation rather than a life of fertility and joy. This was how she felt, Brice Habersham knew, and as a result it had become her habit over the years to rely on him as a servant and a nurse-maid since she didn't want him as a husband. He wasn't sure whether or not he made her physically ill, but whether physical illness led to her dependence, or her dependence led to a belief in physical illness, the result was the same—Brice Habersham had to be there to care for Helen because she could not stand the thought of suffering all alone.

So the agency had found him this assignment and set him up as the proprietor of the gas station/convenience store, where he put in some time each day to maintain the appearance of legitimacy, and in fact he had become somewhat interested in the details of the store's operation, the inventory of odd items like pork rinds and engine lubricants, the conversations with the delivery people, the regulations concerning fuel dispensing, the relationships with his employees, etc. And then there were the meetings in private locations with the local and state police and the few community members who were privy to certain details of the operation, and there was the time spent gathering all of the various pieces of information he had obtained from others or obtained through his own surveillance, all done in his office at home alone, with one ear out for Helen and her bell.

So Thursday Night Dart League was a simple opportunity for relaxation, although tonight it would be much more than that. Tonight, at some point prior to, during, or immediately follow-ing Brice Habersham's singles match with Russell Harmon, he would excuse himself, step outside, take out his cell phone, and call the police. Then, when Russell Harmon (and possibly one or two of his friends, judging by the look of things) made his way out of the 321, he would be searched, arrested, and charged with possession of narcotics. Russell Harmon would be the bottom feeder, the first and lowest link in a chain of arrests that would lead, hopefully, to the breakup of a large smuggling ring operating out of the small towns in northern Idaho and eastern Washington and across the Canadian border. This was the plan, but already a complication had arisen. This particular complication had walked through the door a little while ago—Vince Thompson, sitting at a table in a corner, nursing what appeared to be a facial injury (blunt force trauma, apparently), and demonstrating signs of agitation that the police should be informed about, but which weren't worth the risk of blowing the entire setup by making a phone call to someone he knew at the station. Vince Thompson was not supposed to be here at all, and what Brice Habersham needed was not a reason to have him arrested, but a means of getting him safely out the door and on his way to somewhere else. Vince Thompson was supposed to be arrested later, after Russell Harmon and perhaps his friends had provided enough incriminating evidence on Vince Thompson to help the charges stick, if in fact it came to that. Whatever species of no good that Vince Thompson was contemplating on this particular evening would have to take place somewhere else and be left up to chance in the matter of its resolution, which was regrettable, because Brice Habersham had a particular aversion to the vagaries of chance. But regrettable or not, Vince Thompson and all of those people unfortunate enough to cross his path tonight would have to fend for themselves. The problem was that he seemed to be here on account of Russell Harmon, which was going to make it difficult to get him to leave.

The best course of action at this point, Brice Habersham decided, was no action at all. He had time, for now, to wait and see if the situation changed. There was not much to do, therefore, but wait for his turn to play Russell Harmon in the "showdown." Brice Habersham stood at a table behind the foul line, feeling an impatience that was registered only by the clacking of his flights and an occasional glance at his watch. The match tonight was lasting longer than it should have due to the delayed start, which was unavoidable since a gas station proprietor must appear to care about the theft of his gas, and due to Russell Harmon's prolonged absence after his doubles match, which was probably unavoidable only from Russell's perspective, and which Brice Habersham suspected might have something to do with the arrival of Vince Thompson. The length of the match was of some concern to Brice Habersham, since the longer it lasted, the more anxious Helen would become, and if the match continued long enough it might even lead her to pick up the phone from the bedside table, and, claiming later that she had forgotten his cell phone number, dial 911 to talk to the police. The few occasions on which she'd done this were sources of great embarrassment to Brice Habersham, never far from his mind now when he sat with members of the local force examining evidence. Or, even more embarrassing, he might find her, as he had once before when he'd come home late from work, wandering the neighborhood streets in a pathetic shuffle, barely dressed, her arms crossed in front of her, shivering from the cold, saying that she assumed he had abandoned her. Yes, Helen was making it difficult to do his job these days. He had explained to her in as vague a way as he could about what would be required of him tonight, and how it would take some extra time and how he might be home fairly late, but the whole process was being slowed already, and he would undoubtedly have to call her at some point, either before or after his call to the police.

Now the second singles match was nearing its completion, and Brice Habersham stifled a yawn. Vince Thompson still sat at his table, his eyes glued apparently to the back of Russell Harmon's head. A sad situation. Russell Harmon owed Vince Thompson money, that much seemed clear, and it squared with the fact that Russell had stopped buying from Vince Thompson some time ago, Brice Habersham knew, at which point Russell had dropped off the radar, whomever he was buying from now (because they knew he was still buying, the nervous clenching of his jaw at this very moment telling the whole story, although the nervousness itself could also have something to do with Vince Thompson) not being important enough to come under observation. But when it came time to start questioning, Russell Harmon was the man Brice Habersham intended to begin with, because he knew Russell Harmon would talk, and talk freely, because he saw himself as nothing more than a casual user, probably, and would be scared to death. He was exactly the sort of happy-go-lucky fool who would wander right into something like this unsuspectingly, and who would tell everything he knew as soon as he found himself in trouble. He would be charged with possession. They would scare him with the gravity of the charges and then let him talk his way down to a misdemeanor. Then Vince Thompson would be placed under arrest, and the real work would begin.

To Brice Habersham, Vince Thompson was an interesting character. As far as they'd been able to discover, he was dealing only in cocaine and a little bit of pot, a tangential and rather archaic figure in the new narcotics game along the border, which involved the shipment of coke to Canada in exchange for kilos of what was called "B.C. Bud," a potent form of marijuana grown in the backwoods of British Columbia and smuggled in as of late, the DEA suspected, via hastily constructed tunnels. Vince Thompson was just a conveniently placed pawn, a minor piece who had, nevertheless, a long association with one of the primary suspects, according to sources, a shadowy figure whom Brice Habersham knew quite a bit about through secondhand information, but had not yet been able to locate or name. That would be Vince Thompson's job, and whether Vince Thompson went to prison would depend on how much and whom he knew, and Brice Habersham had begun to hope, strangely enough for Vince Thompson's sake rather than his own, that he knew a lot, and would be willing to spill it.

Because there was something about Vince Thompson that Brice Habersham had almost started to like. He had conducted several casual conversations with Vince Thompson at the convenience store, where Vince often came to buy beer, and had found him an animated and knowledgeable (if somewhat angry) commentator on local history, events, and trends, including the growing problem of meth addiction, interestingly enough. Partly, this was no doubt the result of Vince Thompson's "business" interests—with homemade meth labs popping up all over the county, there was little demand for his commodity anymore—but he also seemed to feel a genuine moral repugnance at the thought of parents using volatile chemicals to cook up drugs while their babies crawled around on the floor, and at the droves of burnouts now winding up in the jails and prisons, costing the taxpayers money with their rotten teeth. Was it possible to be a virtuous drug dealer? Was there such a thing as a "classic" pusher, a throwback to some nostalgic past of the illegal drug trade? If so, Vince Thompson was established in Brice Habersham's mind as the prime example. He kept regular hours, going to his job at the apartment complex on Cedar Street five days a week at the same time every morning. He was a regular at several local bars, but never stayed out past midnight. He sold his cocaine almost exclusively to a fairly consistent group of customers who came to his apartment during daylight hours. He was very likely crazy, Brice Habersham knew, but even his craziness had a sort of consistency to it—a constant pent-up bitterness, a dam that could be burst open by the employment of any number of simple phrases such as "How are you, Vince?" or "Are you enjoying this nice weather?" And the flood of expletives would ensue. Vince Thompson's volatility was so predictable, in fact, that he could almost be Brice Habersham's alter ego, the yin to his yang, both of them rigidly self-defined in completely opposite fashion.

Thinking along these lines while the current singles match dragged out interminably, Brice Habersham found himself even more puzzled by Vince Thompson this evening. There sat Vince—beerless, bleeding, alone, and (perhaps most alarmingly) silent. What did it mean?

It occurred to Brice Habersham that, if he actually were who he pretended to be here in this small town, he could simply go over to Vince Thompson and ask. But he wasn't who he pretended to be. And Vince Thompson wasn't who he pretended to be, either. Vince Thompson was a drug dealer, and almost by definition a drug dealer was someone who led a double life, who spent part of his time selling drugs and the rest of his time pretending that he did no such thing. Brice Habersham's life was much the same—he was a drug enforcement agent who spent most of his time pretending to be the proprietor of a convenience store. So there was really no honest ground on either side from which to approach Vince Thompson.

Brice Habersham focused on the dartboard, watched the darts of the two mediocre opponents in the second singles match continually go astray. He looked at his watch again. It was already after ten o'clock, and there was another singles match to get through after this one, and then his match with Russell Harmon. Dart night was dragging along, and perhaps if he let it continue to drag, didn't make his phone call until everything was already completed but the beer drinking and the post-match talk, Vince Thompson would get bored and go find someone besides Russell to threaten.

He let out an uncharacteristic sigh, picked up his beer glass and took a sip, removed his glasses and wiped them with the handkerchief. There was no escaping what he felt—these moments of sadness crept up on him again and again these days. It was something about this town—about the moonlit water of Sand Creek he saw through the window, about the cool night air coming in the open back door, about the first few notes of the guitar he heard. Everything about this place felt like the small Midwestern town he had grown up in, except that with the lake and the mountains it was much prettier here. It was too pretty, in fact. Even in the short time he'd lived here, Brice Habersham could see where things were headed—the logging industry in steady decline, the farmland encroached upon by development, the property values shooting through the roof, the traditional downtown businesses—the hardware store and the five-and-dime and the local grocery—muscled out of the way by corporate superstores and retailers who catered to the tourist trade. Pretty soon there wouldn't be much left here for the likes of Vince and Russell and Matt, who nevertheless continued to go about their business as if their hometown wasn't being swiped out from under them. Vince Thompson coming into the store to buy lightbulbs or duct tape or an extension cord, whatever small items he needed for whatever small jobs pestered him that day, grumbling ad nauseum about Mrs. Krum, tossing around his casual and, insofar as Brice could tell, unconscious racial slurs. Russell and Matt arriving in the early evening from the woods, covered head to toe with dirt and sawdust, the pungent smell of sweat and engine exhaust and new-fallen timber trailing them down the aisle to the beer cooler, always laughing about something while they wiped their dirty faces with their dirty hands, Russell asking Brice questions about his dart trophies.

Brice Habersham had never felt sorry for the people who lost their freedom as a result of his work. They were lawbreakers, defilers of the stern code. But somehow he couldn't see why Vince Thompson had to go to prison. Somehow he couldn't see why Russell Harmon had to be branded a criminal on the one hand and an informant on the other. He couldn't see why he might have to drag a couple of these other boys—because that's all they were, mere boys, even Matt who ran his own logging operation, even that agitated young man talking to the pretty brunette, his foot tapping out a coked-up drumbeat beneath the table—into the proceedings. These boys, at least, were too young to know what they were doing with their lives, and it was a shame to see them headed in the wrong direction in such a pretty place. But who was he to give advice, really, even had he been able to, if he had not been bound by the requirements of the job he had to do? He had no children of his own, not because he and Helen couldn't have, as far as he knew, but because they had never had sexual intercourse, not once in twenty-five-plus years of marriage. What would he—childless, still virgin in late middle age—say to them? *Cleave to the straight and narrow path. Perform the duty that lies in front of you.* These were the rules that had guided him always. And yet tonight he stood here among all these people younger than himself, even sad Vince Thompson in the corner, and he envied them. Yes, *envied* them, even knowing the trouble that was headed their way. Envied them for their youth, even envied them for the risks they chose to take, the errors of chance they courted so recklessly. He had begun, Brice Habersham realized, to feel his life stretched out behind him rather than in front of him. And there was not enough behind him, not as much as he had hoped for or counted on, of which to be proud, and not enough enjoyment to recollect. And though he loved Helen, loved her deeply, he could see nothing in his future but his wife and her imagined illnesses, the greater and greater burden she would choose to become.

What he would like more than anything, he decided, would be to really be the gas station/convenience store proprietor. That way, Vince Thompson would be a real customer instead of a drug dealer, Russell Harmon would be a real opponent in a real dart match instead of a simple possession charge, and he, Brice Habersham, would be a real person instead of an undercover agent for the DEA, and he wouldn't have to spend yet another night of his life in a roomful of people who didn't really know him at all.

¿Como
Se
Dice?

There was something Tristan Mackey wanted to say, something pressing on him more and more as time passed, and it was important that he say it to the right person—not, for instance, to Russell Harmon, to whom he had been tempted to blurt out something just an hour ago. It was that sort of unwise impulse that had sent him in search of the proper audience before it was too late, and of all the people in his acquaintance, it seemed to him that Kelly Ashton might be the one person who could respond to what he had to say both sympathetically and with something approaching actual understanding. So he had called her, and here she was. But sitting with her here at the table, he couldn't come up with any words. It was like that sometimes now. He could be doing anything—walking down a street, maybe—and he would look at the things around him and they would all fall away, disappear, and he would see nothing and hear nothing, as if he were sinking into some deep part of himself where everything was quiet and dark.

And then someone might come up to him on this street and say hello. He would attempt to say something in response, he could feel his tongue stuttering at the words, but as often as not they would want to come out in a different form, and the things on the street would suddenly seem to want to assume some different form as well, unfamiliar and foreign, and he would find himself looking at the things in his own hometown and thinking of them in Spanish—*calle*, *acera*, *tienda*—and the thing the person said would sound like something else entirely, like his name, as if the person had said the word *Tristan* instead of merely *hello*, and inflected the name upward into a question, the same question Liza Hatter asked, so that it was as if he were the constant subject of a one-word interrogation. And often it seemed like Liza Hatter herself had approached him and asked for some difficult translation of the word—*Tristan?*—and he wouldn't know the answer or how to offer it and he would simply wave his hand and smile and move on down the street, wordless. And so he had decided it was time to put an end to these difficulties.

"*Es tiempo*," he said to Kelly Ashton now. He poured beer into his glass, and the last of the pitcher into hers.

"Tristan," she said, in the voice of Liza Hatter, "you're talking in Spanish."

"It means, *it's time*," he said. He looked at her in her chair. Her face was pretty and her eyes flashed intelligence, but he couldn't feel anything about that, and it was important that he feel something about it, because why else was he speaking to Kelly Ashton instead of some other person? It had been easier for a while, after the coke. But the coke seemed to be wearing off. Maybe he could get some more from Russell Harmon.

"I know what it means," she said. "I just don't know why the hell you keep doing it."

"You know Spanish?" he asked her.

"I took two years of it, remember? I sat right behind you. Mrs. Whitley yelled at us for talking all the time." She folded her arms below her breasts and her crossed leg began to sway. This meant she was perturbed, he knew. "*¡Callete, Tristan y Kelly!* Remember? Does it ring a bell? Hello?"

"Shut up," he said.

"Right," she said. "Shut up. Tristan and Kelly. We used to talk all the time."

"*Las memorias olvidadas.*"

"Right," she said. "The forgotten memories." She nodded, a sullen look on her face. "Forgotten," she said. "I guess."

That was, in a sense, what the whole thing was about—memories. It was this very thing, Liza Hatter's memories—who she *was*, in other words—that made him want to speak to Kelly Ashton. It was the idea of Liza Hatter's memories that had led him to spend hours on the Internet in search of her. Every entry he found was about her disappearance, all except one—a brief article announcing that she had been voted to homecoming court at her high school in Salmon, Idaho. And so, lacking any more direct information about Liza Hatter herself, he had studied the small town she came from. He knew its tourist attractions and its local businesses and the members of its city council. He knew its yearly rate of precipitation and he knew the year of its founding and all of its red-letter days. And yet all he knew about Liza Hatter, still, was that she had been twenty-one years old and that she had been a member of homecoming court and that her parents were David and Carol and that a teacher, Mrs. Courtland, said she was "a bright student who kept in touch and was doing well at college," and that she read *Lucky* magazine and liked to cuddle and wanted to be a veterinarian, and that she'd had a crush on Tristan Mackey, whom she'd died right in front of on a night in May, her wide eyes reflecting the moon. And that was insufficient, because he had come to have strong feelings regarding Liza Hatter and needed to know more about her and her memories. Even his own memory of her was fading, and it was for that reason that he had been led for the first time to dig up her grave.

It was early in the morning and the day was still cool and there were long shadows from the trees on the hillside where he'd buried her. It had not taken so long to dig her up with the shovel, because he was only interested in her face. Two feet down he grew careful, because he didn't want to injure her. He dug with his hands until he received the initial shock—the pretty face had begun to decay, and the eyes in particular, which were liquidy and gray, and there were maggots and beetles and ants on her mouth and her nose and her ears, and, feeling sick, he had picked them off one by one and then shoveled the dirt back in.

Back in front of the computer, he switched his study to the decomposition of bodies in earth. He studied the horrifying effects of putrefaction, learned that the body ate itself from the inside out, that the insects came along quickly to help. He was sickened by the photographs of rotting human corpses, the bloated bodies of pigs. But he learned one valuable piece of information—that he could slow the process by burying her deeper, to keep the insects away. Now she was four feet down, and it took forever to unbury her and bury her again, which he had done several times, uncovering her until he could see her face, until he could sit with her, trying to ignore the evidence of her transmutation, the cheesy, loose consistency of her skin, the shriveling of the eyeballs that held just the barest trace of the look he had seen in them, sucking back into the sockets, soon to be gone forever.

"Why did you ask me out tonight?" Kelly Ashton said. What business did she have sitting next to him, looking so pretty and healthy? And yet she had asked the right question. He had called her because he wanted to tell her about Liza Hatter. Liza Hatter was dead, poor Liza Hatter who had been beautiful for one moment in her life, and someone had to know about it, had to know her story. That seemed to be what she was insisting on every time he heard her say his name, and Tristan was the only person who could tell the story, and Kelly Ashton, because of some lingering feeling he had for her, was the person he had chosen to hear it.

"There was something I wanted to say," he told her.

"Then say it," she said. "Why are you acting so weird?"

What an effort the whole thing was, almost too trying to believe. He was losing her, he could tell, and if he wanted to hang onto her he would need to be the old Tristan for a while, and now that the coke was wearing off it seemed so difficult and pointless to whip that old Tristan into shape, make him say clever things and smile. He would have to give it a try, but his mouth hung open soundlessly, his tongue pressed against the back of his teeth.

Then Kelly Ashton did something surprising—she reached across and grabbed his hand. It was the first hand he'd held since the day he carried Liza Hatter up the hill, and Kelly Ashton's warm pulse made him remember Liza Hatter's cold fingers. "You know," she said, "I've got a limited amount of time here. I don't have, like, three days."

But he couldn't respond, and she pulled her hand away, and he could feel a tingle in his palm. Then she started telling him a story, something about did he know what it was like to lose somebody close to you and did he know what it was like to have someone who depended on you entirely, and he wanted to say, thinking of Liza Hatter, yes he did, yes he did know, both of those things, but the words wouldn't come, not a single word would come at all, it was as if he had lost some sort of internal pressure, almost lost the capacity to breathe, and he began to drift off while she talked about a drunk mother and a dead-end job and then something about the stars. But there was a gleam in her eyes as she spoke, a teary reflection of the bar lights, and it reminded him of how he used to feel about Kelly Ashton, and it reminded him too of Liza Hatter's eyes, and it made him think that, yes, Kelly Ashton was the right person after all, and that he would have to find a way tonight to say this thing, for Liza Hatter's sake.

And since he didn't have a way to say the thing right now, didn't even seem to have the capacity for speech, couldn't be the Tristan that Kelly Ashton seemed to want and remember, he tried to fend off her stories the best he could by holding up a finger, a way to say excuse me, and he walked to the bar to get another pitcher of beer.

And he set the pitcher on the bar silently and waited for the bartender to fill it, and he thought of all the strange things he felt and how he had no words to say them anymore, not even the Spanish ones, and how the world seemed to be floating away from him, or vice versa, how he couldn't feel connected to anyone or anything other than the body of Liza Hatter in the grave up on the hill. The bartender grabbed the pitcher and, to avoid conversation, Tristan Mackey looked up at the small TV on the ledge behind the bar, and there was something familiar there, some scene he should recognize right away, something stored in his own memory, but it took several moments before he understood what he saw—a reporter standing in front of the library of the University of Idaho. The sound on the TV was off, but he could read the caption at the bottom of the screen—*New Clue in Case of Missing Student.* There were people walking in and out the door of the library, and it was as if Tristan could see himself and Liza Hatter leaving there together, walking away. And then there was a loud noise he couldn't quite place and everything went dark.

Candles

What mattered to Russell Harmon, here in the middle innings, you might say, of this particular dart night, this particular Thursday evening, which was turning out to be a strange one, wasn't so much that Vince Thompson still sat at his corner table, the blood more or less dried on his face, it looked like, one eye nearly swollen shut, his hands laid out flat in front of him as if he intended to crush the table on which they rested, his one good eye fixed like a tracking device on Russell's every movement, one or another of his guns, no doubt, tucked away in the camouflage pants, not even to mention the knife in a case attached to his belt. And it wasn't that Tristan Mackey had lost his singles match to the worst dart player ever in the history of the Garnet Lake Dart League, leaving Russell in the position of having to beat Brice Habersham if the 321 Club wanted to wrap up the championship this week, or even that Tristan didn't seem to care about this one way or another, his back turned toward the dartboard, talking to Kelly Ashton, and now having left the table to go to the bar without even looking in the direction of the scoreboard, as if the fate of the 321 Club dart team, of which he was a member, held no interest for him at all. It wasn't that Kelly Ashton seemed to have forgotten Russell's existence, that she sat there now staring out the window, her gaze maybe just three or four inches to Russell's left but still not taking him in, or the fact that he'd just seen her, a minute or two ago, when he stepped back from the line after completing his turn, put her hand on top of Tristan's hand, as if she hadn't even thought about Russell standing there watching, hadn't thought about the fact that he was, after all, *human*, that he had feelings too, for Christ sake, even if, as he had to admit, they didn't exactly play a major role for him most of the time, hidden down underneath the happy exterior where Russell's thoughts were usually located, skimming merrily along the surface. And it wasn't that Matt still had the first bindle in his pocket, or that he'd headed to the men's room at least three times by Russell's count, or that he was catching the occasional glance from Tristan, either, the glance that told Russell he would probably be laying out more of his stash in that direction, for the amusement of the incompetent asshole who was stealing Kelly Ashton and couldn't even beat a drooling retard in singles. It wasn't even that he was having to play the most important match of his life with that *boom-tisk-booming* drumbeat in the background.

No, what mattered to Russell Harmon at the moment, just prior to the end of the first game of his own singles match, was this—he'd discovered that he wasn't as good a dart player as Brice Habersham. Brice Habersham was, beyond dispute, the king of the Garnet Lake Dart League. And, no longer the king of the Garnet Lake Dart League, Russell Harmon now wasn't anything. If he couldn't be the Dart League King, if he couldn't be the best player in town, then he was just a twenty-three-year-old local boy who'd never done shit, who'd moved around from job to job, a fixture of the bar scene, unmarried, unattached, unwealthy, not having taken advantage like some people his own age, even, of the local real estate boom or the expanding tourist trade, scooped up by his more successful friend Matt who kept him on (at least for now, because Russell had lately been seeing the signs he recognized from other unsuccessful endeavors) to do a job he couldn't stand, insisting he keep learning to operate the skidder when he was clearly no good at it, scaring the shit out of himself most of the time and the other guys on the crew occasionally, out in the woods that he never liked going to anyway, too dark and moody, the tall evergreens swaying in the wind that came down the mountainsides. At 6 a.m. he would be back out there, hungover, tired, beginning the worst day of his week. His Thursday night highs were supposed to offset those awful Friday mornings, but tonight he was sinking lower and lower, and there was no telling how bad it would get tomorrow.

He had known at the start of the cricket game that, well, maybe he had drunk a little more than he should have or normally would have, and maybe those last lines with Tristan out in the truck hadn't been such a good idea. And he had also taken into account the presence of Vince Thompson and how Vince Thompson scared the shit out of him too, possibly even more than the skidder, and he had taken into account the distraction Kelly Ashton caused, and at first, when he started losing, he blamed it on these factors. But the truth was that as the game progressed, everyone but Vince and Kelly and Tristan crowding around and offering encouragement, everything else faded away and he felt just fine at the line, exactly as he had imagined he would, and he had to admit to himself that none of these other things had much to do with it and that he was in fact playing, if not his best, at least very well. Yet every time Brice Habersham took his turn, the gap between him and

Russell widened.

It had started off with Russell losing the cork, and Brice Habersham stepping to the line and throwing, on his very first turn, what was known in darts lingo as a "ton"—five 20s. This put Russell in an awful spot—one whole number and 40 points down. Brice Habersham's teammates clapped politely and said, *Good job, Brice*, like they were used to seeing this all the time, and from his own team all Russell heard was James say, "Oh, shit." And right away Russell felt in his slightly ample gut something growing, like an ulcer or a tumor. But he was the Dart League King, and as the Dart League King there was one thing he never did—"chase" an opponent in a cricket game. No, not even Brice Habersham.

The strategy—and everyone on the 321 team knew the strategy, because Russell had devised it and taught it to them—went like this: In a cricket game, it was better for the weaker player to keep the game short, not get points involved. If you started shooting points, the game got longer, and the longer the game went on, the more darts you had to shoot, and the more darts you had to shoot, the more likely it was that the skill of the better player would prevail. So, conversely, it was in the interest of the stronger player to stretch the game out, particularly if he happened to fall behind. And the way to stretch the game out was to get ahead on points so that the weaker player had to make a decision—either keep shooting his own points to catch up, which he would probably fail to do, eventually, or "chase" his opponent, closing out numbers that the opponent had already closed, hoping to keep the game close enough to pull off an upset in the end. Applying the principle to Russell's current situation, then, the weaker player would be better off, probably, trying to close the 20s in order to keep the stronger player from scoring further—"chasing," in effect.

Come hell or high water, Russell decided as he stepped to the line that first time, he was not going to admit to his team—if in fact it was true, which he hadn't decided yet—that he was the weaker player. So he told himself, *Don't chase Brice Habersham on the 20s. Shoot, if you can*—highly unlikely, but not impossible—*seven 19s.* That way Brice Habersham would be behind on points, and he would go back to the 20s, and Russell would keep shooting the 19s, and he would shoot better than Brice Habersham and eventually wear him down to the point that Brice Habersham would have to chase *him* and shoot the 19s. This is what Russell actually forced himself to believe, right before he stepped to the line and hit not seven but three 19s—which after all was pretty good but not enough.

Brice Habersham then hit a triple 19 on his first dart, which meant no chance for Russell to score points *there*, and then two single 18s, which meant there wasn't much use in taking *that* route *either*, and the tumor in Russell's gut grew bigger and more agitating. But he *would not chase Brice Habersham.* He stepped to the line and shot five 17s. And while Matt and James roared their approval, Russell looked over toward Tristan to find him holding Kelly Ashton's hand. And then Brice Habersham hit his final 18 and all three 17s, leaving the double 17 for last and hitting it with a certainty that made Russell nearly queasy. Halfheartedly, because he was still pretending to be the stronger player even though the reality, in both the form of the rock-hard tumor and the increasingly lopsided score taking shape on the chalkboard, was quickly establishing itself, Russell threw at the 16s, hitting two singles, his first slightly subpar turn. Other than that, he'd thrown very well. And then Brice Habersham calmly and coolly hit three single 16s. And so Russell, dragging himself to the line by this point, his arms and legs feeling at the same time both heavy and rubbery, shot a triple 15 and two near misses at the bull's-eye.

The board looked like this:

BRICE H.		Russell	
40	O	20	34
	O	19	O
	⊗	18	
	Ó	17	O
	O	16	X
		15	O

And Russell knew what was coming. He felt it ballooning inside of him, and he wanted to close his eyes. And in fact he did watch from one eye as Brice Habersham stood placidly at the line in his silly stenciled shirt, his old man's hair parted just so, his glasses reflecting the bar light, unaffected by the fake drum going *boom-tisk-boom* and the guitar playing chords that sounded to Russell like maybe James Taylor, although he couldn't recognize either the tune or the words, which sounded like they were being sung in Chinese, and hit triple 15, single bull, double bull, bringing the game to an astounding and rapid conclusion. And Brice Habersham's teammates clapped politely and said things like *Wow, Brice, that's some good shooting* and patted him on the back while Brice Habersham modestly accepted their congratulations. And Matt and James stood there with their mouths hanging open. And Russell realized that he was a loser and always had been.

But he wasn't a *quitter*, at least when it came to darts, at least that was what he now tried to tell himself. The match wasn't over—just the cricket game. If he could beat Brice Habersham in 301, he could force a tiebreaker, and then if he won at Around the World he could be, once again, for the third year running, the Dart League King. But Brice Habersham had just closed out cricket in—count 'em—*five turns*. It was the best dart game Russell Harmon had ever seen anyone shoot.

And as if to commemorate the event, this miraculous and dumbfounding happening, there was a flash of light, and thunder boomed so hard it rattled the windowpanes, and all the lights in the 321 Club went out, as if they marked the Dart King's passing.

Suddenly Russell found himself in a nearly pitch-black room with a couple of dozen people in a state of general confusion, and one of those people was Vince Thompson, locked and loaded, possibly deciding that this was the ideal moment to locate Russell there in the darkness, pop him once or twice in the gut or in the spine, leave him to bleed to death while he, Vince Thompson, made a beeline for the safety of some foreign country with a funny name, like Saskatchewan.

And even though Russell had decided he was maybe the

biggest loser in town, outside of Vince Thompson himself, he wasn't ready to die just yet. There was all this laughing and chattering and shuffling of bodies and in the midst of it he could barely see his hand in front of his face or separate one sound from another, and he didn't know who might be Vince Thompson and who might not be, and if at all possible he didn't want to find out.

His first impulse was to bolt for the back door, but as he started to make his way there, knocking into a table, hearing a glass crash to the floor, it occurred to him that it might not be a good idea to head off somewhere alone, so that if Vince Thompson were lucky enough to find him he could shoot him without any witnesses, not that anyone could witness much at the moment, but still. It was probably best to stay in the bar. Russell had spent enough time in bars to know the best course of action when all hell broke loose, when the fists started flying and the pool cues started breaking over people's heads, and even though that was not the problem right now, he decided that the same rule applied, so he made his way carefully with his hands out in front of him, saying softly *excuse me excuse me* when he bumped into something, whether person or inanimate object, over to the wall next to the dartboard, and when he reached out and felt the cool brick surface, he got his back firmly against it and his darts in hand, just in case he needed a weapon.

The laughing and the chattering continued, and the drunks at the front of the bar let out a whoop that was picked up by some other drunks, setting off a rattling in Russell's skull that made his lips buzz and his teeth clench, and he wondered where Vince Thompson was, and if he was one of the people yelling, letting loose his murderous war cry.

Then there was someone standing in front of him. Russell's eyes were beginning to adjust, and by the dim light through the back window he could make out that it was someone about Vince Thompson's height, and his blood thrummed through his veins with the coke, and he thought about how disappointed his mother would be when the autopsy revealed the presence of drugs in his system.

"Russell?" It was Brice Habersham.

"*Quiet*," Russell said. "Please."

There was a pause, and the bar had calmed down a little, and then Bill the bartender yelled out for everyone to stay put while he got some candles. Russell wondered why he hadn't announced this before, but then realized that it had been only thirty seconds or so since the lights went out, even though it seemed like two days.

"Why?" Brice Habersham said, in a bit softer voice that almost hinted at sympathy. "You in some trouble, Russell?"

"Maybe a little bit," Russell whispered. "Nothing too much."

"Sorry to hear that," Brice Habersham said. "A young man like you . . . " he said, and then didn't complete the thought, leaving Russell to wonder what sort of young man Brice Habersham meant. The kind of young man who had just received an ass-whupping at cricket, probably. Brice Habersham had no doubt seen a lot of those guys. "What would you like to do?"

There were maybe a lot of things that Russell would like to do if he lived to see tomorrow—find a way to pay Vince Thompson the money he owed him chief among the things that came to mind—but he couldn't think of anything he wanted to do right *now*. "Uh," he said, "I think it might be best if I just stand here."

There was a little glint of light along the gold frame of Brice Habersham's glasses. "I mean about the dart match," he said.

The dart match. It rose up suddenly, a beacon of hope, something that Russell could get his mind around, something familiar, even if he was getting his ass kicked. "I want to finish it," Russell said.

Russell saw Brice Habersham's arm move, and then there was a small blue circle in the dark, a light from Brice Habersham's watch. "I've got about a half hour, hour tops," he said. "Let's hope they get the lights back on soon." He reached out and put his small hand on Russell's shoulder, patted the shoulder gently, then turned around and walked off. The pat had been so delicate that it made Russell want to cry, even if Brice Habersham turned out to be a fag or something.

Then came Bill the bartender with a candle, and there was a circle of yellow light from the table nearest Russell, and he sank back against the corner of the wall. The tumor in his gut gave him a violent stab, but then he saw something amazing— the table where Vince Thompson had sat was empty. In a minute Bill had candles lit all around the back room, skinny white candles sticking up out of glass globes, rather classy Russell thought, and he grew happier and happier at having the leisure to think such things as the light reached farther and farther, revealing that Vince Thompson was nowhere to be found. Matt and James came up to him and Russell started to explain about the dart match, about the half hour, hour tops, and then in the warm candlelight there was Kelly Ashton approaching—not smiling, but deliberately approaching him nonetheless. She stepped between Matt and James and, without a word, took Russell's arm in her soft hand and led him to the back door. Russell hesitated just a moment, scared of what might be waiting for him out there in the dark. Kelly Ashton opened the door and pulled Russell after her, and as Russell scanned the bar one last time for Vince Thompson, he fell prey to a rare flight of fancy—the candles looked like tiny men with their heads on fire, waiting for someone to save them.

Where
We
Put
Our
Socks
and
Shoes

Tristan had wandered off to the bar, and he hadn't come back, and so now Kelly Ashton's eyes and thoughts turned to Russell Harmon, because *something* was going to happen tonight, she'd determined that much, and after all Russell had always been, somewhere in the back of her head, Option B, or Option C, or Option D, one of those options further down the line in the space below Option A, which most of the time remained a bit hazy and undefined, just something *more*, but which had lately come to be Tristan Mackey. But with Tristan acting so strangely tonight, Russell was at least worth investigating. She hadn't seen him in a long time, and maybe he had changed, or maybe he hadn't—she wasn't sure which she was hoping for. But it was worth finding out.

By the time she had taken his hand and led him out the back door the rain had almost stopped, the last few big drops splashing down in scattered fashion as if, having completed its work of knocking out the lights in town, the storm could now die peacefully or rumble off to some other place. Still, she was getting wet, and her hair would be a mess, and she didn't want Tristan following her, supposing he gave a damn. So she guided Russell past the wooden chairs and tables and out across the lawn and through some knee-high shrubs into the parking lot.

"Where are we going?" Russell asked.

"Your truck," she told him.

Russell's truck smelled like empty beer cans and cigarettes and something else she couldn't quite name—maybe sweat, though she had a hard time imagining Russell sweating. At the moment the smells didn't disgust her. They were more or less what she'd expected, the familiar atmosphere of Russell. She set her purse down firmly on the emergency brake, as if she intended to stay awhile.

"What are we doing?" he asked her.

"I'm not sure," she said. Russell rummaged in the jockey box, holding up CD cases and peering at them in the moonlight, then plucked one out and put it in the player, some goopy, mellow music she immediately couldn't stand. Russell Harmon's idea of romance. "Turn on the light," she said.

The cab light came on, fuzzy and dim, and she looked at Russell. His curly brown hair was soft and light, hanging down loosely around his eyes and over his ears and down his neck to the collar of his T-shirt. It was Hayley's hair, exactly. And she could see Hayley, too, in the round shape and rosy color of his face. The pale blue eyes were his own. Hayley's were more green, wider, like hers. The grin that curled up the corner of his mouth was wholly and typically Russell.

"Why'd you grab me like that?" he asked. "We go like two years without talking and then you come and kidnap me." He stretched his heavy legs out around the steering wheel and put his right arm on the back of her seat and turned toward her, as if he expected her any minute to lean over and give him a blow job. Stupid Russell.

"Do we have to listen to this shit?" she asked him. Some guy was singing some horribly maudlin thing about saving time in a bottle, as if you could do anything with time other than fight it, try to stop it from going by so fast.

"Un-unnh," he said. "It's my mother's, anyway. I thought it was something else." He turned the truck key and the CD lights went off and there was silence. He turned off the cab light and it was dark again. "I kind of don't want people outside to see me," he said, and his head took a turn looking out all the windows, bobbing up and down trying to pick through the shadows.

"I brought you out here to tell me a story," she said.

Russell laughed, that loud sort of cocky chuckle that she was supposed to find endearing. And she did, at least a little bit. "What kind of story?" he said.

"You remember, you used to tell me stories." They would lie in bed in Russell's apartment before or after sex and she would drape her leg over his and he would recount the details of his high school football games and there was one story about how when he was a kid he'd peeled and eaten all the Easter eggs before his mother and Uncle Roy had had a chance to hide them and one about seeing the Garnet Lake Monster when he was out fishing with Uncle Roy and one about a hunting trip, which was her favorite. "You remember you told me once about the first time you shot a deer?"

"Yeah," he said. "Sort of." He was looking at his big hands on the steering wheel.

"Tell me that story again," she said.

So he did, he started telling her, and she remembered why she liked the story, which was because it had made her like him. How he felt like he hadn't even been shooting the buck, like he wasn't even out in the woods, like it wasn't even happening, and then how when the buck lurched he had thought it was because of the noise, and then its white tail had flickered and it had started to scamper uphill, but then its legs didn't seem to work, and they crumpled up under him suddenly, and then he rose but the legs crumpled again, and he lay down on his side and you could see his belly heave, and Russell had wanted to cry but he couldn't because his uncle Roy was there. Yes, she remembered the story, and yes, it made her feel the same old way, but she grew impatient before he could get very far.

"I want you to tell me a different story, Russell. I want you to tell me a story about me."

He laughed again. "What do you mean?" he said. "I don't know any stories about you."

"You don't?" she asked, looking at the curls of his hair, the only thing she could make out about him there in the dark.

"Once upon a time there was a girl named Kelly Ashton," he said, "who always burned the bottom of pancakes."

She sighed. It was impossible to get what you needed from people. "I want you to tell me a story about you and me," she said. "I want you to tell me a story about how you and me and Hayley would live in a little house, a nice clean little house, right here in town, and what we would do there."

"Whoa," Russell said.

"Tell me *that* story, Russell," she said, her head burning now, beginning to get angry. "You *tell* it to me."

"OK," he said. "*Jesus.* Calm down." Then he tapped his thumbs on the steering wheel. Then he looked out the windows again, bobbing his head up and down. What the fuck was *wrong* with people tonight? They were just sitting and talking. They weren't even doing anything. "OK," he said finally, and sniffed hard and tried to clear his throat. "You and me and Hayley—is that your baby?"

She was tempted to say it—say the word *your*, say the word *our*. "Yes, that's my baby. Only she's really more a toddler now."

"What's the difference?" Russell said.

"She walks and talks. She *toddles*."

"OK," Russell said again. "You and me and Hayley, we would live in a nice little house right here in town." He stopped, looking over at her, checking to see if he was getting started correctly.

"Go on," she told him.

"It would be a clean house," he said. "Because we would keep it clean." He stopped again. It was like pulling teeth. She thought of him with the notebook wire stuck up his nose that day in English class, while Tristan Mackey was sitting somewhere in the back of the room, thinking about destiny.

"Well, you and Hayley would hang out there during the day while I was at work. You would, you know, play stuff, like little games. Then late in the afternoon, or like in the winter when it was already dark outside, I would come home." He grabbed at his pants near his crotch and tugged on the seam, getting himself comfortable, she supposed. At least he seemed to be trying to think. "I would take off my boots and socks and leave them by the fire."

"Would we have a fireplace or a woodstove?" she asked him.

"Um," he said, "a fireplace?"

"OK," she said. "Keep going."

He rested his elbows on the steering wheel and stared out the windshield. "Then I would maybe sit on the couch and you would sit in a rocking chair that we would have. And then . . . oh, I guess this is maybe before you made dinner. Which would be pancakes." She could feel him smiling at her. "Then, like, Hayley, she would kind of walk around between us, back and forth, and she would talk. And we could maybe watch TV. And I would have a couple beers."

He leaned back in his seat and dropped his hands to his sides and his head was pointed down. That was the end of the story, then.

"That's it?" she said. "'We could maybe watch TV,'" she said, mimicking him in a way that made him sound, she knew, more than slightly dumb. "'Maybe have a beer.' Russell, you're describing every night with my mother."

"Well, *I* don't know," he said, raising one hand in the air, the fingers spread. "What the fuck are you asking me this stuff for? What's going on here?"

"Use your imagination," she said. "Come on. How hard can it be? 'I would come home, Kelly, and we would have a nice antique couch and we would lay on it with you tucked up under my arm, and Hayley would climb up on top of us and lay there, too, and we would all laugh and enjoy each other's company. And we would get Chinese takeout, and then later when Hayley was in bed we would split a bottle of wine and watch a foreign movie, and then we would listen to music together or read a book to one another, and then we would go to the bedroom and make love, and we would be happy.' Why don't you say *that*, Russell? Why don't you tell me *that* story? I wasn't asking where you'd put your shoes and socks."

For a second she could sense him looking at her, dumb-founded. "Yeah," he said then, in a softer voice. "All right. That's a good one. I kind of like that story." And he stopped talking, staring again out the windshield. And just when she was about to give up, just when she was about to open the door to go back inside and find Tristan Mackey, he said one more thing, uttered the magic words. "We would live in the little house and we would all be happy and I would never leave."

She still couldn't see him there in the dark but now she wanted to, wanted to see his round face and his red cheeks, wanted to feel the rather soft feeling that he always gave her, something safe and plain, not like the wild rambling of Tristan and the craziness and fear of things she didn't know, places he would take her where she had to wander blindly, trusting in his obscure intelligence and emotion, his elusiveness, the disappearing man. And before she knew it she was kissing Russell's face, his cheeks, his eyes, his nose, and then his lips, and she was over on his seat sprawled up against him, his back leaned on the door while his hands fumbled at her waist and then beneath her shirt, twisting anxiously at her bra strap, and after a little while he said, "There's a mattress in the back." She crawled through the window of the canopy, and Russell, too big to get through, went around to unlock the hatch and throw down the tailgate. He climbed up next to her and she could hear the pattering of raindrops from the birch leaves, and then he had shut them in and everything was quiet except for their breathing.

It was just like when she used to have sex with Russell, just like all the times in his old apartment, just like when they'd conceived Hayley. Here in the truck bed the lumpy mattress, the rattle of beer cans, the discarded T-shirts, the smell of motor oil—slightly different from his apartment, but not that much. And all of it was welcome to her, so different from what she'd considered at the time the romance of Tristan's lake house, the high rectangular windows and the sweet smell of the cedar woodwork and the sighing of the pine trees by the lake. Being with Russell was so easy, because you didn't have to think of what he thought of himself, you could believe in the simplicity and purity of his pleasure there in the dark, not like Tristan and his calculated sexual intimacies, the way he had left the lights on to stare at her face, and she didn't know what the look in his eyes meant. Russell was sweet, Russell was always surprisingly tender. She could forget Russell and lose herself in her own pleasure. With Tristan there had only been Tristan. Now she had eased into the rhythm of her own body, and her mind became lazy and dreamy, and soon she came, squeezing Russell's shoulders and shouting out in the truck, embarrassing herself for a moment but then quickly losing the embarrassment, because this was Russell.

Within seconds, it seemed to her, she was almost sleeping, but then Russell began searching around the truck bed for something and soon came up with a flashlight, and they found their discarded clothes and got dressed. She reached back in the truck cab and grabbed her purse and had Russell hold the flashlight while she used a mirror to fix her hair. As she put the mirror back in the purse, her hand settled on her wallet.

"What do we do now?" Russell said. "I mean, that was great, but I have to go back in."

She ignored him. She opened the clasp on the wallet and flipped through her pictures, stopping at a recent studio portrait of Hayley that she'd had taken at Wal-Mart. Hayley wore a yellow dress and held her favorite stuffed animal, a purple giraffe she called, for some reason, Mopey. She flashed an open-mouthed grin at her mother, just to the side of the camera.

She took the photo from the plastic and gave it to Russell. "Look at her," she said.

Russell pointed the flashlight, angling the picture up and down. "Cute," he said, smiling a little uncertainly, as if he weren't sure what one was supposed to say about children.

"She's yours," Kelly said.

Russell looked over at her, his mouth slightly ajar. "You mean you want me to keep it?" he asked.

She sighed. "Look at her hair. Look at the color of her cheeks." Russell aimed the flashlight again, squinting. "She's *your* daughter, Russell."

That was the story she could tell, the one she could say right out loud. About the last night she'd spent at Russell's apartment. About how when she found out, she was confused and unhappy and hadn't wanted to see him afterward. About how Aaron, her boyfriend, came along and took Russell's place, and how everyone but him thought he was Hayley's father. How she hadn't felt right about that, had started to hate Aaron for it after a while. About how she'd had to work so hard as a single mother, how it made the stars seem out of reach. Even how she'd slept with Tristan and gotten her hopes up. About how she was here now with Russell, though, and it was up to him what he wanted to do about it, whether he wanted to make the story about the little house and the fireplace and the happy family come true. But even as she told this story, her story, looking at Russell's face still leaned in over the picture, the serious and melancholy set of his features, which she hadn't expected and which made her heart go soft, she had to wonder how long she could go on telling it—not to Russell, but to herself.

A
Fucking
Perfect
Opportunity

Vince Thompson's head hurt like a
son of a bitch, a condition that could have been improved, no
doubt, if he'd had access to even a single alcoholic beverage
of one goddamn variety or another during the course of the
last fucking hour or so, but no, even such a simple pleasure as
that was going to be denied him tonight, apparently, what with
goddamn Bill eyeing him from behind the fucking bar like he,
Vince, was a goddamn cattle rustler and Bill was John fucking
Wayne, and so it was starting to look like he was going to have
to shoot Russell fucking Harmon stone-cold sober, and Jesus
Christ Al*mighty* his head hurt like that asshole Clint Harmon
had hit him with a two-by-four, I mean was it his imagination
or was his fucking head actually *lopsided*, I mean if you looked
at it from that one particular angle, if you squinted just like
that, was it actually fucking *lopsided*, like swollen up on the left
side so it looked like his brain was ready to leak out his left
ear, or was that just a fucking optical illusion caused by the
fact that the old goddamn left eye was even more screwed up
than usual? Vince Thompson pondered the question while he
stared at the bathroom mirror, at the same time sticking his

hand under the faucet and dribbling water up onto his throb-
bing nose and upper lip, thinking more at the moment about
Russell Harmon's asshole father than about Russell Harmon,
and how it might not be a bad idea, after blowing Russell fucking Harmon's underdeveloped brain to smithereens, because
when you got right down to it who would really give a shit
anyway, to walk right back up the street to fucking PJ's and
shoot the asshole air force colonel father and Russell fucking Harmon's asshole father too, thereby ridding the world
of two more useless fucking jerks. But, you know, Vince you
old fucker, Vince fucking Thompson thought, you've created
a little problem, haven't you, because, well now they'd all seen
him, hadn't they, everyone in the whole goddamn place, all
bloodied and shit and hanging around with nothing to do but
glare at Russell Harmon with what no doubt looked like homi-
cidal rage, which, OK, you had to look at at this point and say
that that hadn't been such a good idea, had it, because, well,
who the fuck was going to come under immediate suspicion
when Russell turned up dead other than good old Vince, crazy
whacked-out Vince who everyone in the entire fucking town
had just been waiting around for years to see snap, probably
taking up money for a goddamn pool, he wouldn't doubt it a
bit, well in that case he was going to give them their money's
worth. The thing to do was figure out a way to make sure as
shit it looked like he was dead too, like in the fucking movies
how people were always faking their own deaths, right? Like
leaving behind all sorts of bloody evidence and shit and then
disappearing, which shouldn't be too hard, now should it, considering he already had the bloody part taken care of, and as he
splashed more water on his face and at the same time tried to

determine whether the pounding in his goddamn skull meant
he actually might be hemorrhaging, he tried to work out in his
head the details of a drug deal gone bad, something where he
and Russell fucking Harmon would both be shot and he, Vince,
would be dragged away from the scene and dumped at some
undetermined location, and there was a *boom*, like a mortar
round or some shit, and then the bathroom was totally black.
Vince Thompson's hands were in the water and he turned his
palms down and there wasn't any water then and what was
so surprising suddenly, son of a *bitch*, was that there was no
Vince fucking Thompson either, Vince fucking Thompson had
completely disappeared, his hands were in the air somewhere
and his body wasn't touching the sink and he wasn't in contact
with the goddamn earth at all except for the soles of his boots
on the floor, and holy shit it was like he was floating, like he
was suspended in this dark, like floating or sinking, he couldn't
tell which, and it was almost like even his goddamn head didn't
hurt now that he couldn't fucking see it, and he started laughing to himself, *laughing*, what an asshole, and he took a step
back from the sink he couldn't see and the face he couldn't see
and it was like he was free of the whole thing for one goddamn
second, one fantastic second where he didn't feel all weighted
down and shit, all pissy and morose, and he started doing a
pinwheel motion with his arms like swimming or maybe goddamn flying, Vince fucking Thompson was going up into the
dark and flying off to the fucking moon, Jesus what a stupid
asshole. It just went to show what sort of weird shit you got
yourself into when you were essentially a fucking social outcast who spent way too much time on your lonesome and then
found yourself in this kind of situation, in the total fucking

pitch-black hole of Calcutta darkness, imagining all kinds of crazy shit like how you were kind of two different people, like you were one person who was standing there in front of the mirror looking at his goddamn lopsided head and then all of a sudden you were this other person whose head wasn't lopsided at all, and how maybe when the lights came on everything would be cool and you could forget about all this other crap and you might even suddenly look like Brad Pitt. Good fucking *God* it was dark. Vince fucking Thompson came back to himself and splashed one last handful of water on his swollen face and felt around in the dark for the towel dispenser until he found it and took a handful and wiped his face and then aimed the towels in what he thought was the general direction of the goddamn wastebasket, and then with both hands he felt one more time his pathetic lopsided head, and then he went back out into the fucking bar, the thought beginning to grow, beginning to dawn now, that this would be the perfect fucking opportunity, right while nobody could see a goddamn thing, to locate Russell Harmon somehow and stick the Beretta in the back of his skull and force him outside where he could then figure out how to waste his pansy ass.

But out in the bar it wasn't dark, goddammit, not dark like in the john, it took him a minute to actually comprehend that he could actually see again and shit, that there were all these fucking *candles*, and no matter which way he looked, no matter which direction he turned in performing his fucking reconnaissance, there wasn't any Russell Harmon. Russell Harmon, goddammit, was gone. Up at the front of the bar he saw that goddamn Matt walking toward the restroom, like he thought he was going to do a line of coke in there, what a fucking idiot, like he could even open up the bindle in the goddamn pitch-blackness, use your fucking *head!* And there was that Tristan dude, who he would have given more credit, actually like sitting in a chair and *listening* to the goddamn musician strumming his lame-ass acoustic guitar, Jesus, Vince Thompson hated that asshole, *Oh maybe we could crank up a little "Puff the Magic Dragon," oh could you please play us your fascinating rendition of "Where Have All the Fucking Flowers Gone."* It was enough to make you want to pull out the Beretta and shoot your fucking *self.* And there were more of the idiot dart players. And there were the two fags. And here in the back of the bar, all alone, was that crazy convenience store owner, still standing there at the fucking dartboard, still throwing his little darts plunk, plunk, plunk into the fucking board, the dude was fucking creepy, it was like you never even saw him half the time, it had taken Vince about half a dozen goddamn trips to the store before he could even remember who the hell the guy was, and looking around at all these assholes Vince Thompson was happy as shit to get the hell out of the bar, and he knew just where to go, because he knew just where Russell fucking Harmon would go, right out to his truck to do some blow. Stepping outside he found the night relatively quiet and inoffensive, even if it was black as a nigger's ass at least the rain had stopped, and the air was cool, and he could hear the sign on the mountain bike shop next door banging in the wind, and he was so fucking *tired* all of a sudden, life made you so damn tired, it was almost too much to bear to stay so angry all the time, and wouldn't it be nice to just forget the whole damn thing and go home sober and collapse in bed, but no, there was business to attend to, there was the goddamn Beretta in the pocket, give it a little pat,

OK, and there was the hunting knife on the belt, and there was the pain and shit in the lopsided head to keep up the old resentment, and so it was off to the parking lot, crossing the deck on the proverbial fucking cat's feet, don't give yourself away, and approaching the shrubs under the birch trees, feeling ahead carefully in the dark, and lo and behold there was Russell fucking Harmon's truck right there, but squinting into the goddamn blackness Vince Thompson couldn't see anything, couldn't see the outline of anyone in the truck, son of a bitch maybe Russell Harmon wasn't there, maybe he was sneaking up stealthily on an empty fucking truck, that would be just about par for the goddamn course, just about a summary of the whole fucking glorious evening, but then he heard something, he heard the truck's shocks give a little squeak, and you could see the truck move, right *there*, you could see it rocking a little bit on the frame. Holy shit. It occurred to Vince fucking Thompson that there was someone else he hadn't seen in the bar on the way out, wasn't there, son of a bitch, old Russell Harmon was out here banging away on that Ashton chick, what do you know, the last fucking supper so to speak, the final request granted the dying man, and Vince Thompson leaned on a fence post and felt what was it, relief? That he wouldn't have to do it right now? Because he couldn't shoot Russell Harmon's head off in front of a hot-ass chick? Pride? Like a surge of goddamn pride, he supposed, like the thing that went through his head was *way to fucking go, Russell, you old shit-for-brains son of a bitch*, like the fact that Russell Harmon had actually hung out over at his place before and drunk his fucking beers and snorted his fucking lines and basically taken advantage of him from the word go somehow reflected better on him, Vince? Like if

Russell Harmon could get his ass laid by a hot fucking chick that meant there was hope for Vince fucking Thompson too, by association, like he might be able to get some woman that wasn't just a pussy on a computer screen? That was pathetic, the most pathetic thing he'd ever imagined of himself, and he stood there leaning on the fence and wondering how he'd slipped so far, because he'd been normal once, hadn't he, he'd had a truck like that one, not as nice, maybe, but a truck, and he'd had a girlfriend, her name was Summer, this was a long time ago back when he worked for the city maintenance crew, hanging out down at the city shop with all the old farts drinking their coffee and smoking their cigarettes, and Vince always the first one to take a job, wasn't he, they used to laugh at poor Vince because if a water main burst or a road needed grading or a pothole needed to be filled or the snowplows needed to go out in the early morning dark he was always the first to volunteer, ready to go, actually fucking eager, but they liked him too, didn't they, they would pat him on the back every once in a while, one of the old guys, say *You're doing a nice job, Vince*, and back then he'd had Summer to go to every night, but her parents had been goddamn hippies and she was used to moving around, so she'd talked him into saving up money to buy a camper and quitting his fucking job, which was the only real job he ever had, and going on the road to fucking California with all the other goddamn hippie freaks. But it had been worth it, hadn't it, Vince Thompson thought now, hearing the noises from Russell Harmon's truck and looking up at the white stars, which were out now in abundance, just like they were in that camper with Summer, putting out the campfire and going to bed, maybe cooking up a little something on the tiny stove and pulling a beer from the refrigerator, crawling up into the space over the cab where the bed was and lying there talking to Summer for hours, sometimes until you could feel daylight creeping in. Summer, how long had it been since he'd thought of her, or how long had it been since he'd let himself acknowledge that he thought of her, that she was always there behind the pictures on the screen, always her actual flesh somewhere deep in his goddamn memory. She hadn't been much to look at, Summer, nothing like that Ashton chick who he could hear now crying out in the truck, good old Russell, who'd have thought, mousy brown hair and a plain face and thin as a fucking bird, a goddamn vegetarian of all things, but she was the sweetest girl he'd ever known, sweet even about his goddamn deep-seated insecurities and what fucking ever and his shitty moods and his bitter goddamn memories, she had put up with it all, at least up until the time that the drugs got the best of him and he'd gone back home without her, leaving her in some small California town that he couldn't even remember the name. He could listen to her talk forever, back in the good days, and he loved to hear her laugh, loved to hear her soft throaty voice that was what a robin would sound like, he always thought, if it could speak. She'd written him a letter once, after he was long gone, and he had read that letter over and over again trying to find that voice in it, but finally it too had gone away.

The thing was, he realized, that he didn't want to kill Russell Harmon. The thing was that he didn't know if he could kill anybody. But the thing was also that if he couldn't kill a man, what was it that he *could* do. That was the upshot of his upbringing. Sometimes you've got to take a life to save one, like his asshole father used to say, and Vince Thompson knew pretty well whose life he'd be saving. So he turned from the fence and made his way back through the bushes and across the grass to the deck and he thought again of how it would be, how he could picture the scene, how he could work up the anger, because the anger was always there, wasn't it, and there had to be some use for it, so he would put the fucking Beretta to Russell Harmon's head and say, just before he pulled the trigger, *You should have been my fucking friend.* And then he walked back in the 321 and he ignored the convenience store dude who was still there at the dartboard, and why was the fucker staring at him, it seemed to Vince, and he turned up the quarter-full pitcher of beer that was left on Russell Harmon's table and drank it, wincing at the shooting pain behind his swollen eyelid, and he went to the bar to order his own beer because what the fuck did he care after all about fucking Bill and if Bill didn't want to serve him Vince Thompson would just like to see him go ahead and try to say so, and then he stood there in fucking amazement, looking at the newcomers to the bar. *Well, well,* Vince Thompson thought, and he couldn't help smiling a bit despite the pain. *Would you look at what the cat dragged in.*

The
Music
of
the
Spheres

So someone had seen her at the library. That much Tristan could be sure of. Whether he'd been seen with her was another question, one that he found immaterial. Now that the news story was out, there would be someone— one of the shuffling figures who passed through the stacks while he sat with Liza Hatter and she thumbed through her magazine, the red-haired librarian he'd noticed at the desk on the way to the door, one of the several faces they'd passed after making their way out into the warm afternoon—who would remember seeing a tall auburn-haired girl (yes, the one in the pictures!) in the company of a tall handsome guy with long wavy hair, a regular student, no one you would have suspected. And there would be one person behind one of those faces who had, say, taken a class with him, maybe Chemistry 101 way back in freshman year, and who remembered his name. And when they came looking for him, there would be no way to hide it, he wouldn't find the right words to hide it if he found any words at all, and in fact he no longer wanted to hide it, didn't want to deny Liza Hatter in the face of a direct question. No, he knew what he would do—he would take a deep breath, and slowly his arm would rise from his side and point to the hill where Liza Hatter lay buried. Between that moment and this one there was only time.

And in this moment he felt quite relaxed. There was no need for talk, no need for explanation. There were no words he knew how to speak, in fact—he had become, as nearly as he could tell, perfectly mute. He tried now, again, to say a word, any word, just to test his capacity, but all that came when he opened his mouth was the quiet wordlessness of breathing, and he was satisfied. It was comforting not to speak here in the yellow light of candles, the light reflecting in long streaks on the table where his elbows rested, the cool air that came in the open front door following the storm. And no one spoke to him. He had it seemed achieved anonymity, perhaps invisibility, except to his friend the musician, who sat on the stage strumming chords and looking at Tristan from one eye occasionally, a peaceful smile on his face. This was the man who had taught him to speak the language of music, who had converted Tristan's love for the sounds into the ability to speak them through his fingers—awkwardly, stammeringly as yet, a baby's inarticulate approximation of the sounds he had long recognized: G chord, F chord, G. This was the man who, himself, spoke the language so hauntingly, in a way that no one but Tristan could hear. Not one of the other customers in the bar had ever understood this man, had ever heard in the subtle phrasings and almost hidden melodies the presence of a genius for hearing the world, its ambient sounds and rhythms. This man's music, Tristan had known from the first time he heard it, spoke the language of ticking clocks in empty rooms, of cars passing at night outside the window, of unseen birds in the treetops, of dry leaves skittering on the pavement at dusk when the streetlights buzzed to life. It was the language of unpopulated spaces. That was why people couldn't love it or hear it. When the musician sang "Heart of Gold" or "Lay Lady Lay," the crowd would grow attentive, hearing the sounds they already knew, but on the few occasions when he used his instrument to speak the strange language, the crowd would grow impatient, talk to the ones they came with, turn to the bar to order another beer.

At first, Tristan tried to put words to the music. For the two weeks he was home prior to the night with Liza Hatter, he toyed with the musician's strange understated melodies and loose rhythms. And each time he went to the musician to learn the language of fingers and strings, he showed the musician the words he had produced, and each time the musician looked at them and put them away, and Tristan felt that he had failed. Only now did he see that there was no failure—there was simply nothing at which to fail. The music of human absence and silence would by definition admit no words.

Tristan no longer cared. That was the musician's failure now—looking at Tristan while playing the guitar, thinking that Tristan was still involved in the insoluble riddle of the music, perhaps thinking that Tristan had been avoiding him because of his failure to solve the riddle. And in fact Tristan had been leery of the musician and his ability to hear things, penetrate things—until tonight, until now. Because what the musician didn't know was that the music now meant nothing, at least in and of itself. Nothing meant anything to Tristan except Liza

Hatter, the fact of her up there on that hill, a fact that only Tristan knew though there were many others searching to know it. And since only Liza Hatter mattered and only Tristan knew, a chasm yawned between Tristan and the world, and into that chasm all the words had been poured, *las palabras que desaparace*, so that he could do nothing but sit mutely amid the candle flames, and the musician and his odd song meant something only for this reason—that they were in the process of teaching Tristan where he had gone wrong. Of *course* it was impossible for him to tell Liza Hatter's story to Kelly Ashton; Liza Hatter's story, like the musician's song, was one of absence and silence, so there were no words in any language with which to tell it. He, Tristan Mackey, could not serve as translator.

And yet the story was still in his head while he sat listening to the music, as if the story and the music had intertwined. *Liza Hatter was born and raised in Salmon, Idaho. Liza Hatter was in homecoming court. Liza Hatter was a conscientious student at the university. Liza Hatter loved animals and wanted to be a veterinarian. Liza Hatter had strong feelings for Tristan Mackey and went with him one spring evening to the lake, where her feelings were strong enough to pull her too far into the water. Liza Hatter in her last moments appealed out of the strong feeling— love?—to the only person who was left to her. Liza Hatter's eyes widened, she took one last breath, and she said that person's name, in the form of a question—"Tristan?"*

He had heard the word so many times in the weeks following Liza Hatter's drowning, heard her calling it in that soft, frightened voice, that it had begun to set up a kind of echo in his head—*Tristan ((Tristan)(Tristan))*—calling to him from a line that divided the Tristan he had been before that night and the Tristan he had been ever since. And although he had come to love Liza Hatter in a way, he was growing tired of the voice and wanted to put it to rest, and to do that he had to fulfill his obligation to her, had to get her story told. But he had discovered in listening to the musician's song about absence and silence that he could not tell her story himself. It wasn't a question of words, it was a question of that body lying under the ground on the hill. The only person who could tell Liza Hatter's story was Liza Hatter. And that could be arranged.

He would need to speak three words to one more person when the time came, before he walked out the back door into the moonlight, three words that would lead to the telling of the story that would reach just one more person's ears, so that someone else could hear in Liza Hatter's silence the echo of his name, which sounded, strangely, like the song the musician was playing now, as if the musician *had* penetrated everything, knew everything after all, his sharp eyes glowing now and his lips curling into a smile for Tristan, who smiled back this time, hearing the sound like the inside of his head, like the vibrating space between the limitless stars, like the lungs' and the mouth's last breathing.

Whirlpools and Sea Monsters

The candles had a curious effect. Because his head was slightly uptilted when he looked at the numbers on the board, Brice Habersham's glasses caught the dancing candlelight, which threw a tiny glare, like sunspots. It was a mild inconvenience, not an actual handicap. After all, he could often hit what he wanted even with his eyes closed. But for the time being he occupied himself with measuring the candlelight's effect, throwing his three darts and plucking them out and throwing them again, calculating the subtle shifting of the light across the bull's-eye and the flickering glint off the silver wires. He imagined, as always, the dartboard as a vortex, his release point as the vortex's widest circle, the space between the release point and the board a sort of funnel, his chosen target the concentric point where the narrowing circles met, where the dart would be sucked in. It was interesting that the optical tricks played by the light off his glasses altered his throwing motion just slightly, just the tiniest bit, a tightening in his fingers and his wrist and his forearm, as if the well-trained mechanism didn't want to operate with the target not clearly defined. There was, indeed, a measurable difference in the results.

Amusing himself with the task of learning to throw by candlelight helped him not to think of the things he should have been thinking at the moment. He felt a vague indifference, for instance, to the fact that Russell Harmon had left the bar with the pretty brunette, that he was probably someplace close by snorting cocaine with her. He wasn't overly interested in Vince Thompson's departure, even though it might represent some danger to Russell, though he doubted Vince Thompson would try anything stupid with the girl present. Actually, now would be the perfect time to slide out of the bar himself, ascertain Russell's whereabouts, and, if Vince Thompson weren't around, make his call to the police. They could pick up Russell and the girl, maybe one or two of Russell's friends, and he could go down to the station and supervise the questioning and get the statements he needed to arrest Vince Thompson, and then he could go home to Helen and a decent night's sleep, provided Helen would let him have one. But the idea of making the call slipped further and further away, and he told himself that there would still be plenty of time, that the lights would come back up and they would all reassemble, hopefully without Vince Thompson, and finish the match before the unpleasantness began. Only one thing needed to be taken care of in the meantime—the phone call to Helen.

He called home on the cell phone and walked out the back door onto the deck and stared out over the dark water while he waited for Helen to answer. The phone rang six times before she picked it up from the bedside table.

"Brice," she said. "*Brice*," as if it were a demand rather than a question. The person on the other end of the line *had* to be him.

"It's me," he said.

"Oh, God," she said. "Thank God. I thought you weren't coming home. I thought you'd forgotten me."

"Of course I haven't forgotten you," he said. "How are you feeling?"

"*Miserable*," Helen said. "Completely *miserable*. Are you on your way home?"

"What's wrong?" he said.

There was a silence on the other end of the line and then a bumping sound and he could hear a little clang from Helen's bell being knocked over on the table and then he could hear her gulping water from a glass and then setting the glass back down and adjusting her pillow against the headboard. She sighed deeply. "Are there lights where you are?" she said. "Because there are no lights here. Where are you? Do you have lights? Electricity?"

"No," he said. "The lights are out here, too."

"Here where?" Helen said.

He told her the 321 Club and she asked if that wasn't a bar and he explained to her again, in a quiet voice, as much as he could about what he was doing tonight.

"When the lights went out, the dogs started barking," Helen said.

"Which dogs?" Brice Habersham said.

"All of them," she said. "All around the neighborhood. They haven't quit for a second and my head is pounding. Can you come home now? There's a crackle—an electric crackling, that's the only way I can describe it—behind my left eye. Have you ever felt that before?"

Brice Habersham said he hadn't.

"That's the only way I can describe it," she said. "It's going to get worse. If the dogs don't stop, it will get worse. If you're not here, I'll have to do something myself," she said.

He waited for her to say that she would call the police and he prepared to tell her not to do that, please, and that he would be home as soon as he was able to come. But she was silent on the other end of the line. He heard her sigh and then she started to say something and he heard her voice tremble and she stopped again.

"Helen?" he said.

"Brice," she said, "it's so dark here." She was quiet again and he waited for her to say that she was afraid. "It reminds me of that time in the mountains, you remember?"

"Yes," he said.

"It was very dark there, too, just like this, with no street-lights anywhere, and we opened the windows to let the fresh air in and you could hear the wind come down the mountains through the trees."

They had taken a vacation in the Adirondacks one year, and it had seemed to relax Helen. They'd stayed in a cabin. It was for the most part a good memory.

"I remember it exactly," he said. "Just the way you describe."

He heard her sigh again. "I know I'm a lot of trouble," she said.

"You're no trouble," he said.

"I'm a lot of trouble," she said.

"I don't think of it that way."

"I'll get well and then I won't be so much trouble to you," she said. Silence again. "Do you hear it?" she said.

"No," he said. "What?"

"The dogs stopped barking," Helen said.

"Good."

"I think I can sleep now," she said. "I feel tired."

"Good."

"Stay as long as you need to," she said.

"I won't need to stay too much longer," he said.

"I can sleep," she said. She was quiet for a moment. "But come home soon," she said.

They said good-bye and he looked out toward the mountains for a moment and walked back in the bar and began to practice his throwing again, and as he fell into the rhythm of throwing and retrieving, he found himself thinking, as he did occasionally, of Ellen Murchison, a girl from his hometown in Indiana, and what had happened to him a long time ago during a party at her house one afternoon.

He was fourteen and small for his age, late in developing, and had just reached the time when he had begun to feel a sexual urge toward the girls he knew, Ellen Murchison especially. Her parents were away for the weekend, and had left Ellen in the care of her older brother Ken, a senior. No sooner were the parents out the door than Ken had abdicated his responsibilities, leaving the house to Ellen so that he could go camping with his friends and rendezvous with some girls from school. It was summer, and there was not much to do in the small Indiana town, and naturally enough Ellen Murchison had organized a party, calling her friends to come over, asking them to stay the night if they could fool their parents. Brice Habersham knew that he had probably been the last of Ellen's phone calls. His popularity had slipped steadily from the time he had begun to wear glasses, from the time that the other boys had begun to mature without him, from the time that his painful awkwardness at sports had become apparent, and from the time that he had begun to grow shy as a result of all these inadequacies. Ellen Murchison had felt just barely enough of her old loyalty to him, as a neighbor and a childhood friend, to invite him along with the others.

It didn't help matters that his father had just taken him to the local barber for his annual summer crew cut. This time he had howled in outrage, but there was no way to resist his father ultimately. This was the year the Beatles came to America, and he hadn't exactly wanted a mop-top, which would have been a little too defiant for his sensibilities, but he didn't want to look like Johnny Unitas, whom he'd just seen on *Toast of the Town* the week before, either. And so he prepared himself for Ellen Murchison's party by donning a tight white T-shirt, Levi's with the cuffs rolled up, and his black Chuck Taylors, and he tried to disarrange his hair, but without visible effect. It was the best he could do, and he knew it wasn't enough. There was no chance that he would be one of the cool kids at the party.

Telling his mother he was going fishing with Tommy Linden, he left the house with his tackle box and fishing pole and made sure to go all the way around the corner in the direction of the creek before doubling back and cutting through the school yard, where he left his things behind the hedge that circled the gymnasium. Ellen Murchison's house was just on the other side of the school yard, and he walked there humming "Love Me Do." Not a musician himself, Brice Habersham nevertheless was an authority of sorts on the latest hits, listening assiduously late at night to the Top 40 radio station out of Indianapolis, carefully shifting the dial when the radio faded or squawked. He was always the first to learn the new songs and the new performers, and he had an uncanny knack of predicting which ones would rise to the top of the charts. He was known at school, insofar as he was known at all, as "the music kid." Secretly, though, he grew bored with the music easily, its simple arrangements and rhymes, and would have preferred listening to his father's Beethoven records, or maybe nothing at all.

There was Ellen Murchison's house, bright, white, the first in the neighborhood with a new invention called vinyl siding, also boasting an expanded garage that housed the Murchison's second car (since they'd bought their Lincoln Continental), a Chrysler New Yorker station wagon that Brice Habersham had actually ridden in many times when he was younger, on the way to the municipal swimming pool, with Ellen in her bathing suit. Approaching the house of the wealthy Murchisons, looking at their old car, he felt a curious mixture of past and future pleasure, a feeling that he would never experience in quite the same way again. He connected the innocent happiness of riding with Ellen in the station wagon, noticing even at that age that she was pretty but not feeling any anxiety or passion at the sight of her prepubescent body in the swimsuit, blue with a daisy pattern just above the right hip, he remembered, with the not-as-innocent pleasure of seeing her at the party, perhaps wearing a skirt that showed her leg above the knee, a tight blouse that exposed her round arms and her white throat, and he could see ahead of him the possibility of enjoying the charms of Ellen Murchison or another girl much like her, the possibility that he would grow out of his awkwardness and his perturbation, maybe even on this very afternoon or evening, though he would have to make sure it happened before dark, when he had to be home. Looking back on it now, releasing the dart yet again from his hand, noting carefully the flash from the candlelight and attempting to compensate with a tilt of his head, he could see opening Ellen Murchison's front door and going inside as his last real moment of hopeful anticipation—even his wedding night with Helen was not the same, encroached upon as it was by the knowledge of past defeats, half expecting the defeat in the midst of his anticipation.

There were junior varsity football players at the party. That was the first sign that made his heart sink. Fifteen and sixteen years old, muscles bulging from their T-shirts, surrounding Ellen Murchison and her friend Patty Mooney. They were drinking beer. Ellen waved at him and smiled, but he was shunted as if by a conveyor belt off to the other side of the living room, near the record player, where he talked to Tommy and his friend George Halbert and a kid he knew named Mikey and two girls with glasses and flat chests, Alice Atterburn and Gloria Penfield. That was what he had known it would be like, really, before the brief fantasy he entertained while approaching the door.

Then one of the football players, raucous and backslapping, took it upon himself to bring the group by the record player a round of beers. Brice and Tommy and George and Mikey and the girls had accepted them without comment, reluctantly, playing the role that they seemed to be required to play, the hangers-on who benefited from the football player's largesse. The beer was in a squat brown bottle, rather warm, and Brice Habersham drank it trying to keep down the bile in his throat and a sense of dread. By the time he had nearly finished, another was placed in his hand, and by the time that was nearly gone, the scene had been magically transformed. The sunlight through the window imbued the Murchisons' living room with a yellow glow and a pleasant heat, a moistness he could feel on the skin of his forearms and the space between his toes, a sleepy, languid feeling of romance. Ellen Murchison was beautiful there across the room, and it didn't seem impossible that he would talk to her. Out the window, the houses of the Indiana town hummed their way across the flat land to the cornfields, which Brice Habersham could imagine if not actually see. Even Alice and Gloria were part of the new mood, fun girls whom you could talk to, who laughed and made you feel good. The only wrong note came from the record player—Tommy had, in his ignorance, put on an old Elvis Presley tune.

Downing the last of his beer in two big swallows, Brice Habersham stepped confidently toward the record player and the stack of records next to it, mostly Ellen's brother's, he suspected. It was a smorgasbord of the latest songs, all the music he listened to when he was supposed to be asleep.

He knew all of these—the Beatles, of course, and Paul Revere and the Raiders, and the Beach Boys, and the Supremes, and the many dozens of others. What must it be like to be Ken Murchison, who obviously received an allowance large enough to buy whatever records he liked? Brice Habersham got only enough each week to buy one or two records, if that's how he chose to spend his money.

One after another, he placed the records on the turntable until there was a fat stack of 45s waiting to drop. He hit the switch, and the player arm rose slowly and tapped the bottom-most record, which fell into place and commenced spinning.

Then the song was playing—"Deadman's Curve" by Jan and Dean. "Hal Hartman Plays the Hot Hits," Brice Habersham said out loud, to no one in particular, in the voice of the crazy nighttime DJ from Indianapolis, which he could bring off almost perfectly.

He was surprised to hear someone behind him laugh. "Hey, that's pretty good," he heard one of the football players say, the same one who had distributed the beers.

"This one's so hot it sizzles, gang—*sssst!*—Oww!" Brice Habersham said, still not knowing quite why he did so. "Let me spin this one for you while I go find the Band-Aids," Brice Habersham said. "Holy smo-o-okes! Where's the fire extinguisher?"

Now there were more people laughing, almost what you'd call an audience, if you were thinking of it in that way. "That's pretty good," the football player said again. "Hey, listen to this!" he called over to Ellen Murchison and her group. "This kid sounds just like Hal Hartman."

And so they all gathered around Brice Habersham, and each time a new record dropped he did the routine, aping lines he'd heard Hal Hartman use. And everyone laughed, and while the songs played, they danced, and soon he found himself actually dancing with Ellen Murchison, and he regretted that he hadn't put on any slow ones. The air in the room grew stifling, though, from the summer sun and the exertion, and Brice Habersham's head felt a little dizzy and he suddenly needed to pee, and he excused himself for the last song and went in search of a bathroom. Going out of the living room and past the front door, swelled with a sense of well-being—Ellen Murchison had danced with him!—he remembered that there was a small bathroom at the top of the stairs, so he walked up holding on to the banister. He was now feeling almost desperate to relieve himself, so he shut the door without locking it, an oversight that he certainly would not have committed were it not for the two beers. When he finished, he buttoned up his pants and buckled his belt and washed his hands at the sink. Something pink caught his eye, and instead of opening the door he turned to look. There was a bra hanging over the shower rod—a pink, lacy bra, something girlish about it, not a bra, Brice Habersham guessed correctly, that Mrs. Murchison would wear. Imagining Ellen Murchison unhooking the bra before she stepped into the tub, he felt himself stiffening in his pants. Slowly, carefully, he lifted the bra from the rod, examining the padded pink cup that held Ellen Murchison's tender breast, the strikingly hard wiring underneath—that would be uncomfortable, wouldn't it?—the complicated mechanism of hooks and straps. Again, carefully, he placed the bra back over the rod as he had found it, but looking down at the floor now he saw a pair of pink underwear, just to the side of the bath mat near the wastebasket. He felt blood rush to his head, and he put one hand on the edge of the sink. Did he dare? The panties had clearly been worn recently, tossed down carelessly in haste—probably when Ellen Murchison took a shower just prior to the party. He could see the panties' white lining over what must surely be the crotch, and a slight discoloration there. His hands were shaking. He looked quickly around the bathroom. He could still remember to this day the white soap dish on the sink, the blue bath mat and shower curtain, the delicate flower pattern of the wallpaper. He was alert enough to take in all these details and preserve them. But he did not think to lock the door. Bending over, he picked up the frilly panties and felt the soft fabric in his fingers. Was that actual silk? He closed his eyes and brought the panties to his face and breathed in the tangy scent of Ellen Murchison. Transported, it took a moment for him to realize the door had opened, and when he looked up he saw Ellen Murchison standing over him, aghast, her mouth open to reveal her white teeth, her pretty nose crinkled up and the lines showing around her squinted eyes, so that she looked rather like a pig with fangs. Then she screamed and ran back out the doorway. Brice Habersham dropped the panties and lurched backward, hitting his head on the corner of the sink. Ignoring the pain, he righted himself and rushed out to the staircase just in time to see Ellen turn the corner into the living room, screaming her head off. When he reached the front door he could still hear the screams just as forcefully, as if Ellen's head had literally become detached, and was still there at the bottom of the stairway wailing piteously while her body went on ahead. Then, finally, staggering to the sidewalk, he heard Ellen's frantic voice raised against him and a couple of the football players laughing uproariously and the other girls mewling in disgust.

While he ran across the school yard gasping for breath, Brice Habersham quickly ticked through the list of possible excuses, and realized there were none. Even worse, he knew instinctively that Ellen Murchison would embellish the story, and that those who told it afterward would embellish it further. His life was over. He would never be able to hold his head up at school again. He would be an outcast, a pariah. And although, stopping by the hedge to retrieve his fishing gear and then sitting down and letting the tears come, he could not have predicted the trajectory of his life from that point on, he came pretty close. There was nothing for him to do, he decided, but dig into his studies, use his brain to achieve whatever he could. And when he went to college he would find some field of study that would take him out of his Indiana town forever, and in all matters he would choose safely and correctly, minimizing the chances of anything so horrific happening ever again.

And this was largely how things went. He earned straight A's through high school, except for the B he received intentionally in his senior English class so that he wouldn't have to go onstage at graduation to give the valedictorian's speech. He kept to himself, ignoring as best he could the taunts and the giggles and the whispers—which, he knew, would still continue today in certain quarters if he were ever to return home. His adolescence was marked by the pain of isolation and shame, and he wondered now, tossing the darts again and again, waiting to see if the lights would come back on, whether what he had done in that blue bathroom so long ago was actually all that unusual or bad. He had no knowledge of sex, really, other than his private imaginings and the occasional glimpses over the years of Helen in the nude—and the wedding night, the harrowing wedding night, there was that—but it seemed to him that many fourteen-year-old boys would have reacted in the same way to the discovery of Ellen Murchison's undergarments. He wondered if Ellen Murchison had ever thought of this. According to the last report he had received from his mother on "the Murchison girl," she had married an architect directly out of college and moved to Boston. Did she ever remember the incident in the bathroom, and, remembering, did she think to herself how it wasn't that serious a crime for a young boy to commit, and feel her own sense of guilt and shame at what she'd done to him? Did it occur to her, all these years later, that she could simply have lowered her eyes and closed the door and walked quietly away?

It wasn't that he'd never gotten over it—he had, of course, eventually. He had moved away and he had made a career for himself and a life, such as it was, for himself and Helen. But in thinking about that day now and how vividly it had always been impressed upon his memory, his imagination, he began to wonder—rather uncharacteristically, because Brice Habersham didn't much go in for idle speculation—whether almost everything he had done afterward could be traced back to that one point, to that terrible embarrassment and how he reacted so strongly against it, vowing never to let it happen again. For instance, there was the decision in college to take up criminal justice, which he pursued with a zeal that often wore out both peers and professors. Here was the extensive set of rules to guide behavior, here was the painstaking attempt to define the nature of wrongdoing, an area of study Brice Habersham could sink his teeth into. There was no wild youth, no period of experimentation—rather, there was strict regimentation. He looked only to the future, and his future was secure.

He was settled both financially and professionally, already an agent in the relatively new Drug Enforcement Administration when, just before turning thirty, he met Helen McSweeney. She was a clerk in a department store in Chicago, working in the area of home furnishings. Brice Habersham had recently bought a home in the expanding suburbs, in order to gain more space away from his neighbors than he could have in his downtown apartment. It was summer, and he was enjoying the upkeep of his neatly trimmed lawn during his hours away from work, but it occurred to him one day that the house's interior was threadbare. It was to Helen McSweeney that he applied for help.

She showed him blenders and microwave ovens and silverware, dinette sets and sofas, bed frames and draperies. Most of what she suggested, he purchased. She was not friendly, but neither was she impolite. The same age as Brice Habersham, he would later learn, she was not pretty, but neither was she unattractive—straight brown hair very neatly cut, a thin, rather nervous body, a plain face with regular features, tiny hands and feet. She didn't look like the love of anyone's life. Maybe, in some way, it was the setting. Brice Habersham watched her move through the simulated environment of a home. She was dour and solemn and timid and somehow sad, and that also helped. She struck him as someone who would not judge his careful ways harshly.

He kept returning—buying napkins, steak knives, a lamp. On his fourth visit he lowered his head and smiled rather shyly and asked her to dinner. Six months later they were married in a Catholic church on the north side, her father wearing a Cubs cap to the ceremony. For the honeymoon, they rented a bungalow on the Outer Banks. It was early spring, and the weather was not in a mood to cooperate. A nasty squall blew up from the gray ocean, slashing the windows with rain. They went to bed early. Helen wore a plain yellow gown that reached to her ankles. She lay on her back with her arms at her sides. Brice Habersham kissed her and received no real response, and, not knowing what to do, finally lifted her gown carefully and ran his hands over her small, soft breasts. There was nothing from

Helen but her heartbeat and her breathing. Soon he became agitated, and began prodding at her awkwardly, his fingers in the strange curly hair of her pubic area. Helen's mouth began to emit an odd sound—it did not seem to come from Helen herself, the Helen he knew—a gurgled kind of whistling, and for a few moments Brice Habersham mistook this noise as a sign of pleasure.

Then came the most terrifying minutes of his life. Brice Habersham had walked into rooms with armed men who would have killed him if they thought they had the chance, but there had always been a way to analyze the possibilities and outcomes of these confrontations, to place himself at a calculated advantage beforehand—he was known in the agency for his ability to defuse potential violence. His work required courage and skill, but it was a courage and skill that could not help him with Helen. The whistling sound became a piercing scream reminiscent of Ellen Murchison's, and Helen's tiny hands clutched his own with such ferocity that he thought his bones were cracking. Suddenly she was standing over the bed, a looming silhouette in the window frame, spewing language so foul that he felt it could not be directed at him, mild-mannered Brice Habersham, and could not come from the woman he knew, his quiet wife, Helen. He was a fucking this and a goddamn bastard that and a cocksucking so and so if he thought that she would ever let him touch her, if he thought she would ever let him put his disgusting penis in her cunt. Brice Habersham lay motionless on his side throughout, crying hard with his eyes shut tight, until Helen locked herself in the bathroom, where he heard her weeping on the floor. He did not try to go to her. After a while, for some reason, maybe to comfort himself, he masturbated, and then he felt ashamed.

In the early morning hours he woke from awful dreams to find Helen back in the bed with him, slowly rubbing his bruised hand. She was sorry. She hadn't meant the things she'd said, but he should never have married her. She was not what he thought she was. She had pretended to be someone else. Really, she was a pathetic woman in love with a man named Nolan Bridges, the supervisor of the men's clothing department at the store where she had worked. Nolan Bridges had swept her off her feet, he was handsome and charming, but he was not a good man, he had cheated on his wife and made Helen promises and taken advantage of her and then dumped her with no more feeling than he would have had for a discarded pair of shoes. She was glad that she was married to a good man now—but he would have to give her time.

At this moment, at precisely 11:32 p.m. according to Brice Habersham's wristwatch, on a Thursday night in June in the year 2007, looking around the bar at the suspects all reassembled, all the poor characters in the drama, the ones who would have to be arrested, who would have to be shamed for their transgressions, and feeling so low that it was as if the monster stenciled on the back of his own shirt were trying to swallow him, he had given Helen nearly half his life, over twenty-seven years.

One Last Dart in Hand

Russell Harmon sat alone in his truck cab, looking at the photograph of the little girl. No matter how he angled it under the dome light, it was still his own face looking back at him.

Kelly Ashton had gone back into the bar to "give him a minute to himself," but how he was expected to use this minute remained unclear. His brain seemed to him a little bit numb, even more so than usual. He could do a line of coke, he supposed, but he couldn't work up much enthusiasm for it all of a sudden. He supposed that, having just fucked Kelly Ashton, having just discussed the possibility of cohabiting with her— *tell me* that *story, Russell*—having just found out that he was the father of her child, it was best to go back in the bar and try to think of something to say.

There was a distinctly new feel to the air outside, an atmospheric shift following the storm, but whether it was warmer or colder Russell couldn't tell. His body seemed to have undergone a temperature change, as if he were connected to another beating heart—tucked away in the wallet in the pocket of his shorts now—that either warmed him or cooled him, he didn't know which. He even *looked* different to himself. His large feet in the Birkenstock sandals, for instance, looked strangely like an alien's. As he walked through the open door of the 321 the first person he saw was Tristan Mackey, who Kelly Ashton had slept with just recently, who had invited Kelly Ashton out tonight for reasons that escaped Russell, who sat now all by himself listening to the open mike guy strum his guitar, some sort of crazy music that didn't sound like music at all. The candles were still out. The lights hadn't come back on. He should have known that from the darkness on the street, but he hadn't paid any attention. He went to the bar and ordered a beer from Bill. He headed toward the back, and the first two people he passed were his own father and Vince Thompson's. As usual, his father refused to acknowledge him. Russell noted the ridiculous muscle shirt, the outdated feathered hair, and he felt a little embarrassed. Other than that, what struck him most was that his father's face was very much the same as the face in the photograph. Then as he came nearer the dartboard there was Vince Thompson himself, a cartoon version of Vince Thompson sporting a puffed-up, discolored eye and dried blood on his face and a lump on the side of his head, glaring steadily not at Russell but at his father, or at Russell's father, Russell couldn't tell. And there was Kelly Ashton, sipping a glass of red wine and talking on her cell phone. Russell tried to smile, more or less how he thought he was supposed to—but how was he supposed to, under the circumstances? What kind of smile did the occasion call for? And there was Brice Habersham, looking at Russell from over by the dartboard. He was still here.

And there was Matt, sitting at a table with a pitcher of beer, grinning at him conspiratorially, knowing he had left the bar with Kelly Ashton. Reliable old Matt. Something about looking at Matt now made Russell Harmon want to cry, but he hadn't cried in such a long time that he wasn't sure he could remember how to get started.

Once, when they were maybe twelve or thirteen or fourteen or so he and Matt had ridden their bikes down to City Beach on a summer day. They had just quit the baseball team so they would have more time to look at girls, and City Beach was the place to do that. All of the girls were junior-high or high-school age, lying around on towels, applying sunscreen. Russell and Matt dropped their bikes in the grass and sauntered a bit self-consciously toward the beach hut, where you could buy hot dogs and sno-cones and soft ice cream. They stood digging through their shorts to figure out how much money they had between them when Russell's father came strolling out of the hut, wearing nothing but a Speedo and a thick gold chain around his neck, checking out all the young girls lying in the grass and peering down toward the sand and the water to make sure he wasn't missing any. He didn't see Russell and Matt until he was right next to them. A hitch in his step, just for a moment. "Boys," he said, nodding, and walked on past while Russell tried to record the sound of his voice, so that he could recognize it if he ever heard it again, upon answering the telephone, for instance, maybe. His father's retreating thirty-something-year-old ass sagged a little bit sadly in the Speedo despite all the hours in the gym, and Russell knew who he was, knew what he was supposed to mean, watching him walk off like he had a number of times before, always seeing him from behind, it seemed, feeling a kind of rolling in his gut, and Russell turned his attention back to counting the change because he didn't know what else to do, only to find that Matt was gone. Russell found him around the corner of the beach hut by the men's restroom, sitting there on the concrete, bawling like a baby. That was the kind of friend Matt had been for all these years, the kind of friend who would do your crying for you, if necessary. He would be the first person Russell would tell.

But not now. Right now Russell Harmon couldn't tell anybody anything. It was as if he'd walked through a revolving door and was now busy holding it shut behind him, so that he could see and almost hear people trying to get in but no one could, not Vince Thompson, who might be trying to murder him and who he'd been so scared of half an hour before, not his own father, who didn't seem to matter much, not Brice Habersham and the dart match, not even Kelly Ashton. He was behind some sort of glass door that separated him from the world where other people moved, alone with the picture he carried in his wallet, which seemed to absorb all his attention even though he couldn't see it anymore and didn't know what to think about it or how it made him feel.

Brice Habersham approached him. "You ready?"

"For what?" Russell said.

Brice Habersham looked confused, rotating the darts in his hand, the flights clacking. "Our dart match?" he said.

"It's dark," Russell said.

Brice Habersham looked over at the dartboard. "We could scoot those tables closer," he said. "There's light enough with the candles."

What a strange man Brice Habersham was, thinking about

darts at a moment like this. Why was it so important to him? Hadn't he said he needed to go home? Didn't he know that Russell Harmon had responsibilities? For God's sake, the proof was right here in his wallet, a three-by-five glossy of a little person with his own face and hair. Russell sighed. "Give me a sec," he said, and he sat down next to Kelly Ashton, who was still talking on the phone—*But how do you know she's asleep, Mother? All I'm saying is would you please go back and check . . . Mom, you're smoking in the house, aren't you? You're* smoking. *Yes you are. That's why you won't go back there. Put out the cigarette and go check. You're* drunk. *Yes you are. All I'm saying is go check on Hayley.*

Go check on *his daughter*. The woman was *smoking in the house*. She was *drunk*. "Do you need to go home?" he said.

Kelly Ashton shook her head and held up a finger to say hold on. She shook her head again—*Good. OK. Don't fall asleep on the couch, Mom. Go to bed. Yes it does make a difference it* does. *You'll fall asleep on the couch with a cigarette and burn down the building. You'll . . .* listen *to me, Mother.*

The woman was *burning down the building*. Shouldn't someone be alarmed? Russell made a dart-throwing motion and did a little pantomime with his fingers, like the Indians used to do to explain things to the white men in the old Wild West movies—walk many moons, reach land over the mountains where buffalo cavort in the long grass—to show himself walking to the board, playing darts with Brice Habersham, then coming back to Kelly Ashton and *taking Kelly Ashton home*, or if not taking her home then at least participating somehow in the process of home-going. Kelly Ashton went into a head-nodding routine, as if this all made sense to her. "Are you sure—" he said, but she nodded again and put a finger to her ear so she couldn't hear what he was saying.

He turned stiffly to the dartboard and some sort of bustling ensued, people choosing seats to watch the show. Then he was playing darts with Brice Habersham, what he had come down here for tonight. They were playing 301. He'd lost the cricket game, and if he lost 301 he'd lose the match. No individual championship, and the team championship would still be at risk next week. He told himself these things, but they were part of some forgotten belief system, some religion for which he'd worn out his fervor. Russell Harmon was dimly aware that he was losing, and he didn't really care. He had a vague recollection of doubling in to start the game, of shooting darts and subtracting numbers on the chalkboard. But the photograph was burning a hole in his shorts. He couldn't think about anything else.

He stood at the line, darts in hand, and he stepped back for a moment and looked at Matt, who puffed out his cheeks and raised his eyebrows. *Tough going*, his look seemed to say. Russell turned around and looked at Kelly Ashton. She met Russell's gaze and smiled politely. Bored. He thought about calling the whole thing off, just quitting. Look, he would say to all assembled, I just found out we—he would indicate Kelly Ashton—had a baby together. But her mother is burning down the building. I think I better see her home.

Then Matt started clapping. A steady clapping, like the hoofbeats of a horse. "Come on, Russell," he said. He nodded at Russell, who stood at the line with his arms at his sides. "You can do it, buddy." He quit clapping and cupped his hands around his mouth, as if he could direct the words straight into Russell's ear, and said a little more softly, although still loud enough for everyone, including Brice Habersham, to hear: "Remember you're the fucking Dart League King." Then he clapped a couple more times for emphasis, as if he were reminding Russell of who he was and what it was that he could do if he could remember how to do it.

Almost the whole back of the bar was filled with spectators, standing with their arms crossed or sitting at the tables with the candles lighting their faces. Even his father had been drawn from the bar by whatever was going on, most likely not realizing that Russell was involved, but holding his ground now along with Vince Thompson's dad, both of them yucking it up over some stupid joke, trying their best to make it look like they weren't paying attention. Probably they were scoping out Kelly Ashton, whose chair they were standing behind, and Kelly Ashton's breasts, which they could conveniently get a peek at. And right to the side of Kelly Ashton, Vince Thompson had pulled up a chair. No one sat at his table with him, for obvious reasons. He was grinning at Russell out of the side of his mouth in a way that Russell didn't particularly care for, but he didn't look like a guy who was ready to shoot anyone at the moment. In fact, strangely, he resembled someone watching a dart match.

All these people, all these faces, turned to him expectantly while he stood there with the darts in his hand. Even the faces of Brice Habersham's teammates seemed to be encouraging him, as if those teammates, despite their dart-league affiliation, were secretly hoping that Russell got the job done: *Out-of-Town-Guy-Former-Professional Moves to Area, Buys Out Convenience Store and Nice Home in Nice Neighborhood Poor Local Losers*

Can't Afford, but Can't Buy Victory over Dart League King (or At Least Not So Easily).

So they wanted him to throw darts, that much seemed clear. So OK. Maybe he could do that. Russell turned to the board, let his eyes adjust to the candlelight, raised his arm and made the little circle with his fingers around the fat part of the 20, and then let the dart go. The board thupped. A single 20. He closed the circle around the triple 20 and threw again, and, almost without waiting to see the result, again. Each dart had hit where he aimed it. 140 points. How easy it was. You just let the dart go where it wanted to. You could just about go to sleep. When he used to come back from hunting with Uncle Roy, cold and wet and smelling of dirt and sweat and damp wool, they would go to PJ's for a "relaxer," according to Uncle Roy, and Russell—twelve years old, fourteen years old, sixteen— would go to the back where they had the old beer-stained pool table and the beat-to-shit dartboard, and while Uncle Roy drank at the bar, talking to the worn-out fake-blond bartender (Uncle Roy's "girlfriend")—Russell learned to play darts, throwing and throwing while his boots steamed away by the baseboard heater where he'd placed them to dry, slowly becoming mesmerized by the easy repetition of the motions involved, barely able to keep his eyes open but still plunking darts into the board. That was what it felt like now, almost. One time in particular when he and Uncle Roy had come back to town without having managed to shoot anything, Russell woozy as an old dog, throwing darts like a sleepwalker, one of the old guys had come back to challenge him. "Hey, Roy," Russell heard the guy say after the game was done. "Too bad he can't make a living shooting darts, your nephew." It was the first time Russell remembered feeling that he knew how to do something right.

And Brice Habersham seemed to be struggling, at least for Brice Habersham. He kept tilting his head at odd angles when he threw. He wasn't finishing the game off as rapidly as he should have. And now, as Russell fell into the pattern of stepping up to the line and throwing, it wasn't as if he were actually *thinking*—no, but he was beginning to feel something, something opposite from the constriction in his chest and his arms that he'd felt earlier in the evening, something in the center of him that involved the memory of throwing those darts in the dim and musty bar when he went with Uncle Roy, the peaceful dizziness he'd felt in the truck cab on the way there, half sleeping while the snow swept up at the windshield, spinning him gently into space while the rattling heater and the hot chocolate in the thermos his mother always packed warmed him outside and inside, something old and half forgotten, a comfortable feeling in his body's memory that he could do this thing, the thing that lay before him, in this case beat a man whom he knew he was no match for, not as a dart thrower and not as a person probably, either, a steady polite man who never got ruffled or angry and who said things like "Good darts" to you when you were beginning to kick his ass—as Russell seemed to be doing now, strangely enough—a good man, probably, who took both his victories and his defeats quietly without resorting to boasts or excuses, who certainly wouldn't need all the pandemonium that was breaking out around Russell now to make him feel good, even though Russell was glad to see that everyone was on his side, it was nice enough to see, but this growing feeling was of more importance, more important than the fact that Kelly Ashton still seemed vaguely uninterested,

more important than the fact that his own father was apprais-
ing him in earnest now, possibly for the first time, or that he
had absolutely no idea what the look on Vince Thompson's bat-
tered face meant, no, the feeling was more important than all
that, because if the feeling that he could do this thing, that he
could beat Brice Habersham, held true, then maybe he could
do other things too, maybe he could actually be the Russell
Harmon he'd imagined when Kelly Ashton had told her story
about the cozy house and the little girl who would climb on his
chest, put her head down there and go to sleep. Maybe he could
actually be that man and not the one who sat in the truck cab
afterward looking at her picture and feeling, he knew now, that
there was so much distance between the Russell Harmon he'd
become and the little girl that it could never be covered, that his
intentions would carry him only so far, and that it would not be
enough to change his life or hers. Maybe Russell Harmon did
not actually think any of this, but he felt it in the slow raising of
his arm, the eyes that sought the target each time he threw.

And before he really even knew it, he had beaten Brice
Habersham in 301, and the match was all even. Matt was behind
him, grabbing his shoulders, slapping him on the arm. Russell
didn't want to look at anyone else, though the back of the bar
sounded like it was full of happy people who were excited by
what he'd done. Matt was the only one who understood, Matt,
who had talked strategy with him all week, who had helped
Russell keep his confidence up, who had given him the easy
job running the backhoe today so he wouldn't be exhausted,
who, win or lose, would be there at Russell's at 5 a.m., idling
the logging truck on the street—the only alarm clock Russell
needed—while Russell struggled blearily into his dirty jeans,

his ragged T-shirt, his pitch-stained work boots, Matt, who would tell him good morning and hand him a cup of coffee when Russell climbed into the cab. If Matt thought he could do this thing, then maybe Russell thought he could too.

But Brice Habersham nodded to him to throw a cork for Around the World, and as Russell toed the line he couldn't help it if a little of the nervousness crept back up, because the cork would make all the difference here, Around the World was a simple game, you just had to hit numbers 1 through 20 and a bull, not a game for a former professional, a bit of an embarrassment, really, a concession to the poor quality of the league itself, a way to keep the evening moving faster than the proper game, 501, would, and because it was a simple game the competitor who threw first had a distinct advantage, the problem with Around the World was that if you went first you never had to stop shooting, if the third and final dart of each turn hit the appropriate target, you were rewarded with three more darts, so, theoretically, and very literally in the case of an excellent shooter, a former professional, say, with a shiny trophy from Cleveland on the shelf above the drive-thru, it was possible to complete a game of Around the World without ever allowing your opponent to shoot (Russell had come very close to doing this himself on a couple of occasions)—it was all running through his head now, a latent cognizance of worst-case scenarios . . . and Russell was shocked to find that the cork had already left his hand. He had thrown when he wasn't concentrating. His dart was lodged somewhat crookedly an inch down and left of center from the bull's-eye. Brice Habersham could beat that throwing between his legs.

Briskly, almost *unfairly*, Russell Harmon thought, because

on some level he was beginning to care now, because he hadn't *meant* to throw the damn dart right at that particular moment and was maybe thinking of inquiring about the possibility of a do-over, although that would certainly have been against the rules, Brice Habersham stepped in, squared the toe of his shoe along the line, tilted his head in that funny way that Russell couldn't figure out, and zipped one of his darts into the green single bull's-eye. It was the deciding game of the match, and Brice Habersham had won the cork.

It wasn't so much that he wanted it for himself, he thought as he watched Brice Habersham shoot, score with his third dart, pluck the darts, shoot again, score with his third dart, pluck the darts, beginning to make his way from number 1 to number 20 with alarming speed now, the head-tilting still going on but apparently he'd found the right angle, and Russell realized what it was now, that the man couldn't *see* . . . it wasn't something he wanted for himself anymore, not especially, to be the Dart League King, which seemed like a childish and almost improper title for the father of a baby girl, but it seemed to be something that other people wanted, that *these* people wanted, the ones sitting in the chairs and standing by the tables, the ones he'd known all his life, some of them, and if they wanted it, it seemed like something he should give to them, like a pat on the head, like a piece of candy, a simple response to a sim-ple need, what a father might give to a child, for example. But there was this impediment—this man with the slicked-down hair, the shiny glasses, the fiery dragon on his shirt, whirling back and forth in the candlelight from the board to the line to the board to the line like a little red demon, refusing Russell Harmon his opportunity. And Russell Harmon felt kind of pasty, suddenly, there was a clamminess to his skin, like he was being embalmed with the sweat from his own pores, because it began to dawn on him that he was really, truly losing, *reallytrulylosing* yet again, at one more thing that, at least, used to be important, and maybe still should be.

And then the board took a hard spin, as if it were one of those whaddayacallit wheels in Vegas, one of the things you dropped the ball into and crossed your fingers, hoping for luck, and Russell took a step back and leaned his arm on a chair to stop the spinning. Brice Habersham had just done something shocking, hadn't he? He had thrown his second dart right square in the heart of the single 20. Russell had one second to glance at Matt for confirmation, and he could see it on Matt's face, a look of disgust, because to Matt it would seem like blatant arrogance, wouldn't it, like a form of disrespect, but to Russell it seemed very brave, something to admire. Brice Habersham—even knowing that he was playing the Dart League King, that if one person in the entire league, the entire town, even the entire state of Idaho, maybe, could run the board on him in Around the World, go from zero to bull's-eye without giving up his turn, he was playing that one person— had thrown his second dart into the single 20, leaving himself just one dart in hand to hit the bull's-eye and win the game or forfeit his turn, when he could have, should have, thrown his second dart off the board and then hit the 20 with his third, giving him another turn in which he would have three chances to hit a bull's-eye and win the match. Russell Harmon had just enough time to lean on the table, look at Matt, think all these things before Brice Habersham's third dart thupped the board, a millimeter outside the bull's-eye. Brice Habersham walked calmly to the board and pulled his darts, wrote "20" on the chalkboard, stepped off to the side, and folded his arms, looking at the board, waiting. Russell Harmon would have his turn.

After all the shouting had died down, at the tail end of the show of faith, Russell stepped to the line and threw without thinking. He couldn't allow himself to think, had to do this with the unthinking part of himself that had done almost everything in his life, because if he started to think now (hitting the 1 with his first dart, missing the 2 with his second, hitting the 2 with his third, hearing as if from far away a collective sigh of relief), if he started to think *now* it was all going to grow too big, it was going to get as huge as that lake out there, it was going to be like trying to swim all the way across that lake one tiny stroke at a time (which was how he was making his way around the board, making the circle with his fingers and throwing a single 3, a single 4, a single 5), it was going to be like that deal Kelly Ashton had told to him once with the butterfly wings, how they flapped somewhere and set off a hurricane, if he started thinking he was going to think about how everything reached out to something else, how if he failed there would be people disappointed, and how that disappointment, even if it was a tiny one, even if it was like one time, say, when a father failed to speak to his son when he saw him in a crowd, and that son had not been able to sleep that night or for many nights afterward, lying in bed fighting the dark hours and feeling emptier and emptier and more and more alone inside until the inside disappeared altogether, and it had made that son a different person than he might have wanted to be if there had been an inside left in him to do any wanting, how the disappointment might be enough to make one of these people who wanted something from Russell Harmon now argue with a girlfriend, maybe, and this argument would come back years later to cause somebody pain, maybe even cause the children of those somebodies pain in some small or very large way, maybe all these people would leave this bar on this summer night with the disappointing feeling that Russell Harmon had lost this match and was no longer the Dart League King and in a series of little words, little actions (like the slight movement of his hand now, and the dart sneaking fortuitously, because his aim was a little off, into the triple 7, which nudged him along to 10), would set off a chain of disappointments that spread far beyond the confines of this town and lasted for generations, if he started thinking now and let the pressure build and lost, it would be one more thing he'd lost at in the eyes of Kelly Ashton, one more thing to show that he was unfit, that he would always lose, and it would look that way to his father, and his father could once again find a reason to turn away, and worst of all, biggest of all, if he started thinking now instead of just letting his hand do what it had to do (releasing the dart now, watching it settle softly into the triple 12, now the single 15, it was going very smoothly and very quietly for him despite all the noise, the fact that Matt was standing on his chair now and shouting, that there was someone who insisted on clapping him on the back), it would grow inside starting from this time and going on, that in the one thing in the world at which he'd been pretty good he wasn't good enough, and that a person who wasn't good enough at even one thing couldn't hope to be good at something else, something larger and more important, something complicated and mysterious like being a father, say, and especially if one had never had a father oneself but only an Uncle Roy, who was really more of a fishing and hunting buddy than a father, and if you had always thought to yourself over and over as a child in a kind of obsessive daydream that if you were a father you would take your child somewhere else, teach your child to do something other than catch things and kill things, talk to your child more about the world of children, their world of desperate love for the things they didn't have, and how this would be even harder if you added the complication of the child being not a boy, which is what you'd always imagined, but a little girl who didn't even know your name, if he started thinking about that now, how every time he let the dart go (a double 17 with his third dart, thank God, because his hands were beginning to shake, and he didn't know how much longer or further he could go) it was like he was releasing his whole life into the air, there would be no way to keep going, to do this thing, which was the first thing before the next thing and the next. And so he refused to think about any of that as he stood at the line with his second dart in hand, the first dart jutting straight out from the single 19.

He had come to the same place as Brice Habersham. There he stood with his second dart in hand, and he could go the safe route, waste the second dart and shoot a single 20 with the third, provided he didn't miss, and then have three shots at the bull's-eye. Or he could, as some phrase stuck in his head from somewhere long ago, maybe some English class, suggested to him that he might, screw his courage to the sticking place and throw the 20 with dart number two, leaving him one shot at the bull's-eye, just as Brice Habersham had done. The thing was to keep not thinking about it, just do what his body said to do, but he was pausing, he was waiting for something to tell him, and Matt was definitely trying to, he could hear Matt over there saying *Do* not *even go there, Russell, do* not *be stupid, don't do it*, and his hand was moving now, he was trying to listen to something in the air and what he heard for the first time, oddly enough, since it had always bothered him so much before, was the musician's song, unplugged this time from the annoying drumbeat, just an isolated plunking note or two that settled in his heart and washed into his bloodstream, and the dart, which was supposed to fly above the board and settle harmlessly into the red felt backing, instead described its arc and wobbled precariously into the upper-right corner of the single 20.

Which left Russell Harmon with one dart in his hand. And that hand was raising already, because he couldn't stop to think, and that hand was now releasing the dart, and Russell felt all the breath go out of him as if it were his breath and not his hand that set the silver ball onto that wheel, sent the dart into the air, where it twirled ever so briefly, like the bright burst of a single lifetime measured against the stars, the flights spinning gently in little flames of candlelight, blond twists of a small girl's hair, and before Russell Harmon had time even for the lowering of his hand he saw the dart stick firmly in the red heart of the double bull's-eye, as perfect a throw as he or Brice Habersham or anyone else in the history of the world had ever made, and looking at that dart in the board's dead center his relief was so great that he would have burst into tears if he'd remembered how. He barely heard the air around him erupting with cheers.

And then unexpectedly his feet left the ground and he wondered if he was flying, but there was a crash against a table and whirling candlelight and glass and his body going down, down, till his elbows hit the floor, sending sparks up his arms into his shoulder blades, and in pain he wrenched around to find the face of Vince Thompson looming over him like a dark moon eclipsing the sun.

The Point at the Center of the Universe

Vince Thompson had the whole menagerie assembled right in front of him, Russell Harmon and his asshole father Clint Harmon and Vince Thompson's own asshole father, and he had a gun in his pocket and a knife on his belt and he could lay waste to the whole goddamn joint if he felt like it, just come up stabbing and firing right and left and then jet into the night, make a beeline for his folks' place and grab his money box and then maybe stop at the gas station on the way out of town for some Tylenol, which he could sure as hell use right at the moment, since his whole fucking head felt like it was ready to explode or just drop right off his neck and roll onto the floor. What he found himself doing instead, though, was watching that son-of-a-bitch little convenience store guy, little what's his name, Bruce or Boyce he couldn't remember, his brain didn't work worth a shit any-more, but anyway watching this little guy with the neat haircut and the shiny glasses and the silly dragon shirt throw some fucking darts. The dude could *throw* some fucking darts, Vince Thompson could tell. It wasn't like he was exactly a dart expert or anything, Vince Thompson, in fact he found the game point-less and stupid, but he'd played some motherfucking darts himself once upon a time, he'd logged enough fucking hours of his tragic misspent youth hanging around bars and killing time at the dartboard, enough to know what the hell was going on at any rate, and he knew a shooter when he saw one, and even though this little convenience store guy wasn't actually playing the best he'd ever seen anyone play, you could see it in everything the guy did, the precise movements that were the same every time, the total concentration, the calmness, that this guy was a fucking pro, and now that you mention it there were those trophies, weren't there, he'd seen the fuckers at the convenience store, that's right, but he hadn't assumed *this* little dude had won them, he didn't know why. He had actually had this experience many times before, running into some quiet little guy at a bar, generally some dude just trying to mind his own fucking business but Vince Thompson would keep both-ering him, because he liked bothering people who were trying to stay out of his way, and generally little guys were better because they wouldn't punch you, although he'd had that hap-pen a few times too, and then finally the little guy would start talking and you'd find out he actually had some fascinating tal-ent or whatever, he'd turn out to know everything there was to know about jazz, for instance, or he'd be a rare stamp collector and he'd pull out a bunch of stamps and show them to you and explain their history, stuff like that, the little fascinating details of nondescript people, stuff that would make Vince Thompson envious because he'd never been able to focus on one thing long enough to really know it like these people did. And so here was this quiet Bruce guy or whatever who turned out to be a badass dart player, who'd have thought, but there was some-thing wrong with him, too, he kept moving his head back and forth like a fucking Tourette's patient or something, but it didn't take Vince fucking Thompson long to figure it out, given his own history with the fucked-up vision thing, the guy couldn't see the goddamn board, that was his problem, he was probably just about blind as a fucking bat without his glasses and now it was too dark in the room or the candles were screw-ing with him or something, but still the guy was shooting up a fucking storm, putting an ass-whupping on Russell fucking Harmon, who had always bragged to Vince Thompson about his supposed dart-throwing expertise, he was the champion this and the champion that for thus and such number of years. Yeah right, well *that* was about to come to a sad conclusion. Compared to the little Bruce dude, Russell Harmon shot darts like a fucking girl, and Vince Thompson took a lot of pleasure now in watching how Russell's shoulders seemed to stiffen every time he turned to the board, probably imagining a bullet thudding into his fat ass, he, Vince Thompson, was glad to have a hand in Russell's undoing, so he made sure to smile in a mysterious way each time he caught Russell Harmon's eye so that Russell would think he was a lunatic. And so when Russell Harmon calmly threw a single and two triple 20s, Vince Thompson was at first annoyed. The dangerous grin was no longer having its desired effect. But as Russell Harmon kept shooting, as he actually started shooting *better* than the little Bruce dude, and even though you had to take into consideration the problem with the Bruce dude's impaired vision, Vince Thompson began to have that same odd feeling he had when he found Russell having sex with the Ashton babe in the truck, a feeling that suddenly made him want to turn to someone next to him, one of those other fucking geeks with the dragon on his shirt, maybe, and say, "I *know* that dude, he buys drugs from me," which of course wasn't a thing it was possible to say, but he wanted there to be a connection between him and Russell Harmon, something to link him to Russell and the evening's exploits, and by the time Russell had *won* the fucking 301 game, Vince Thompson was asking the dragon guy at the next table all about the situation, and he heard all about the league championship and the individual championship and how Brice, which turned out to be the little dude's name, used to be a professional, and he realized that Russell Harmon was in the match of his life, that the scope of this thing was beyond what he, Vince fucking Thompson, had imagined, and he felt ashamed of himself for the trouble he had been causing Russell Harmon, who was here trying to win the dart league championship against a serious fucking badass dart player, a *ringer* more or less by Vince Thompson's estimation, some guy who'd been brought in unfairly from out of town, *ashamed* that he had been distracting Russell Harmon with the threat of physical violence and sudden death, he felt bad about this, and now that asshole Brice was shooting the lights out in Around the World, it was impossible to make the guy miss, Vince Thompson tried coughing loudly a couple of times right when he went to throw and it had no effect, he just kept plunking in single after single, and Vince Thompson felt like standing up and letting the Brice dude have it with the Beretta in the back of the fucking head, *that* would put a stop to him, and then pretty soon the Brice dude had come to the fucking bull's-eye, and Vince Thompson had scooted forward to the edge of his seat and he closed his eyes and held his swollen head because he couldn't watch, couldn't look, and then there was noise and he looked up and the Brice dude had missed, had *missed*, and Russell was at the line and Jesus, he looked a little shaky, didn't he, and Vince Thompson felt his hands start to sweat and he was hot in the camouflage pants even though they were still wetter than shit and he'd been freezing his ass off just a minute before, but Russell was keeping it going, a wild shot here but a single there, making the shots when he had to, and then he started finding his rhythm, it started going more and more smoothly, and Russell Harmon looked to Vince Thompson like a Greek god there at the line with his curly hair and his goddamn gut pushing out the front of his T-shirt, he was like a blaze of light in the fucking darkness, and Vince Thompson could barely contain himself, he started looking around at the other faces to see if they saw it too, and goddammit that Ashton chick didn't look like she had a fucking clue, just sitting there swinging her leg under the table, and Clint fucking Harmon and the asshole air force colonel father just talking, talking, laughing, laughing, *ha fucking ha*, like they weren't fucking impressed, the cocksuckers, and Vince Thompson couldn't stand it anymore, there had to be something for him to do, so he was up out of his chair and over behind Russell and he started slapping Russell on the back in between turns, saying shit like *That's my boy!*, causing some visible alarm among Russell's friends, it looked like, but not to Russell himself, who didn't seem to notice where the slaps or the words were coming from, even, so totally wrapped up was he in the brilliance of what he was doing, a triple, a double, and finally, with everything on the line, with the pressure built up to its most extreme point, so that Vince Thompson felt the climax of Russell's performance would be that Vince Thompson's own pounding blood would spew right out of his fucked-up head, Russell fucking Harmon threw a goddamn dart right in the middle of the fucking bull's-eye, a throw so fucking perfect that the dart sticking straight out from the very goddamn center of the board looked like it had arrived somehow at the core of the entire fucking world. It was the most beautiful thing Vince Thompson had ever seen in his entire fucking miserable life and there was nothing he could do to hold himself back anymore in the expression of his sheer his utter fucking joy, it had built up inside him now to such a point that there was abso-fucking-lutely nothing he could do other than tackle Russell Harmon as hard as he could from behind and knock him to the floor. But when Russell Harmon turned to see him it was with a look of, what, maybe terror, and Vince Thompson felt so bad that he started almost crying, saying softly *I'm sorry, I'm sorry*, but then the next thing he knew he'd been kicked in the ribs and it wasn't by Russell who was after all underneath him but by that same son of a bitch Clint Harmon, who, oh, *now* all of a sudden wanted to claim Russell as his fucking kid or something, now that everybody was congratulating him and shit, but it was too goddamn late for that, too late for the deadbeat dad, and Vince Thompson grabbed for the knife to stick it in Clint Harmon's gut while Clint Harmon got on the floor and started pounding him *again*, god*damn* was there never any end to this fucking night, he was going to wind up in the hospital by the time it was through, and he got the knife unsnapped but before he could get it in his grip it had clattered loose and his knuckles were being rapped on the hardwood floor, it was the asshole air force colonel father unit, saying *piece of shit* and *crazy* and *waste of human life* and shit like that, Jesus he and Clint fucking Harmon were like a whole fucking SWAT team between the two of them, and his head knocked on the floor from one of Clint Harmon's punches and the bar went kind of blurry and tilted and surreal so it was hard to know what exactly happened next but he was lifted up from the floor and set against the wall where he was standing, leaning, wobbling, and there was his fucking *friend*, his fucking *good friend* Russell Harmon, the best goddamn dart thrower Vince fucking Thompson had ever seen, shoving his own father out of the way and saying *Get the fuck* off *him, man, that's* enough, shit like that, and then Vince Thompson was trying to clean the fresh blood off his face and Russell was talking to someone, saying *Wait right here*, and then he was telling goddamn Bill the bartender, *All right, all right, I'll get him out, don't call the cops*, and then he and Russell Harmon were out on the sidewalk and the air on Vince Thompson's face was like cool cool water. And after he had gotten done telling Russell thank you over and over and he had gotten done telling Russell that he was his friend and that he wouldn't ever let that asshole father upset him ever again, he'd go right back in there and shoot him right between the fucking eyes all Russell had to do was say the word, and after he'd gotten done telling Russell that the bull's-eye he'd thrown was the greatest thing he'd ever seen, it was like the sudden alignment of all the fucking cosmic forces orchestrated by a godly higher being, no *shit*, he was *serious*, motherfucker, don't *laugh* at him like that, Russell was holding him by the arm and helping him stagger down the street to his car, which Vince Thompson kept trying to point to in a roundabout sort of way but it was *hard*, goddammit, he was seriously beat to shit now and he kept getting confused and not seeing things correctly, the street was dark as piss, he just wanted to make it to his car and go home and fall asleep and in the morning he'd clean the bloody sheets, he didn't give a rat's ass right now, he was just so incredibly fucking tired, but when they got to the car finally and he'd gotten the goddamn thing cranked and was telling Russell Harmon out the window that he was OK, he was fucking OK, Russell was his friend, he suddenly didn't want to go home anymore, he didn't want Russell Harmon to leave, so he offered the only thing he could offer, the only thing he'd ever been able to offer for a long, long time now, and Russell Harmon looked around the dark night as if he was searching for something and his big hands squeezed the window frame and Vince Thompson held his breath because it mattered so much to him right now, he was so fucking lonely, go ahead and admit, and he might have even said it out loud, he couldn't tell, but then Russell was in the passenger seat and Vince Thompson was making a U-ey in the street and not even giving a shit about checking for cops and he was driving leaned up over the steering wheel trying to see out of his fucked-up face with Russell guiding him and they made the block and came around and crossed the bridge over Sand Creek and Vince Thompson pulled the car to a stop in the gravel parking area on the other side. And when he went to grab a bindle out of his pocket he put his hand in the wrong one and found the Beretta instead, and he realized with a kind of horror that, just like the uncanny perfection of Russell Harmon's final dart throw, everything had turned out exactly like he'd planned.

Distance

Tristan Mackey had said the three words, and now, if he could help it, he wouldn't say much of anything else. He sat in his truck in the parking lot behind the 321, staring out over Sand Creek and the bridge, the mountains on the far side of the lake, the moon in the sky and all the space beyond it.

Right after he had spoken to Kelly Ashton, said *Come with me*, there had been as if in some strange answer to his request bodies tumbling to the floor, shouting, fighting, and a knife that skittered on the hardwood, a knife that Tristan, blocked from getting to the door, had picked up for no other reason than to get it out of the way. When things had settled down he had begun again to walk toward the door, not saying anything to anyone, and Russell Harmon, saying *Wait right here* but not to Tristan, had slipped something into his hand. It was not until he crossed the parking lot that he realized he still held the knife, and now, in the other hand, a carefully folded paper containing Russell Harmon's cocaine.

Having nothing to do for the moment, he placed the knife securely under his seat next to the whiskey bottle, and he looked around to make sure the coast was clear, and he turned on the dome light and rolled a dollar bill and opened the paper carefully and snorted as much as he could, which was quite a bit, it seemed, as there wasn't that much left. So he went ahead and did the rest of it, and he leaned his head back, and for a while all he felt was the luxury of his breathing and the racing of his heart.

He smoked a cigarette and waited. It must have been at least five minutes now. He would wait a little longer. The wonderful thing about this drug, which he was beginning to wish he'd discovered earlier in life, was that it made everything crystal clear. His thoughts came to him with perfect precision. There was no difficulty with words, with speaking, with playing a role if need be. He could talk to Kelly Ashton if he had to, play the part of the fake Tristan she seemed to admire. And if Kelly Ashton did not come out of the bar and get into his truck, there was nothing to be done about that, either. After all, he had tried. It would actually be much nicer just to drive to the lake house, grab the shovel and the lantern and make his way up the hill, uncover Liza Hatter's face and sit down next to her, staring up into the vast sky.

With that thought, Tristan Mackey let his mind go white, and only when he heard Kelly Ashton's footsteps did he seem to arrive again there in the parking lot, resituated in time and space, retrieved from some great distance in order to witness a curious scene being played out on the bridge across the water, yet another odd drama in this rather unusual evening, and he realized he'd been watching it all along but not understanding. Now it seemed oddly illuminated—the streetlights had just come on. The raindrops on his hood glistened like tiny diamonds, and the lights from the marina caught the waves of Sand Creek running slow past the boat slips. Kelly Ashton's footsteps were coming closer, they were almost to the truck door now, and there on the bridge was Russell Harmon, lumbering along the sidewalk by the guardrail, his long shadow striding in front of him, thrown there by the streetlight on the far side of the creek. And there across the bridge, backing away from the light, moving out of the yellow glow into the safety of darkness, was Vince Thompson, both arms held out in front of him, pointing a large handgun toward Russell on the bridge. How strange it was that in the world outside his own quick breathing, his thrumming heart, in the night breeze beyond his windshield, out there suspended above the water, lit like a Hopper painting and swirling to the musician's tune he still heard somewhere in his head, there should be this other story going on, and that the characters should be people he knew. In fact he found the prospect of seeing Vince Thompson shoot Russell Harmon mildly interesting, but Kelly Ashton was at the truck door now, and it was time to open it and let her in. But she was standing back from the door, staring off toward the bridge at Russell Harmon. For a moment he thought things might take an unexpected turn, that she would shout to Russell, take out her cell phone and call the police, and he might end up actually involved in the scene in some way, and probably not one that would lead to any good. But her mouth was set in a straight line, her eyes just a bit vacant and sad. She didn't see Vince Thompson, obviously. Looking at her pretty face, he felt a quavering inside him, a slight hesitation caused by the way he'd felt about Kelly Ashton in the past. But he had gone way too far out now to get back there.

He would not say anything, or he would say as little as possible. While she buckled her seat belt, he would smile at her warmly, to show how glad he was that she'd made this decision. Silently, he would drive out of the parking lot and onto

First Street. He would make the turn onto the highway, and they would cross the long bridge over the lake, the dark water skimmed by moonlight. On the far side of the bridge he would make the turn to the lake house, the headlights shining on the ghostly birch trees. If she tried to talk, ask him what was wrong, why he was being so strange, he could pass it off with a few words, or maybe he would just smile mysteriously. *It's a secret!* his look would say. He would put a CD in the player if he had to, though he would rather listen to the music in his head. They would glide along the road beneath the evergreens, the tires whispering. At the top of a hill they would see the lake and the mountains and the stars. They would pass the summer cabins along the shore, and the opulent houses of millionaires blazing with lights on the cliff sides. They would reach the gravel road, and they would ascend the hill, and looking out the windshield they would see the lake stretch toward the darkness of the far shore miles away, the silent mountains rising like dark flames.

He would lead her quietly from the truck and down the long driveway to the shed, still smiling mysteriously. In the shed he would grab the shovel and the Coleman lantern. With the lantern still unlit, they would scramble up the cliff side in the cool air. When they came to Liza Hatter's grave, he would light the lamp, and she would see the dirt mound. He would not say anything. Then he would begin digging. When he had uncovered Liza Hatter—that would be the hardest part, he knew. Because then she would cry and plead, then she would do her best to reach the old Tristan Mackey, the one she thought she'd known all those years. And Tristan's only fear was that she would succeed, that somehow in her piteous state, her hair like a halo in the lamplight, the warm curves of her body, the glistening tears in her large eyes, the tremendous fear and sadness in her voice, she would locate somewhere inside of him the Tristan he used to be. But he believed he was safe. He believed that part of him had fully passed away.

He would do what he had to to calm her down. And when she had finished screaming, if in fact she did scream, and when she had finished crying, because she would almost certainly cry, they would kneel there under the wide northern sky looking down on Liza Hatter's lovely face. And then Liza Hatter could tell her silent story, offer her mute testimony, her dead eyes staring into the lantern light.

Maybe it would work that way and maybe it wouldn't. Maybe, in order to get her there, he would be forced into a premature explanation, but if so, that was fine. Explanations were just so many words. They didn't cost you anything. One way or another, Kelly Ashton was going to see Liza Hatter, that much he knew. And somehow he would have to make her be still and listen, so that the three of them, all together, could feel the universe brushing their faces, hear the dying suspiration of the stars.

Velocity

Vince Thompson's hand was still on the gun when Russell Harmon opened the car door and acted like he was ready to get out, and so he asked Russell what the hell he was doing, and Russell Harmon started shaking his head in a goofy way and saying *I can't do this, man, I'm sorry, I've got someone I really need to go meet, I appreciate the offer, seriously, I'm glad we're friends again, I'm going to get you your money soon, too, I swear, but I really can't do it this time, I'm serious* and shit. Vince Thompson's skull started bang-banging and the blood rushed up into his swollen-all-to-fuck eye and he didn't want to say anything, he didn't want to make a fool of himself in front of Russell Harmon any more than he already had, but this was the *wrong* thing for Russell Harmon to be saying right now, it was just *exactly* the wrong way to get started making amends, people were always misunderstanding Vince Thompson, they were always misconstruing his impulses, and he was getting fucking sick and tired of it if you wanted to know the truth, and so even though he banged his hand hard on the steering wheel once, then held his hand up in the air to signal OK, OK, everything was all right, just a little bit of tension and frustration exhibited there, it had been kind of a rough night but everything was fine, no reason to get all worried and excited, he still couldn't help the words coming, couldn't help fucking saying *Not good enough for you, huh, is that it?* because they both

knew that's what they were talking about here, right? Good old
Vince fucking Thompson was fine to have around when you
needed to rip him off and snort his blow, but when compared
to a hot chick like that Ashton one and his fucking friend Matt
and all those other assholes back in the bar, old Vince just
couldn't measure up, could he, he wasn't Russell's favorite sort
of dog and pony show, isn't that what they were saying here?
And you'd think, you'd seriously fucking *think* that when he,
Vince Thompson, was the only one who'd really understood,
the only one who'd really had the capacity to *get* what Russell
Harmon had done back there in the bar when he'd shot that
fucking bull's-eye, who really fucking *knew* how hard it was to
beat the little Bruce dude or whatever his name was and that
Russell fucking Harmon had had to be better right at that
moment than he'd ever been in his whole goddamn life, and
he'd had to do it with that asshole of a father sitting there, and
being afraid that he, Vince fucking Thompson, was going to
shoot him and shit, which he still regretted by the way, he was
sorry that had happened, goddammit, but how all of that just
made it even more amazing, and then the whole time the
Ashton chick had just sat there like she couldn't give a flying
fuck, like she couldn't even fucking *see* what was going on, why
was *she* the one who deserved Russell Harmon's loyalty, why
not *him*, Vince Thompson, his fucking friend who understood
him? All of this was implied, Vince Thompson hoped, by the
words *not good enough for you, huh?*—all of that was what Vince
Thompson meant, but he could see when he said it that it
wasn't going to make a goddamn bit of difference, Russell
Harmon was still leaning toward the car door, and the thing to
do was *waste his ass* like he'd planned to earlier, it was like fuck-

ing destiny or they wouldn't be sitting here now just the way he had imagined it, and Vince Thompson's hand went back into the pocket but it obviously made no impression on Russell Harmon, who didn't even cast a glance, the fucker thought he was *safe* now because of all Vince's goddamn blubbering and shit, well he would let him know otherwise about *that* real quick, wouldn't he? And yet he still couldn't seem to pull the gun out, still couldn't seem to bring it out in front of Russell Harmon's face, couldn't stand, he fucking supposed, to see the look there, the fear, the sense of betrayal, whatever, but he had the gun right there in his grip and Russell Harmon said, *No, man, that's not it I swear, Vince, I like you, you're my friend, but it's really important, I've got to go back there*, and when he said it he had this sincere fucking look on his face and Vince Thompson could almost believe him. And so he let Russell Harmon get out of the car, and he watched him start walking to the bridge, all blurry and shit there through the windshield because of his, Vince Thompson's, beat-up face and shit and maybe because he was starting to cry, a forty-two-year-old man sitting there in his piece-of-shit barely operational Ford fucking Escort crying to himself because some goddamn kid wouldn't snort a fucking line with him, and to top it off it was *his* fucking coke, Russell Harmon was getting the goddamn shit for *free*. This thought stirred Vince Thompson's anger and outrage sufficiently enough for him to open the car door and get out and reach in his pocket and bring out the Beretta and point it at Russell Harmon's back as best he could in the fucking dark and with his damp clothes hanging on him like lead and his teeth starting to chatter now in the cool air and especially what with his eyes all messed up, goddammit, and with his left hand he touched his face gingerly to wipe away the tears and he could see a little better. But still he let Russell Harmon keep on walking, his finger tight on the trigger but not tightening all the way, even though he could almost feel the kick of the goddamn gun in his imagination, and then the fucking streetlights came on all of a sudden, Jesus who'd have figured there would be so much trouble concerning fucking *lighting* in trying to take care of this business, because now he could see Russell Harmon better, sure, but he was also standing right under a goddamn light in the parking area with a fucking gun held out in front of him for the whole fucking town to see, so he retreated back behind his car door and when he got there and was leaning on the window to help him balance and get lined up again Russell Harmon had come to a stop on the bridge and he was staring out toward the other side across the water. Now was the fucking time. But he needed to nudge his anger up just a little bit more, just enough to make the difference in the pressure on that trigger, and to do it he closed his eyes and squeezed them tight and tried to imagine all the money Russell Harmon owed him, but instead what he saw was Russell standing at that line, his red cheeks and his roly-poly gut, letting that last dart go and the dart making its slight arc and sticking right the fuck in the *middle* of the fucking bull's-eye, it was the coolest fucking thing Vince Thompson had ever seen, and it was making him feel something all right, but not exactly what he had hoped for, no, it was making the blood rush to his fucking severely wounded head and everything was spinning and he felt again like he had in the bathroom in the dark, like he was floating, like he had disappeared, left with no fucking body but just this crazy stream of thoughts coming from somewhere in the air, and the thoughts going why, why, *why* exactly was he doing this, *why* was he getting ready to shoot the very person who had made him so goddamn happy just a little while before, it was because he was so fucking lonely and lost and depressed, wasn't it, and because Russell Harmon wouldn't fucking *help* him, that was why, and because you didn't fuck with Vince Thompson and because sometimes you had to *take a life to save one*, but those were the goddamn asshole air force colonel father's words, not *his*, not Vince Thompson's, and why should he be listening to the goddamn asshole etcetera right now when he'd fought, fought, fought against him his whole fucking life, not like his asshole brother who did everything right with the goddamn squeaky-clean life and the squeaky-clean family, Vince Thompson had gone his own fucking route, for better or worse, he had been his own fucking man, and you couldn't think, for instance, you couldn't say that with all the goddamn fighting and all the goddamn anger and all the goddamn time he'd spent making sure that above all else all the people in this town knew he wasn't the sort of person to fuck with and that if they couldn't exactly respect him they would at least know enough to be afraid, you couldn't say that in devoting himself to that cause he had actually brought about just the opposite fucking result of the one he had intended, that he had actually only succeeded in giving the asshole father what he wanted from Vince Thompson all along, someone to look down on and belittle, someone who wasn't as big a fucking man, the thoughts in the air went could you say *that*, for instance? And the answer came back, yes, you could. Yeah, Vince Thompson thought, he guessed you could. He guessed maybe that was just about the fucking gist of the thing. And he also guessed it was true that he had never really wanted to be the sort of person you didn't fuck with, not deep down, not when you got to the very fucking center of all this blackness and found yourself there, in the middle of this floating feeling washing you along, washing you almost all the way to sleep.

Vince Thompson opened his eyes to see that Russell Harmon had started walking again on the bridge. Maybe he should let him walk. Maybe he should let him get to wherever the fuck he was going to. It was his life, and maybe Vince Thompson, when you got right down to it, was happy to let him have it. He, Vince fucking Thompson, had spent almost his whole life in this town, and that poor Russell Harmon bastard out there on the bridge was the only friend he had to show for it, at least if you could believe what the son of a bitch said, goddamn Russell Harmon with his own fucked-up piece-of-shit father and the same problems Vince Thompson had.

Maybe just say screw the whole thing. There was nothing left for him in this town. Soon he would have to move out of his place above the hardware store and into the apartment complex. And nobody wanted cocaine anymore, they all wanted to fry their brains on crank, and the high school kids didn't even want to smoke pot, they all wanted Darvocet and Oxycontin and shit. The world wasn't what it used to be, that was for sure. And old Mrs. Krum would probably fire his ass from his job managing the apartment complex, too, as soon as she got a good look at his fucked-up face tomorrow morning. Old Mrs. fucking Krum, riding around on her motorized grocery cart or whatever the fuck it was. She'd miss him for a couple of days, until she found someone else.

Maybe the thing to do was drive to the goddamn folks' house, march right in the goddamn door, no sneaking around. Grab the box, have it out with the old man, then hit the fucking road. Do it fast, without thinking. Staring down the barrel of the gun, still keeping Russell Harmon's back in line as squarely as he could, Vince Thompson didn't remember the name of that little California town, and it was absurd to think a girl he left there so long ago would still be hanging around, after all he wasn't a fucking fool, but it had been a nice little town regardless, and once he was cruising down the highway as fast as his piece-of-shit car would let him, he'd bet you he remembered it. Or, if not, he'd bet you he could pick it off a fucking map. All he had to do to make it happen was ease his finger off that trigger, but still he held it there, kept squinting down the sights at Russell Harmon on the bridge, the seconds ticking down, the time revved to such a speed that there was no room in his head for thoughts or decisions, the story of his fucking life, it was all up to his goddamn finger, finally—tighten or loosen.

Weight

Kelly Ashton sat in her chair, turning the candleholder around and around with her thin fingers, weighing the two phrases of three words against each other. *Wait right here. Come with me.*

Oh, if she had only stayed home tonight, said no to Tristan's call, she could be in bed right now in her little room, Hayley asleep in the crib right next to her. Or she could, right now, be taking Hayley out of the crib and bringing her into the bed and holding her in her arms, feeling Hayley's breath against her neck and the soft curls of Hayley's hair against her lips. How nice that would have been.

But she had put herself instead into a difficult situation, and it seemed that she was being called upon to make a decision, and it was very likely one of the most important decisions she would ever make, and she had had one too many beers and one too many glasses of wine.

Tristan had left his cigarettes on the table over an hour ago, before he had disappeared, or she had disappeared, she couldn't remember. She took one out now but she didn't have anything to light it with, and she turned to the first person she could find, the muscle-shirt man who'd been in the bar brawl, and asked him. He didn't smoke, didn't have a light, but he'd go to the bar and get some matches, the least he could do for a pretty girl like her. Good Lord. He came back and made a big show of lighting her cigarette and sat in the chair across from her, and she settled down to the business of ignoring him and weighing her offers.

On the one hand, there was Tristan. Tristan was intelligent and he was handsome and he could take her out of this town into a different life if he wanted to, if she could convince him to, but he was, she had discovered tonight, a little more odd than she'd remembered. Several years ago in a high school English class, Tristan Mackey had made her dream, and dreaming was something she needed then, her father lost in the mountains, and it was probably something she needed now. She was sure she had needed it until tonight. Then she had gone with Russell Harmon to his truck—God she couldn't believe she'd done that—and she had told him about Hayley and she had seen the look in his eyes and she had known that, if nothing else, Hayley had a father in this world. And for that she felt very grateful, and it had settled the issue for the moment. But at the same time she had felt—and she knew it was stupid, *stupid*, a feeling born from watching too many dumb TV shows with her mother, from too much time watching herself fantasize in front of the mirror—that she was selling herself short. And then there had been that ridiculous dart game, grown men making fools of themselves throwing their little darts at their little board and shouting and yelling while—Jesus Christ, didn't they notice?—there was a world outside the fucking window, a sky that held so many stars. And Russell at the center of it somehow, much to her embarrassment. And just as it was all over, Tristan Mackey reappeared and approached the table. *Come with me.* And then there had been some huge, senseless brawl, and Russell somehow, some way, for some unapparent reason, had left the bar with that crazy freak. *Wait right here.* It was about what she expected of him, really. Russell Harmon. She knew him through and through. Russell Harmon *was* this town, or at least the part that she'd been trying to leave. He *was* the life she'd lead here. And it wouldn't be the life she'd dreamed of in his truck, the story that she'd told him. The cozy little house of her imagination would in fact be dingy and dark, with two small bedrooms and a tiny bathroom with bad plumbing, cheap vinyl siding on the outside, treeless yard and patchy grass, cardboard box of toys left out to crumble in the rain. But it would be a safe life for Hayley, with a father she could be sure of. And there was something about Russell Harmon that she loved.

So, on the other hand, Russell. She realized, with what she had to admit was a warm feeling inside her, that she was in fact waiting right here.

But then she had waited five minutes, ten. The man was still sitting across from her, though he had stopped talking. His eyes were on her low-cut blouse, and he was turning the matchbook in his fingers, making sure his muscles flexed. He had been the one to jump in when Russell was on the floor.

"How do you know Russell?" she asked.

He looked up at her with some alarm. "What?" he said.

"Do you know Russell Harmon?" she asked. "Do you know where he went?"

He looked down at the table and then out the window, and his mouth opened and closed, and a sour look took shape on his face, the wrinkles standing out around his eyes. Without a word, he left the table and went to the bar to join his friend.

It had been ten minutes, easily. She checked her purse to

make sure her cell phone was in there. She took out the phone and checked the time. After midnight. Too late to call and check on Hayley, because if her mother woke up she would start drinking again. She looked around the bar for Matt but didn't see him. Where was the little man with the glasses, the one Russell had played darts with? He probably wouldn't know where Russell went anyway. Maybe she should just walk out the front door to her car across the street and drive home. She grabbed the matches and lit another cigarette. When she finished it she stubbed it in the ashtray, grabbed her purse, and walked out the back.

The air was cold, the way it could get on clear summer nights, and she folded her arms in front of her and started walking fast. There was Tristan's truck, the engine already running. As she approached the door, the streetlights came on. Standing there, she felt like she had just been spotlighted on a stage. She could see herself clearly, as if she were her own audience—there were the heels, there was the skirt, there the blouse she'd picked out, there the painted fingernails, the version of herself she'd put together so carefully. And yet she saw herself as disgusting and dirty. What was she doing, *really*? Was she actually going to sleep with Tristan, too? Who *was* Tristan but the remnant of an old idea, one she should have already forgotten? He would take her to the lake house, probably, but she didn't really care. And if he wanted to talk, that was fine. And if he didn't want to talk, that was fine, too. She was too tired suddenly to care what happened, just so long as he got her back to town first thing in the morning. There wasn't any dignity left in her position, anyway.

Some movement on the bridge caught her eye, and her hand,

which had reached for the door, dropped by her side. There was Russell, coming this way. He stopped. He had seen her, too. They looked across at one another, each in their lighted spaces. At this distance, she could see his curly hair, almost read the words on his shirt. She wanted to go back in the bar and wait as he had asked her to. He could be there in one minute. Maybe he would hold his hand up right now to say, *I'll be there. Wait for me.*

But that was weakness talking. The thing to do was get in the fucking truck. This was the moment when the losers were born, when the could-have-beens and should-have-beens were made, when the fault was exposed in the underlings. This was the moment when, facing the mirror, one averted one's eyes, denied oneself and all the plans that had been laid.

She wished she were at home right now, looking in the mirror. She wished she could trust herself alone, but she didn't know how to, couldn't seem to get started that way. She didn't want to look at either Russell or Tristan, so she looked off across the lake toward the faraway mountains, and she pictured her father there. He had gone off in his illness, walked into the woods to curl up and die like an animal. Or maybe it had been just the opposite. Maybe he, too, had suffered all those long years in silence, stuck in the house with her mother, maybe he had felt the quiet panic and hadn't known how to end it, maybe in a moment of extreme determination he had stopped his truck on that mountain road and set off up the ridge in his brown suit and his dress shoes, headed for a life on the other side, where he was waiting right now for her somewhere, enjoying a glass of wine, two tickets in his pocket for the theater. The thing to do was quit being such a baby, get in the fucking truck.

She reached for the door handle, but her eyes went to Russell on the bridge. God, the weight of these choices, the options held in a balance, the direction the scales would tip. Even now, she knew, it would take just one gesture from Russell for her will to dissolve, for her to give up everything right in this moment and do what her heart was telling her to. All he had to do was wave.

But here was Tristan Mackey opening the door, inviting her in, saying to her without words, *Come with me, to wherever I'll take you.*

Gravity

Russell Harmon breathed a lot easier once he was out of Vince Thompson's car and into the fresh air. He was glad to have the Vince Thompson nightmare behind him, and as he reached the bridge he was able finally, fully, totally, for the first time during this crazy Thursday night, to relax—to feel, in other words, like the real Russell Harmon. And yet he was a different Russell Harmon, he knew. He was like a new Russell Harmon who had been dug out from under a rock or released from an air bubble to rise to the surface of a stream. He was a Russell Harmon who had conquered his fears by beating Brice Habersham, and he was a Russell Harmon who had learned that he was the father of a baby girl—or a toddler, a year old, two years old? He couldn't figure it out exactly.

But as he started across the bridge he took a few moments to try to get the rest of the evening straight in his head, because that was what this new Russell Harmon was all about, getting things straight. That was why he had broken up the fight between his father and Vince Thompson, that was why he had slipped Tristan the last bindle. Or maybe he had broken up the fight because it was embarrassing and strange and he had realized all of a sudden that it would be a good way to make Vince Thompson like him again and not kill him, and maybe he had slipped the bindle to Tristan because he was afraid the cops would show up. And definitely there was some wavering when he got in the car with Vince Thompson, the idea of a line or two had sounded pretty good, but getting *out* of the car was definitely an instance of getting things straight—so he was confident now that he was headed in the right direction. The first thing to do was go back to the bar and meet Kelly Ashton before she got angry at him and left, which would probably lead to a cold reception when he went to her apartment tomorrow afternoon to see Hayley right after he got off work, or maybe he should take a shower first. Go back to the 321 and meet Kelly, have one last beer and a little chat, maybe discuss his visit with Hayley, come up with a game plan for how to go about introducing him into the family, because he knew it was something that would take some time, then walk Kelly out to her car and get her to go home before her mother, his mother-in-law now in a sense, and probably his actual honest-to-God mother-in-law sometime soon if things worked out the right way, burned down the building. And then after Kelly was gone, he would need to talk to Matt. He didn't think he'd go into the whole explanation, he figured it would be best to save that for tomorrow morning's drive in the truck, but he needed to make sure that Matt had picked up his expensive darts and his dart case, which he'd left behind in the midst of all the excitement. Then he would take Matt home and then he would go home himself and get some sleep, because Friday morning was going to be a bitch like always, even if he had ultimately laid off the coke and the beer more than usual.

Then, starting tomorrow, it would be time to go to work on getting the big things straight. Russell Harmon knew it wasn't going to be easy, he wasn't going to start in on this thing being stupid and naïve, which had generally been sort of a problem in the past. The picture Kelly had painted of the tidy little house and the three of them there together was nice, he was starting to like it more and more, but he knew that wasn't how things would be right at first, it would take a lot of time and effort and patience. There were some things he was going to have to accept. For starters, his job. A family man, the father of a toddler, couldn't just up and quit his job because he hated it, Russell knew. And even though logging was dangerous, especially for Russell, it paid pretty good, and if he ever quit he would have to find some other serious work to do, not some lame-ass thing. Maybe he could go into construction, where compared to logging the industry was booming. He knew how to pour concrete and lay a foundation and frame a house— he'd done that with Uncle Roy when he built his new place. So that was a start. At any rate, there were also some things he'd have to do differently. No more coke, keep the drinking to a minimum . . . and no more dart league. What would be the point of it, anyway? He had nothing left to prove. Yeah, right, Brice Habersham had had a little problem with his glasses. But it wasn't like Russell hadn't had a few distractions of his own. He'd won fair and square. So what he would do, maybe, was one day when they owned a nice house he would set up a trophy case in the basement. He would put his six trophies in there, three team championships and three individual championships. They wouldn't be great big impressive trophies like Brice Habersham's, but one day years from now when he and Hayley were in the basement maybe watching TV, he could point to them and say, *You didn't know your old man once beat a professional. You didn't know your old man was once the Dart League King.*

He could set it all aside like that, he knew he could. Making his way across the bridge Russell Harmon realized that he had been ready for this a long time. What had kept him from growing up and acting like an adult? It was just that no one had ever told him when the serious part was supposed to begin.

He was nearing the middle of the bridge when a strange thing happened. Right in front of him, occurring in just a split second, every light in the town came on, like someone had plugged in a Christmas tree. There was the back of the movie theater and the men's clothing store and the mountain bike shop and the place that sold Western trinkets, their colorful signs visible now, and the lights shining down on the water. There were the birch trees behind the 321 and there was the parking lot . . . and there was Kelly Ashton, getting into Tristan Mackey's truck. She had seen him too, at the very same moment, and her hand dropped to her side right as Russell stopped walking, and they stood there looking at each other. Even from this far away, and even though she was leaving with Tristan Mackey, he couldn't not see how pretty she was.

But that didn't help any. Once again, it turned out he'd been stupid and naïve. Everything he'd been thinking was just a waste of time. There would be no little house and happy family like the one she had told him about. She had obviously decided on a different plan. But that was how it went, wasn't it? Guys like Russell Harmon, he supposed, weren't meant to get the Kelly Ashtons of the world. They were reserved for the Tristan Mackeys, the smart guys with the college degrees, the ones who would wind up pushing papers in air-conditioned offices and lounging back in swivel chairs while they talked on the phone, the ones who would build the huge lakefront houses out of the trees cut down by all the Russell Harmons, if not here then some other place. He felt like a fool for having thought any different. He supposed now the whole thing in his truck had just been a way to introduce the idea of paying child support, the sex a consolation prize.

But why was she just standing there and looking at him that way? What did she want him to do? Offer her his blessing, wave to her and smile, give her a thumbs-up to say everything was OK? Did she want him to run frantically across the bridge, shouting out her name, to stop her from getting in Tristan Mackey's truck? Well, he wouldn't do it. She could make her own decisions. He had some pride, after all. And he had proven tonight that he was just as good as Tristan Mackey or anybody else. Russell Harmon was—still, once and for all—the Dart League King.

And so he started walking again, and out of the corner of his eye he saw Kelly climb into the truck, and his pace slowed. Maybe there was still a chance. Maybe if he started running, right now. For a second it was like he could picture himself there with her in the truck, could see her legs and her hands folded in her lap and the way her brown hair curled down over one eye—he knew her well enough to know exactly how she looked, but he didn't know what she was thinking. They'd known each other since second grade, in Mrs. Henry's class. She'd made fun of him in class once, because he couldn't read very well, and that day at recess he went off by himself and sat on the merry-go-round, and he saw her watching him, and she never made fun of him again. In Mrs. Muldrow's fifth-grade class he sat right behind her, and he looked at her long hair every day that spring, the way it came down over her soft shoulders in the sleeveless dress, the sun shining through the open windows, and on the last day of school he wrote her a note that he had pondered over for hours the night before—*I like you as big as the sky*, the note said. She held it under her desk and laughed very softly when she read it, and Russell could feel the blood come hot to his face, and his fingers trembled when she handed him her response. *Are you sure?* it said. *The sky is pretty big.*

It seemed strange to Russell that they'd known each other for so many years and in so many different ways and had still never figured out what they meant to one another. He thought maybe they'd done that tonight. And what he would ask her right now, if he could, was whether she was leaving with Tristan Mackey because she thought she was supposed to, or because it was what she wanted. But there was probably no time. Tristan's lights came on, and Russell lowered his head and waited for the sound of the engine, but what he heard instead was a car approaching him from behind.

He turned to look and there was Vince Thompson pulling up in his shitmobile, the passenger window rolled down, Vince holding something out to Russell with his hand, which would be the coke, probably. Jesus H. Christ, the guy never gave up. He was slowing down, and his muffler was loud, and Russell had to look up once more to see that Tristan's truck still hadn't pulled away, and he took a step in the direction of the parking lot behind the 321, as if his feet had decided to lead him there. But then he saw what Vince Thompson held out toward him, and everything else disappeared, everything went soundless, it was the Vince Thompson of his dreams, seen behind the barrel of a gun. The world had collapsed in narrowing circles and

Russell Harmon didn't think or feel or know a single thing, his eyes on that black gun barrel moving at a snail's pace, as if it were some dark creature floating through the air on its own, floating toward him, and in the absence of any thought or feeling Russell Harmon did the one thing he knew how to do instinctively—he grinned. It was a grin that said everything Russell Harmon knew to say—that he hadn't intended any harm, not to Vince Thompson or anyone else, not ever in his whole life, that he had always liked Vince Thompson just fine, just like he essentially liked everyone else once he got to know them, that he had enjoyed all those times sitting in Vince Thompson's apartment listening to him rant and rave well enough, just like he enjoyed most things he did well enough, that Vince Thompson was his friend just like everyone was his friend, that he was innocent, that he couldn't be blamed for what he could not help, that, most of all, he didn't deserve to die for his myriad failings, particularly now that he had turned over a new leaf and would do better from here on out, if only Vince Thompson gave him one more chance.

It was the same grin he had relied on his whole life, and, focused so intently on the barrel of the gun that he did not even know he was grinning, it took a few moments for Russell to see that the grin had worked its usual effect. Slowly the gun was pulled away, lowered by an arm, and then there was just Vince Thompson sitting in his car, grinning back. "You goofy son of a bitch," Vince Thompson said, shaking his head. "Russell fucking Harmon." He kept shaking his head from side to side, apparently in sheer wonderment, and then he laughed. "*Adios*," he said. And then Vince Thompson was gone, headed across the bridge and fighting his car into second gear, honking the horn once, twice, and Russell could feel his knees wobbling beneath him. And he turned to lean on the bridge rail for support, and for a while he couldn't think of anything at all.

It was reflex, almost, that made him turn to look at the parking lot, and it was only when he saw the empty space where Tristan's truck had been that he knew why he was looking. But it didn't matter. No matter what she did tonight, he could always see Kelly Ashton tomorrow. The threat of death had a way of putting things in perspective. Russell leaned his back against the rail, his knees still shaking a little, and he ran his hand across his damp forehead, and he shivered a little in the cold air. Crazy old Vince Thompson. Smiling at him. Maybe it was just a joke, then. Maybe he had never meant to shoot Russell at all. A decent guy, really, just a bit insane and a bit too hung up on the whole father issue. Russell's father had actually stepped in to help him at the bar, a gesture of sorts, and he guessed that was enough. The trick was not to expect too much from people. Kelly Ashton, for example.

Oh well, they were gone now, all of them, Vince Thompson and Kelly Ashton and Tristan Mackey. The night was over. Everyone leaving, everyone gone. Good night and sweet dreams. *Adios.*

One thing was still certain. Russell Harmon dug his wallet out of his pocket and he took out the picture and, yep, that was his little girl. Now that Kelly had told him, even if she regretted it, there was no way she could keep him from being Hayley's father. In fact he'd still go there tomorrow afternoon. It might be awkward between him and Kelly, but she would have to show him in, and he would walk down a hallway to Hayley's room, and there she would be, playing on the floor with a lot of girl toys surrounding her, whatever those were. And her mother would tell her to get up and be introduced to this new visitor, and there she would be, this tiny living image of Russell Harmon and Kelly Ashton, toddling across the room. And Russell wouldn't blurt out anything stupid or inappropriate, he wouldn't want to confuse her or frighten her, so he would start off their relationship this way, very simply: "Hi, Hayley," he would say, "I'm Russell," and he would hold her small hand.

It had been, Russell Harmon decided, a good night all in all. And just as he had also decided to go back to the bar and tell Matt everything there was to tell—right now, before any of his good mood faded—there came Matt, trusty old Matt, walking toward him on the bridge. And seeing Matt there on the bridge made him feel like doing something he hadn't done in a long, long time, since he and Matt were kids. And so before Matt could reach him, Russell Harmon kicked off his sandals and pulled off his shirt and, with a little more difficulty than he had ever had in the past, climbed the metal bridge rail, and with his feet on the bottom rung and his hands holding on to the top, he leaned out over the water. When he was a kid, after that time with Uncle Roy in the boat, he had always been afraid the Garnet Lake Monster was under there, and that when he hit the water the monster would rise from the depths to swallow him, Russell Harmon, and maybe it still would, someday, but right now Russell didn't care. He had let go of the rail and he was falling toward the lights on the cold water with the wind in his ears, and he felt like the new Russell again, like he was leaving a lot of things behind him there on that bridge, and he didn't regret it, not any. He only wished it could be like this forever, the thrilling upthrust in his gut, the feel of the world rushing past him.

Release

Brice Habersham was sorry that the last game in his match with Russell Harmon should be Around the World, and that it should be so easy. Russell deserved better—he had played 301 like a pro. But now Brice Habersham stood at the line near the end of a late evening, holding two darts in his hand. He had already decided to throw the next dart at the single 20, to leave himself just one for the bull's-eye. It was unlikely that he would miss, as he felt quite comfortable and honed in now, and it was even more unlikely that Russell Harmon would be able to run the board if he did miss. But giving himself just one dart would allow Russell to go on hoping a little bit longer, and Brice Habersham found that appropriate.

He had also decided, somewhere along the line, that there would be no phone call, that he would simply finish this game and go home. He'd had too much time to think this evening, too much opportunity to consider his actions and ruminate on the past, too much time to wonder about how he might have done things differently, about where he might have made his own mistakes. It had led him to feel a kind of tenderness toward these people, and the idea of making that phone call and having Russell Harmon and his friend Matt and, later, Vince Thompson arrested was more than a bit distasteful. He didn't have the heart—not tonight. Brice Habersham would give Russell Harmon this night, win or lose, because Russell

Harmon had earned it. Let him be young tonight, let him enjoy his friends.

He had not decided what he would do tomorrow. He did not know whether he would make a different phone call, to the agency, and announce his retirement, tell them he was no longer suited for the job. He did not know whether, if he made that call, he might one day soon take the risk of saying a few words to Russell Harmon, offer him a little advice and perhaps a subtle and highly illegal warning that would help him to straighten out his path. He did not know whether he would do something out of the ordinary like, for instance, actually purchase the gas station/convenience store. He did know that he liked this town, and that he sympathized with these people and their small-town concerns, and that he would like to go on living here himself, but he did not know if that would be possible for Helen and him. He did not know if, after he arrived tonight at his dark house, he would slip off his shoes quietly, climb the stairs, walk on tiptoe to the bathroom and brush his teeth and take off his clothes, then slip into bed and try something that normally would have been unthinkable, try to make love to his wife after all these years, in the hope that it was what they both needed.

The candlelight flickered across his glasses, and he tilted his head a little to one side and threw his single 20, and he did not know even as he raised the last dart in his hand that he would decide there was one more thing he could do for Russell Harmon, and for Russell's friends who were gathered around him, and even for his own teammates, who had after all lived their lives in this town and for that reason did not want Brice Habersham to win. And he did not know that he would decide to do this one thing for himself, for this one time at least—that he would toe the line and raise the dart and, at the last possible moment, close his eyes and take his chances.

Epilogue

It is midway through the hours of a short summer night. The stars vibrate out the window of a truck headed south on Highway 95, across the Long Bridge over the shining water, advancing on the dark sky. Kelly Ashton rides in the glow from the moon coming in her window and she lets her thoughts go where they care to, too lazy for thinking, too broken down tonight at the core to see Tristan Mackey's troubled gaze or hear him not speaking or see his fingers knotted on the wheel. And he looks up at the stars that have emerged from the distances of the sky and watches them vibrate to the beating of his heart and thinks of the girl there below the ground and how he and Kelly Ashton will be there soon. There is very little time for turning back now, although the road stretches on and branches in every direction like the veins of a leaf or of a hand—he could easily turn from this one, could turn onto that road or that one passing from the windshield to the rearview mirror, he could simply stay on this road and let it lead them south, leaving the girl to her silence, there underneath the ground with all her secrets. There are a lot of different choices in the world, and a lot of people making them. It is a wonder that the whole town doesn't shudder beneath their weight.

Brice Habersham is home already, sitting on a sofa in the living room in the light of a single lamp. He is listening to Beethoven's ninth and final symphony, the volume on the old record player low. He has not heard any movement from upstairs. Helen is sleeping soundly now, apparently. He feels a cord inside him tighten with love for Helen, love despite her bitterness and her anger and her neediness and her fear, and it does not feel to him like a naïve or hopeless love, based on some pathetic romantic impulse or internal weakness, but a love that has abided in his heart all the time and which has withstood the many trials she has put him through, regardless of whether she deserves this love from him, which she herself might say she does not. But the love feels real to him, and he imagines that there is a corresponding love somewhere deep inside Helen that it might be possible to bring out now after all these years, and yet he cannot make up his mind to turn off the music and climb the stairs.

Vince Thompson has arrived at his parents' house, and he is performing the old reconnaissance again. It seems like he has been checking for danger his whole life. Bomber, his father's black Labrador, has already approached the car, his tail wagging. Vince is familiar enough to him, though it's been a while. Bomber has sauntered off, sniffing around the edge of the driveway for something, but he will return to the car door and start to bark if Vince doesn't move. There are two lights on in the house, one upstairs, one down. The downstairs light is the kitchen light, waiting for his father's return. The upstairs light is his mother, and he can see a blue flickering in the window from the TV. She is probably sleeping with the TV on again. His mother in her modest flowered gown, her silver hair on the pillow. He gets out of the car and pets Bomber and fumbles for his house key.

Tristan Mackey puts on the turn signal, although he still can't believe he will turn. There is a car in the opposite lane, and as the lights come faster he thinks he will abandon his plan, switch off the blinker and go straight, turn around in the parking lot of the lumberyard up ahead and take Kelly Ashton back to town. But now the car is past and he is turning. There are the fir trees towering above the headlights. There is the moon. Kelly Ashton is fighting back tears, but he doesn't see them. She is not thinking of Russell Harmon and she is not even thinking of her decision to come with Tristan, though it already seems like a mistake, the truck so filled with silence. She is thinking of Hayley in her crib, her pink hand balled around a stuffed animal. What will happen when she wakes up and misses her mother? She wants to think of herself as a strong person, one who can face the obstacles she has presented herself in her own life, the ones that have been presented to her, and overcome them, but there is this weakness and this longing that won't seem to go away, which she knows as she rides with Tristan Mackey in the pale light of the moon through the evergreens is connected to that image of her father, the possibility of a life that disappears, the possibility that she herself will disappear and her daughter come to forget her. Tristan Mackey is not thinking of Kelly Ashton any more than Kelly Ashton is thinking about him. He is watching the road spool under the tires and thinking how each short stretch, every curve, brings him closer to the moment of revelation, the body emerging underneath the shovel, the ground like a womb.

Vince Thompson has passed through the kitchen now, and

the living room too, walking on the proverbial cat's feet down the hall lined with photos from his father's days in active service, into his old bedroom. There is the single bed, there the old cassette deck, there the baseball all-star trophy he received before Chuck hit him in the eye with the iceball. Here in the closet is the locked box. Vince Thompson has the key. He turns the key and lifts the lid and it is all there, the cash in fat rolls, secured with rubber bands. How many times he has imagined lifting this box from its position in the corner, carrying it out of the room. But he has never imagined doing it at night in an almost empty house, ghostly with a certain near silence, just the breeze in the maple out his window and a branch scratching the wall, the dim hubbub of the TV upstairs in his mother's room. He has imagined confrontations and rage.

Tristan Mackey is, he estimates, halfway there, halfway from the turn to the lake house, and the idea looms in direct relation to the distance covered—it is twice as big. He thinks in terms of preparation. He will bring the whiskey bottle and the knife along, or maybe not the whiskey. He knows exactly where the shovel and the lantern are. He almost knows the number of steps it will take to climb the hill. He does not know what to expect from Kelly Ashton. She remains silent. They have not said a word. She is thinking that she will refuse to sleep with him. She is thinking that she will roll to her side of the bed and tell him that this is not what she wants, not what she wants after all, this strange loneliness that she feels only when she is with him, Tristan Mackey. Tristan. She almost says the name. It is a different thing in her head than it is in the person it belongs to. She does not know the person it belongs to, but she will tell him to sleep awhile and then drive her home. They are almost there now. She remembers this place where the road turns to gravel. The crunching sound of the tires reminds her of bones.

Brice Habersham is in the bathroom. His heart beats irregularly. Helen is right there, on the other side of the closed door. He has not made a sound to wake her. He looks in the mirror and brushes his teeth. He is a nondescript man, could be described only as tidy in his appearance and habits. How could such a man hope to excite passion? Tomorrow he will announce his retirement. There—he has decided to do it, this thing he has been thinking about for some time now. The work never suited his temperament, not really. It has been a mistake to do it for so long. He rinses the toothbrush and places it carefully in the holder. He bears no ill will toward anyone. He thinks briefly of poor Vince Thompson and Russell Harmon. He hopes they are both safe and sound tonight, that Russell is enjoying his victory. He closes his eyes as he did when he made his final throw, and he holds his hand out in front of him. He opens his eyes and looks at this hand in the mirror. Small, soft, lined with veins that show his age. In just a minute he will place this small hand on the smooth skin of Helen's belly. He does not know if she will scream.

There is something I need to show you, Tristan Mackey says. She asks him, *How long will it take?* They are standing at the shed. The shed is like the road. It is another place where one might change course if he chose to. *A while*, he says. Is it important? Yes. Yes it is. Can't it wait? No. What she would really like right now, she tells him, is a couple hours sleep and a ride back to town. There is the road forking; one way leads up to the house, the cool covers at the conclusion of a long night, sleep, no secrets revealed, no changes. Maybe things can continue like they are, maybe no one will identify the young man in the library. And there is the other way, the objects in the shed, the walk up the hill, poor Liza Hatter who refuses to disappear, who won't leave the minds of the ones who search for her or the one who knows she's there. Not possible, he says. Not now. I am tired of assholes, she thinks. This is the very last time. Then there is a lantern, a shovel, a knife tucked in a belt loop that she can't see. The light he left on in the house, casting shadows, beckoning her in.

It is too dark to walk up the cliff. He goes ahead and lights the lantern, the gas making a soft hiss. He holds the lantern up, he holds the shovel in his other hand, he feels the knife secured against his belly. How can he do anything now but walk to the grave? What else would make any sense? He has narrowed his choices considerably. *Follow me*, he says.

Russell Harmon is home now, in his basement room. He has eaten the leftovers in the refrigerator. He is sated and sleepy. He takes off his sandals and his wet clothes. He puts on clean boxers and a T-shirt. He gets in bed and clicks off the lamp.

Helen Habersham lies in the dark, listening for some sound from the bathroom. She has slept well following the storm and there is no harsh light in the room and she is at this moment free of pain. She is not angry that he woke her. She feels, right now, a certain softness toward him. It has been so many years. Who was the man she loved so long ago, whose rejection of her had felt like death? She cannot even remember his name. She falls back toward sleep, hearing as if in some other time her

husband—*husband* the word goes lazily through her head—
her husband pulling back the covers and slipping into bed,
and there is still no pain from the covers moving against her
nightshirt, and then there is the feel of a hand against her skin,
and she is awake. She gasps. The hand begins to slide away,
but with a quick, involuntary movement she grabs the hand
and holds it where it is. There is something warm inside of her.
She imagines the man the hand belongs to, can picture him
perfectly there in the dark, his plain face and his neatly combed
hair. It has been years since he tried to touch her in this way.
She has wondered at times if he would ever do it again, but she
has always imagined it happening in the midst of the pain, and
at the moment there is no pain, and she tries to reach inside
herself to find the reason for her ancient rejection, and she
cannot find it. This is the man who quietly cares for her, who
anticipates the variety of her needs, who bears the trials she
knows she puts him through without complaining. The disgust she thought she felt for him, has felt for him in the past on
these occasions, is not anywhere. What is wrong with the feel
of his hand, with the picture of him lying next to her? With a
slower, more considered movement, she interlaces the fingers
of the hand with her own.

Vince Thompson sits on the couch with his box of money.
He is waiting for his father to return. There are things to be said
now, things he has harbored for years. He will have his scene.
He has taken one precaution against his own anger, however.
He has removed the Beretta from his pocket and placed it in
the closet where the box used to be. Now he remembers the
knife and he reaches for it to go put it away as well, but it isn't

there. He remembers how he tried to attack Clint Harmon with it. It seems strange to Vince Thompson that he could have been that angry just an hour ago. It is even stranger to him how he feels right now, very cool and collected. He has only been imagining the possibility of his anger, out of habit. He feels no anger inside him anywhere. He has not felt this calm in many years. It will be strange to talk to his father without the anger. But Vince Thompson's father is nowhere close to coming home. He and Clint Harmon have made their way back up the street to PJ's. They still have an hour before closing time. Vince Thompson's father does not think of Vince Thompson at all. He almost never does. And Clint Harmon is through thinking of his son, Russell. There was a moment back there at the 321 when he wanted to speak to him, wanted to acknowledge things officially. Look at how his son was the center of attention, look at how all these people were watching him. He had attacked that piece of shit Vince Thompson in a surge of pride. But then the hot girl had said the name. It was the name that always disgusted him somehow—Russell Harmon. The fucking nerve of his mother to give him that last name when she had never meant as much to him as the nail on his little finger. It had felt good to walk away from it again. Close call. Big mistake almost made. Things are good at PJ's, where he and his buddy can talk in loud voices about the might of the American military, how since World War II it has never been unleashed in all its strength. It's high fucking time, Clint Harmon says.

Kelly Ashton's initial thought was to walk back to the truck and refuse to go with Tristan. Not once during the time she spent preparing herself in the mirror did she consider traipsing through the woods tonight. It is not what she dressed up for. But now, even if a little sullenly, she has grown interested in the shovel and the lantern. Tristan Mackey is going to dig up something. It seems like an appropriate and hopeful metaphor.

He plunges the shovel into the earth and digs up the first shovelful. She has not asked what he is doing. He does not know what he is doing either, but as soon as the shovel hits the earth he begins to be driven by the thought of the face, as he always is, the usual urgency. But this time there is someone watching. He pauses for breath, his back turned to her. His legs feel weak and he needs to urinate. It is not a good idea to go on with this. He scoops up dirt from the pile he has made and the shovel hovers with it. He cannot decide whether to drop it back into the grave. There is the feeling of a strong urge being suppressed.

For the first time she asks, *What are you doing?* But she does not mean why is he digging, she means why has he stopped. So he drops the dirt back onto the pile and begins to dig again. She has taken off her heels to keep from breaking her ankles, and her feet are on the cold ground, and her arms and legs are bare, and her blouse is thin, and she is freezing. But she will see what he digs up. At first she wonders if it is some memento from the past, if, long ago, in a kind of romantic distress, he put all the things that reminded him of her in a box and buried it here. Class pictures, valentines, yearbooks with the things she wrote in them (*I'm so glad you're my friend* and *You were meant to do something amazing in life* and *I hope our stars stay aligned*), a hair band or barrette he picked up from her desk when she wasn't looking. Maybe, in the same way he had always hidden his feelings, he had hidden all of these things, buried them, and now he would show her what she'd meant to him. But in the lantern light she sees that whatever he has covered up here is far too big. The dug-out place is as long and as wide as a grave, even though he shovels just one end of it, going deeper and deeper. A wild thought takes her—he has found her father's remains. He will dig a little further and she will see the tie, the collared shirt her father left the house in that day. Crazy, but she can't put the thought away. He couldn't have buried an actual *body* here. She is getting less puzzled and more afraid. And she is frozen through and through. *What are we doing, Tristan?* she says. *What the fuck are we doing? I'm cold.* He steps back and looks at her, his eyes weird in the lantern light, not speaking, the shovel held crossways in front of him. *Let me dig,* she says.

He stands there looking at her, breathing hard. *No,* he says, *I'll do it,* and turns to the task again.

The night is a fine one, clear and starry. Helen Habersham has opened the blinds and she stands at the window. She feels good, very warm, very comfortable in her skin. It will not always be like this, she knows. The pain will return. But for now it is gone and she knows once again after a long, long time what it feels like to love someone. It is not the same kind of love she felt before, for someone else. It is less insistent but more intimate, wakeful but not restless—maybe *caring* more than love as it would commonly be defined. But there is strength in it, and it is this feeling that has made her come to the window, and it is this feeling that draws her back into the bed, where she slips one arm carefully over her husband's waist and looks at him in the light from the window. He is an ordinary-looking man, a man devoted to routine, unexciting in the usual sense and always has been, but he has great stores of courage and patience. Carefully again, she pulls him a little closer, and he does not move. Brice Habersham is fast asleep.

Vince Thompson gives up his vigil. He is getting tired. It is time to hit the road or he will fall asleep on the couch, and he does not want to be in this house, this town, come morning. Right now, departure is the thing. He will have to live without the confrontation. He stands, and he picks up his box, and he puts it down again. He climbs the stairs to his mother's room and he stands in the doorway watching her sleep. She has slept in this room for nearly fifty years. Vince Thompson looks around at the familiar furniture, the familiar crocheted doilies, the feminine touches his mother has lent to this room all her life as a balance to her husband's bristling manhood. He looks at the photographs on the walls, some of himself, taken at the ocean, in the mountains, in the desert, framed as evidence of the family's few vacations. His mother turns lightly under the covers, her hand comes out and rests on the pillow next to her face. Vince Thompson approaches her quietly and touches his fingers to her silver hair. He turns off the TV and goes quietly down the stairs and picks up his box and leaves the house and locks the door. He pets Bomber and goes to his car and puts the box in. The wind has died down. It is a cold night but a quiet one. He looks around the old neighborhood, where everything is still. He does not know what he would have said to his father, but he knows what he would like to say—*Old man, I'll miss you in a way, you fucker*. He gets in the car and pulls out of the driveway and heads for California, the rattle and cough of his muffler leaving a last trace of him in the dark.

It has gone terribly wrong for Tristan Mackey. Kelly Ashton is watching him dig and there is not much left to dig now and the time is growing short. He has ruined everything. He has put it all in the hands of someone else. There will be no more private world at the lake house and no more silent moments between himself and the dead girl for whom he is responsible. Already words are taking shape in his head. Already a story is forming. Already he can see this life he has lived for the past month, this short turning of spring into summer, from the outside. He is determining where he went wrong. He is labeling himself the guilty party. Everything is crashing down. He shovels automatically, as if he has no choice, and every now and then he glances back at Kelly Ashton in her bare feet and short skirt and sleeveless blouse, rubbing her arms to keep them warm, the lantern showing the light working of her muscles. She is really a beautiful girl, and a smart one, and braver, it turns out, than he is. He thinks of how many times in the past he has thought of her, and he tries to think of how well he knows her and why he asked her out to this place and he tries to find in what he knows of her what she will say when she looks into Liza Hatter's eyes, but all he can hear is that same question—*Tristan?*—and he wonders how he will answer it this time.

There is a chill in the air and the night breeze has died down to nothing. He can almost feel the fog take shape, adhere to his skin in tiny particles. There is nothing in the world but the sound of the shovel, and the cedars with their barely perceptible motion, and the slowly pulsing stars. He has to get on his knees now for the shovel to reach, and he pauses there over the grave. For a moment everything stops, and his eyes are windows through which he can see this frozen moment, feel it on his skin, as if the moment and he himself are separated by some transparent veil between his body and the air, and he feels one last time that he can make his body do something different, that there is still a decision here.

But no alternative presents itself. He goes on digging. The shovel snicks again in the earth. He is going ahead. He judges he is nearly there. He is embarrassed, almost, when he hears her moving behind him and knows that there is a smell. It is something he has grown used to without realizing. *Please stay back*, he says.

And she does. She is very cold but her blood is racing, and she can in fact feel sweat on the back of her neck and under her arms, and as Tristan drops the shovel and begins to dig with his hands she can almost feel the dirt beneath her own fingernails. He scoops the area out wider where the walls he has dug tumble in. He is close, she can feel it, and she is not thinking of Russell Harmon who might as well be a million miles away, and she is not thinking of Tristan Mackey, or even of Hayley, only of what it is Tristan will show her, and she knows that she is still seeing her father's face, that what her thoughts tell her lie just before her are the tie, the shirt, the face just as she used to see it, and she knows this is wrong, that it can't be, and yet she thinks that this discovery is what the night has been leading to all along, that this is what every twist and turn has been leading to, that there is something here that will change her life.

He has come on it, the last of the earth has been scooped away, but she cannot see what it is he's found. With one arm he invites her forward from her place, and as she moves it is not what she sees but what she smells, there is a sickness in the air as she gets down to her knees but still she cannot see it, and with her left hand she reaches back for the lantern, and she holds the lantern over the hole in the earth, and what she sees in the light is not her father's face but her own face, pulpy eyes sunk in their sockets, flesh drawn in toward the bone, greenish and blackened. For a moment she is dead. He has brought her here to see her own death. The blankness, the remoteness, the disappearance. And then the face is not hers, it is a young woman's, it is the face of a young woman who could be her but is not her, and she can't understand what this means, kneeling there with the lamp held in her hand, the light shining on the face, the smell hitting her in wave after wave. She rises to her feet, backs away. *Tristan?* she says, and she feels him behind her, and now she is afraid. The dead girl's eyes seem to warn her, the girl's bloodless lips say a name. Her body wants to scream but she can only choke, a dry, soundless choking, and she feels something behind her, her skin is almost burning, and her arms drop down and her legs give out and she is kneeling on the ground again, her whole body gone slack and numb and motionless, but what she feels is only Tristan's hand on her back, then Tristan's hand taking the lamp from her fingers.

Then she is up on her feet and running. Her legs shake and she can't keep them underneath her and she is just wild motion, not accomplishing anything. There is nowhere to go to—the truck, the house, the lake down below, they are all the same, and he is behind her, and as she falls headlong down the hill and then gets to her feet again he has grabbed her, the lantern crashing down in a gash of light and then going out and everything is dark, and still she cannot get any sound to come out but she turns into his arms and hits him with both fists, his shoulders, his face, the side of his head, and she knows she is crying now, there is the sound of her crying even though she can't feel it coming out. Now he has her arms and he is squeezing tight and he is asking her to calm down, settle down, can she please just let him tell the story, can she please just let him explain, it is not as bad as she thinks. Now he is all talk, all words, and her eyes are closed, and her body is held tight so that she can no longer hit him, and there is something comforting in the tightness, the way he holds her with the words, she feels warm and he is not hurting her, and this is *Tristan*, she wants to tell herself, *Tristan* whom she has known all her life, not some insane character from one of her mother's TV shows. The words keep coming. He needs to tell her. Will she let him tell her. Please.

The lantern is lit again. She looks at him in the light and he is not so frightening. He looks as scared as she is. In his hand the lantern shakes. She can almost imagine that, like her, he has seen the body for the first time, that he had nothing to do with how it got there. He wants to take her to the house, but she will not go. She agrees to be led down to the dock. What choice does she have? He will run to the house and get a blanket. But having him go away is even more frightening than having him not go away. He has seated her on the dock and he is standing and she grabs his arm. She feels as if she's choking still, but she should not be hysterical, there is need for caution here. There must be some explanation. There are logical things to do and say.

"Tristan," she says, "who is she?"

"She's a girl I knew named Liza Hatter," he says. His voice breaks a little on her name. "She drowned in the lake."

He does not say anything else and she rocks back and forth,

her cold hands held to her face, until the crying stops, and now she is shivering. "What happened?" she asks him.

He tells her it is a long story. He wants to get her a blanket. He sets the lantern down and holds his hands out in front of him, as if making the shape of her shoulders can hold her there. "Please just wait," he says. "Please just stay." He walks off a few steps, the boards of the dock creaking and swaying, then turns to her again. He says her name. He tells her it is just him, it is just Tristan, he swears that it's OK.

He hurries toward the house. She is alone with the dead woman on the hill, a woman no older than she is, a woman Tristan brought out here the same as her, probably, and she drowned, and now she is up on the hill in a grave. Liza Hatter—she is, Kelly Ashton realizes, the girl from college who has been on the news.

She wants to call her mother. She has been gone from home a long time and she needs to check on Hayley. That is what concerns her. She knows that means she is not thinking right, but she cannot think any other way, cannot think of what it is she should be thinking. Maybe she should be trying to escape over the cliff. Maybe she should be hiding in the woods. And then it occurs to her that she can tell her mother to send the police. She looks up at the house and she does not see Tristan inside there and the blood rushes to her head and she wonders if she can get up to the truck to grab the cell phone. But she could probably not get a signal. And then it is too late. Here he comes from the house, carrying a blanket. He is back beside her in no time. She takes the blanket and wraps it around herself and it feels so good that she will never let it go. She does not say anything.

He sits and dangles his feet off the dock, into the cold water. She looks out into the cove where the girl must have drowned. She looks up at the sky and she has not seen so many stars in her whole life.

He brought her here the night before his graduation, he tells her. He talks slowly and softly, as if he is unsure that even this simple statement is correct. She had wanted to go for a swim. He had gone out a long way and didn't realize she was still behind him. She called out to him for help. He swam back to her, and he got there in time. He could have saved her, but he didn't. There is something wrong with him, he supposes.

She does not want there to be anything wrong with him. It is frightening. She wants him to be the same Tristan she has always thought he was. She looks over at him, guarding herself under the blanket.

The look in his eyes is painful, as if, even in the face of the evidence, he is surprised to see the question in her eyes, the question they both know is there. "I didn't kill her," he says. He is quiet for some time and then says it again. "I didn't." He looks out at the lake. "But I let her drown," he says, and she starts to cry again, softly, to herself. Maybe he is a coward, he says, maybe there is something missing in him that other people have. He doesn't know what it is.

And she begins to feel sorry. Sorry for the girl, sorry about whatever it is that has happened, sorry that the whole world has changed in some way now, sorry, even, for him. He is staring down at the water and she has never seen him weakened like this, she cannot help her heart from going out to him. This is the Tristan she has always wondered about, the real Tristan down beneath the cool exterior, but he has come to her too late.

"I still don't understand," she says. She pulls her hands from under the blanket and places them in her lap. She is no longer shivering. She shakes her head slowly back and forth. "This is crazy," she says. "*Why* is she up there on the hill? If it was an accident, what is she doing there?"

He moves his feet back and forth in the water. He says he doesn't know. He says that he remembers standing right here on the dock after it happened. He looks out into the cove, his eyes seeming to focus on a certain spot, and she imagines the girl going under there, a corpselike girl, a dead body sinking, not the live person she actually would have been. He was alone, he says. Instead of calling the police, he went to bed. He couldn't understand what was happening. The next morning there was no body. There was no *body*, he says. He stands up suddenly, starts pacing on the dock. He stops with his back turned toward her, framed in the lighted windows of the house. If there had been a body, he says, it would have seemed real. He didn't want it to have happened, so he acted like it hadn't. It was easy when there was nothing but the memory in his head. He stands there with his arms across his chest, his head down. "Thank you for coming here with me," he says. "Thank you. I feel like myself now." He lifts his head back, his face pointed at the sky, so that she can just make out the shape of his jaw against the lights, his mouth moving, as if he were speaking up into the stars. "It's been a species of hell. Really. I didn't even know it, but I've had an awful time. I've felt terrible. But now I feel like myself again."

And she thinks that he'll cry now, having opened up this far, but when he sits down next to her he isn't crying. She wants to comfort him the way she would comfort her own child, but there's still something in him that won't let her. "That doesn't explain everything," she says, though she can't think what else needs explaining.

"I'm very tired," he says. He closes his eyes and sways his head from side to side and puts his hand to the back of his neck. It is like he is almost a dead person himself, a person who has been drained of everything, falling limp. But he goes on speaking. Her body didn't come up for a long time, he can't remember how many days. Weeks. He had hoped it would go away, that *she* would just go away, but then one day there she was. He buried her because he couldn't tell anyone. He thought about it, he tried to make himself, but he couldn't. The police wouldn't have believed him by then. He lies back, on the boards of the dock, and puts his arm over his eyes. She can see his Adam's apple move up and down. He doesn't know what else there is to tell her. He doesn't think that there is really anything more to say. She keeps looking at him. "I'm glad you know," he says. "You're the only person I could tell."

Maybe there is still some hope for him. Maybe this is not the end. What has he done, actually? She cannot quite get it through her head. He has failed. He has failed to save a girl from drowning, a girl who could have been Kelly Ashton, because he was scared. He has failed—because he was scared, because there is something wrong with him, because he has never had to grow up the way she has, to learn that the world makes you take responsibility—to tell anyone, to report the girl's death. He has failed to see that she was a person, that she would not just go away. He has failed to report her body. He has buried her on a hill. In the grand scheme of things, she can just see how he would get away with it. Think how he would appear to the police, to a judge, to a jury. A young man with a bright future, a college degree, a stack of awards and a bunch of admiring professors. He had behaved in a cowardly, disgusting fashion, but look at how handsome, how smart, how charming—it is just such people who get the second chances. She is not afraid of him anymore. She is simply sad. She wants to go home and take Hayley out of the crib and hold her. She wishes she had stayed with Russell. She thinks if it had been Russell instead of Tristan at the lake that night—Russell, clumsy silly Russell, she knows he would have saved the girl.

She looks at Tristan and sees someone who is defenseless. All the barriers are down. "Will you sit up for a second and look at me?" she says. He does—the shaggy hair, the slumped shoulders, the downcast expression. He will tell her the truth now. He has been telling her the truth all along. The question she wants to ask is not important anymore, and she feels guilty for even wanting to know. "Did I ever mean anything to you?" she asks him. "Really—did I ever mean anything?"

His eyes are on hers. His gaze is open. He isn't hiding anything. "Yes," he says.

It could have been her out here with him that night, if he'd thought enough to call her. "Would you have saved me?" she says.

He looks at her and nods his head up and down slightly, not to say yes, but to acknowledge her right to ask the question. "I don't know the answer to that," he says.

She looks around at the stars, the bright moon, the water, the trees on the cliffs, the house with its glistening windows. It is one of the most beautiful summer nights she has ever seen. But she just wants it to be over. She lowers her eyes and looks at her hands. They are not shaking anymore. "Tristan," she says, "we have to go up to the house and call the police." Everything is quiet. He doesn't answer. She glances up at him and sees that his eyes have narrowed, that he is resisting. "You don't have any choice," she says.

But that is a mistaken view, to his way of thinking. Up until now she has made perfect sense, and he has told her everything. He has been in love with her for the past fifteen minutes. "Maybe we could just leave her there," he says. He doesn't hear a sound from Kelly Ashton and he is afraid to look at her face. But feeling so much like himself, feeling so much like the self he used to be, way back before any of this, he does not want to call the police. It does not seem fair to turn himself in. "I don't have any reason to be sure they'll find me—I could just leave town," he says. "You could come with me." And he wants her to. He means it.

But it is the wrong thing. He can tell that by the way she doesn't answer. She isn't saying anything, and he won't look at her. He looks down at his feet. When he puts his toe down just on top of the water, tiny green waves spread out. The water appears almost opaque, more solid than liquid, an interesting effect. She is right, he knows. She is being logical. Of course she won't go with him now, not anywhere. Of course there is only one thing to do, call the police. In her presence he is, for the first time, truly ashamed. But shame is not a good motivation for calling the police. If he calls the police, more people will know, and he is beginning to see that it is better for people not to know. Only one person knows right now, and he is beginning to wish that she didn't, that he hadn't brought her here.

"Tristan," Kelly Ashton says, "you can't think like that. I

don't believe you really mean it. I don't believe you'd just leave her here like that and run away." She is standing over him, looming there, her shadow cast out over the water by the lantern. "I don't think of you like that, and I've known you for a long, long time." That's all she says, as if that's proof enough, as if the length of time she's known him is an indication of anything. And it *should* be, he knows that. The past should count for something.

Now he looks up at her. She nods her head up the hill at the house, the light framing her so that he can't see her face clearly. She is just a silhouette, a voice talking in the dark. "We're going up there to call the police," she says. "I promise I'll stay with you till they're through. And I'll tell them everything you said to me, and I'll tell them I know you're telling the truth. It'll be OK. It's the only thing you can do."

His toe makes tiny waves. In the lantern light, the water looks viscous and green. Here is the strangest thing—she is right, but she is also entirely wrong. He has operated up till now on the mistaken assumption that he has had a choice in the matter. He doesn't. She is right. But she is wrong that the only choice is to call the police. That, he realizes, is not a choice at all. That is not even one of the options open to him. It would be open to someone else, but not to Tristan. He should have seen this coming, he realizes now, from the moment he decided to tell Kelly Ashton. She is who she is and he is who he is and the outcome should have been clear.

He looks at his feet in the water for a moment and considers his situation. It is a practical matter, really. Yes, they know someone was with Liza Hatter in the library, and maybe, by now, they even know it was him. And yes, Kelly Ashton was seen leaving the bar with him by at least one other person. But he still has money, and he still has precious time. A bank withdrawal, a plane ticket, and he is in Buenos Aires. He has a passport. He speaks the language. He can blend in. *Un apartamento, un trabajo, un nombre nuevo*. It could happen. It could work. He could get started right now if not for Kelly Ashton.

He is only slightly surprised to be taking the knife from his belt loop. He recognizes the moment, of course—like everyone else he knows the story, he's seen the popular films, he has read novels and newspaper accounts. This is the moment when the formerly mild-mannered husband, the formerly mild-mannered father, the formerly mild-mannered classmate or coworker or neighbor or childhood friend crosses the line definitively from sanity to insanity, from innocence to guilt. From now on, he can make no excuses. But he finds this line easy enough to cross—he has crossed so many already. He looks at his feet there in the water one last time, at how strange and alien they appear.

He stands and moves closer to her. Is she sure about her decision, he asks. He wants to know if she is sure. There is still time for her to change her mind, he tells her. And she backs away a little. He is close enough now to see the answer in her eyes. He has seen that look before. He breathes in deep and lets his head fall back, taking in the wide open space beneath the stars.

She *does* mean something to him. One part of him loves her, and it is that part right now that could almost break into tears. At one time, Kelly Ashton was the truest measure of his heart's longing—even to this moment he can remember the day she spoke to him in art class, the day she formed in him the desires that made him who he was then—the desire to be recognized, to be admired, to be loved. He left those desires behind. But there is another part of him, and it is still there, and it has been there his whole life. That part is made of baseless pride and boundless selfishness. That part cares nothing about anything but itself. He knows it, he hates it, he hates what it will make him do, but it is the stronger part of him in the end. There is no point in denying what it finally desires—the absence and the silence it has come to know, the only music and language it hears.

As she sees him come toward her, sees the knife he holds out in his hand, it might be that all she feels is fear, that it is all reduced to that, but there are other things beneath the surface of the fear, things that make her who she is, Kelly Ashton. She feels stupid. She has been fooled again. She is the mother of a two-year-old girl, and she has failed in her responsibilities to her daughter, Hayley, and those responsibilities—to protect, to provide for, to love, to *stay*—are more important to her than anything in the world. There is how her father disappeared, and how that changed her life, and how that disappearance might have led her to this place in which she herself might disappear, to be buried on the hillside. There is her mother and how Hayley will be left to her. And then a thought does rise to the surface from under the fear, a thought of Russell Harmon, and she is so glad she told him. He is a good person, and he will do the right things. These are her thoughts as she sees Tristan come closer and she raises her hands against him. She wants to tell Russell: there is a certain way to warm a bottle, there is a way she likes a scrambled egg, there is a way to potty train, there is a way to take her out of the bathtub and dry her off, there is a way to adjust the car seat, there is a way to hold her when she cries, there is a way to put her in your arms at night and help her fall asleep, there is a way to smell her hair, there is a way to receive her smile and a way to smile back at her, there is a way to love her and make her feel loved and make her grow and keep her safe and you, her father, you will find it, Russell, please.

She is the mother of a two-year-old girl and if this man who wants to steal that from her thinks she will not fight him with every scrap of energy and strength she has, he is about to find out different, but the words she says are spoken as if from some other time, on some day long ago, to someone she thought she knew—*Take me home now, Tristan. I need to go home.*

In a few more hours, there is the sunrise. Everything has changed. The town itself looks different to Matt, rumbling along in his logging truck through the mist weaving up from the asphalt, the sky an unusually bright red. The buildings and the traffic signs look altered in this light, and he is the only one to see them, barreling through town on his way to Russell's.

He passes an apartment complex. Inside is a young girl lying awake in a small room. Her mother has left her in the crib all night and in fact her mother is not there. She is not crying, though. She is lying soundlessly in the reddish half-light, feeling a longing and sadness she does not have the words to name. The door to her room stands wide open, ready for someone to enter and take the longing and sadness away.

Russell Harmon wakes to the rumble of Matt's truck outside on the street. As soon as his eyes open he is struck by a terrible thought—when he dove from the bridge, he left his wallet in his pocket. He jumps out of bed and turns on the lamp. He locates his shorts and yanks out the wallet. With trembling fingers he pulls out his daughter's picture. It is not ruined. It was stuck to the back of his maxed-out credit card, and some of the photographic paper has peeled away, and near the edges where it got damp the colors have bled. But the face is still there, smiling out at him. And now that he knows what he knows, there will always be time for more pictures. Russell Harmon looks closely at his daughter one last time. She has his cheeks but her mother's eyes, he thinks. He dabs at the moist surface with the hem of his T-shirt, so that there won't be any further damage done. He puts the picture away in his sock drawer.

It is time for the Dart League King to start another day. He pulls on his jeans. He puts on his boots and laces them. He walks out of his room, but in a moment he returns. He takes the picture out of the drawer and lays it face up on the nightstand. That way, it will be the first thing he sees when he comes back in.

Rules and Regulations for the 2007 Garnet Lake Dart League

GARNET LAKE DART LEAGUE RULES AND
REGULATIONS 2007
(by Russell Harmon, Commissioner)

General Rules:

1) NO ELECTRONIC BOARDS! Garnet Lake Dart League matches will be played on regulation bristle boards only! The team sponsor is responsible for keeping the boards in good playing condition (meaning no "bubbles," bent wires, worn-out areas around bull's-eyes, etc., report these problems to the Commissioner).

2) Each team must be sponsored by a local business that serves ALCOHOL! (Food is optional).

3) Team sponsors must be willing to schedule matches each Thursday night, 8 p.m., during spring/summer dart season (won't have to hold matches every week, since sometimes their team will be "visitors," but should have bar available each week just in case).

4) Team sponsors (or team captains) will make sure all measurements of dart board, foul line, etc., match up with American Dart Association standards (Commissioner will check each board prior to beginning of season).

5) Teams are four players (with one official alternate) each. Matches start at 8 p.m. If a team doesn't have four official players by 8 p.m., team must forfeit if opposing captain says so. BE TO MATCHES ON TIME, guys! We have had only one forfeit in three years, so take pride in your team!

6) Every team will have official team shirts that must be worn to matches (ask sponsors if they will provide shirts).

7) All players should plan to attend the annual Garnet Lake Dart League Awards ceremony on the Thursday night following the final matches (location to be announced. TROPHIES for team champs and individual champs!) *Note—see number 8 to know why it's important to plan on attending the awards ceremony!

8) *Scoring* will be done this way: *Teams*—Win=2 points. Tie=1 point. Loss=0 points. Team with most points at end of the season wins the Team Championship. In case two teams tie, the team that won in head-to-head competition is champ. If the two teams tied in head-to-head competition, they will have a tiebreaker match at Dart League Award night (neutral site)! *Individuals*—Player with most wins at end of season takes the title. Any ties will be decided at Dart League Award night!

9) Some singles matches (at the end) may not be meaningful in terms of the team outcome of the match—ALL MATCHES SHOULD BE PLAYED IRREGARDLESS! They still count for the Individual Standings, and even if you are not one of the players on the leaderboard, you should still be concerned about your individual record! NO FORFEITS! Take pride in your game!

10) The rules and regulations of the Garnet Lake Dart League are designed to be the best rules for THIS PARTICULAR LEAGUE! They may or may not be the same as national or world dart league rules, but they are the same if not otherwise stated. LEARN THE RULES!

Match Rules:

1) Team lineups will be made up prior to match on the official dart league lineup sheets (new this year!) by team captains. No switching places after team captains compare sheets! If you want specific matchups, talk them over ahead of time.

2) All team matches will consist of a doubles section and a singles section. Doubles matches are played first. There will be two doubles matches and four singles matches—each player on the team must play one and only one singles and doubles match, for a total of two matches per player per week.

3) Doubles matches will consist of a Cricket game (with points, also known as "killer"), a game of 301, and a game of Around-the-World, in that order. Best two out of three takes the match. If one doubles team (same for singles also) wins Cricket and 301, that match is over, and you go on to the next match. Each match (doubles and singles) counts *1 point*, meaning there are six points in a match overall. *The team with the most overall points wins, with a 3-3 score meaning a tie for that week's match.* THE WINNING MARGIN DOES NOT MATTER! A 6-0 win and a 4-2 win (or loss) both count the same for the Team Standings. See number 8 under General Rules if there is confusion.

4) Singles matches are the same as doubles matches, except only one player instead of two.

5) Every game of every match will begin with a "cork" (one player from each team throws one dart at the bull's-eye,

closest to the middle wins). The player (team) that wins the cork goes first. Players then take turns, throwing three darts per turn. In doubles matches, teams must alternate turns (player from Team A throws, followed by player from Team B, followed by second player from Team A, then second player from Team B, etc.).

6) All scores will be recorded by the player who scores them at the end of each turn on a chalkboard, so that the score is always known by all competitors and there isn't any arguing about it later! (Make sure sponsors provide chalkboards.)

7) One of the two team captains should report the results of their week's matches to the Commissioner (Russell Harmon) NO LATER THAN SATURDAY by phone (555-2606). (Leave a message if Russell isn't there.)

Game Rules ("Killer" Cricket, 301, and Around-the-World):

"Killer" Cricket:

To win, a player (or team) must close all numbers 15 through 20 plus bull's-eyes (in any order) and have at least an equal number of points as his opponent. Three scores in each number means it is closed. A single counts as one, a double counts as two, a triple counts as three. When a number is closed, and the opponent has not closed that number, the player with the number closed can score that number of points on his opponent by hitting the number additional times (for example, if I'm closed on 20s and my opponent is not, I can hit a single 20 for 20 points, a double for 40, a triple for 60, etc.—a single bull's-eye is 25, a double bull is 50). You can only score on an opponent when he does not have that number closed! When a player (team) has closed all his numbers and the bull's-eyes and has equal to or more points than his opponent, he (team) wins.

The scoreboard should be drawn with 20s at the top and go down to 15s, with bull's-eyes (marked by an X or a B) at the very bottom. Write the numbers down the middle of the board and put the teams on either side. When you score once on a number, mark it with a /. When you have two scores on a number, make an X. When the number is closed, put a circle around the X (if you hit a triple, you can just draw the circle without the X in the middle of it—this saves chalk!) Points are kept track of on the side of the board next to the team that scores them. This is the most skillful game, so if you are a weak player, good luck!

301:

We play this game "double in, double out"—some leagues do not play "double in." The object is to start with 301 points and work down to zero—first player (team) to zero wins. To begin subtracting from 301, player must first hit a double—any double, including double bull's-eye—to get on the board. You begin subtracting from that dart (if it's your third dart, the first two don't count, in other words). Singles, doubles, and triples point values are the same as in Cricket. To complete the game, player must throw the EXACT DOUBLE to get him to zero (for instance, if I have 16 points left, I have to finish the game by throwing a double 8). If the score gets down below 2, it is considered a "bust," and the player gives up any darts remaining in the turn and begins his next turn from the same place he started the last one—the "busted" turn is erased in other words, basically.

Around-the-World:

This is a game not normally used in competition but we use it to keep things moving along (it is fast and fun). We only play this game if the players (teams) split the Cricket and 301 games—it's a tiebreaker, in other words. The game is simple. You hit every number from 1 to 20 (in order) and then finish with a bull's-eye (single or double, it doesn't matter). There are only two basic things to keep in mind. 1) Doubles and triples are scored differently than the other games. In this game, a double means you get to skip the number that comes next (if I hit a double 4, I go to 6 next, not 5). Hitting a triple means you skip the next TWO numbers (triple 4 means I go to 7 next, not 5 or 6). 2) Whenever the player scores the required number with his third dart, he gets to keep his turn (if I'm on 4, and I hit a single 4 with my last dart, I go back to the board and start on 5s, for example). What makes this game interesting is that theoretically a player could shoot all the way around the world in one turn and never let his opponent shoot! Good luck! It's very hard to do and can only be accomplished by an expert player!

Acknowledgments

Thank you to all these folks, who read this novel at various stages of its completion and offered a great deal of help—Steve Almond, Dave Shaw, Jason Durham, Brock Clarke, Angela Morris, Sappho Charney, Will Cathcart, Michael Griffith, and London Morris. I hope I haven't forgotten anyone who had suggestions to offer, and if I have, I apologize. Thank you to my agent, Renee Zuckerbrot. Thank you to Lee Montgomery, Tony Perez, Meg Storey, and all the other folks at Tin House who worked on the book. Thank you to editors Brigid Hughes, Jodee Stanley, Kevin McIlvoy, Stephen Donadio, and Nicola Mason, who have continually supported my work. Thanks to Scott Ellingburg, who assisted with research (we had many excellent conversations about cadavers). Thanks to Nathan Morris, just for hanging around and being cool. Thank you to Krishele. Many, many thanks to my many, many friends, in Idaho and elsewhere—I wouldn't keep trying if it weren't for you.